TIME AND SPACE

Also by Shireen Jeejeebhoy

In Print and Ebook

Lifeliner

She

Concussion Is Brain Injury

Aban's Accension

In Ebook

The Job Sessions: Why Do The Innocent Suffer?

A Nibble of Chocolate

Eleven Shorts +1

TIME AND SPACE

SHIREEN JEEJEEBHOY

http://jeejeebhoy.ca

ACKNOWLEDGEMENTS

Time and Space has been a long time in gestation. I'd like to thank everyone who helped me on the way. It began with me reading books, articles, and websites on theoretical physics and discussing concepts with my friend Andrew Fogg and my father Khursheed Jeejeebhoy. I wrote the outline, and as was my habit by 2011, I reviewed it with my editor Greg Ioannou. We had a long chat about what skin colour people would have in the future once the entire populace of the world had intermingled. But in the end, if the colour I describe in these pages is deemed incorrect, that's my mistake alone. National Novel Writing Month 2011 was the event that drove me to get my outline done on time and to write the entire novel. I'd like to thank the tireless people behind this event, as it's made my book writing possible. As always my Beta Readers—Andrew Fogg, Ann Benoit, Olive Jeejeebhoy, and Khursheed Jeejeebhoy—gave generously of their time and me lots of invaluable feedback. And last, but not least, I want to thank my editor Pam Elise Harris. She strove to ensure she understood my style and FutureSpeak (what we called the way my characters in the future speak—see Glossary), and she created a style sheet that both of us could use in the final phase of editing *Time and Space*. I greatly appreciated her regular questions while she edited *Time and Space* and her comments on the manuscript.

A *final note*: There is a Glossary at the end for FutureSpeak. I also took a bit of liberty with neutrinos and with current theoretical time travel convention. It is a fictional story after all!

1

THE SNATCH

FORTY. Tomorrow, I will be forty. That number echoes in my footsteps as I walk the familiar beat to work.

Time.

That's my name, and ... where did the time go? When did I get to forty? What does it mean?

Beat, beat, beat: my footsteps rap along the sidewalk in time to the music pumping into my ears from my iPod touch. My footsteps distract me. But only for a moment. I think: at my age, my mother still had not had me. That's why my mother and father had called me "Time."

"It was about time your mother got pregnant," my father would say often during post-Sunday-dinner coffee, as he leaned back in his worn armchair lighting his pipe.

"And it was about time you got out. You sat in there and sat in there and would not come out," my mother would retort to me.

"So we called you 'Time'," Father would say. Then he would end the story with: "Seemed logical."

"Seemed appropriate," Mother would counter as Father finally managed to pull a draw from his pipe and emit three puffs.

What a horrid name, I think, as I turn the corner onto Queen. Today, it's made me obsessed with time and with turning forty. I see a people-stuffed streetcar trundle by, and I sigh. It's been awhile since I gave up trying to catch the streetcar to work and reluctantly woke up earlier to get there on foot.

Peggy and Sue have this big birthday lunch planned for me tomorrow at our favourite restaurant. And the boss has generously—I roll my eyes at "generously"—given me two hours off so we can take our time. The whole thing is surreal.

Bzzzttt.

I take my iPod touch out of my skirt pocket and look at it. The screen is dark, and I press the Home button. No notifications. I turn it this way and that to find what created that strange noise. It seems okay. I shrug, slip it back into my pocket, and continue walking along my route.

The morning sun is slanting sharply along the sidewalk in front of me, toward me, pointing at me, that old woman turning forty. I want to hide from its edgy light, but no point in crossing the street into the shadowed sidewalk. I'll only have to cross back again. I hate walking.

Voices interrupt my thoughts, and I glance into a garishly-painted alley and think: Ford Nation has obviously missed this place. But perhaps there's so much graffiti in Queen West alleys, it's worn out Mayor Ford and his fans before they could erase it all. But there's no one loitering or walking in the alley, only solitary people like me hustling along Queen Street, coffee cups in hand. Suddenly, I stop. I look at my empty hand: I forgot to get my morning café latté, no whip, soya milk, half-sweet, grandé. I think of retracing my steps, but then I'll be late, and the boss doesn't like tardiness. He gets in a snit if I'm even one minute late. My feet resume walking.

And my thoughts resume churning.

At my age, my parents had been married twenty years. It would be another five before I was born. They'd both died a decade ago. I have no sisters or brothers. And since both my parents were only children, I had no immediate cousins. As a child, I met these strange adults my parents called "distant cousins" on special occasions like weddings, adults who embraced me in powder and perfume, exclaimed over how much I'd grown, making me squirm. But I haven't seen them since the funeral.

The last funeral.

I've been alone in the world for ten years, yet until today I hadn't dwelled on it, hadn't felt alone. I live in the house my parents lived in. I've been working at the same kind of job since I graduated from university with my English Lit degree and went right into a temping agency. Father tried to get me to think bigger, but what was I good for? I'm bad at math. Numbers confuse me. And science is gibberish. Only eggheads do science anyway. But then who'd want an English grad? I thrust away a stray memory of an interview with ... I can't even remember now. Father had said I'd sabotaged it; Mother had said never mind, I was born to type. And so type I did and have until this day. I thought it'd be temporary until I found my feet. Yet there they are, my feet, attached to the bottom of my legs, and they're taking me to my admin assistant job as they do every weekday.

"Her."

I hear a word faintly from ahead of me but ignore it. I am thinking about my bosses. I had a few different bosses at several different companies in the early days. Every time I landed a new job, I'd think: this time I'll have a better boss. This time he—or she will treat me like a person with a mind. But they're all the same. They boss you around, treat you like you can't think, dismiss your suggestions unless it's about what to get their spouse for their birthday or how to sort their endless paperwork. I stopped thinking for myself. I stopped caring about having someone else think for me. It's been a long time since I've used my brain independently. And so why do I care today? Why does it bother me now? I shake my head. I've been working at the same company, for the same boss, since two years before Mother and Father died. Father was glad I'd landed a job at a prestigious firm—if I had to be an admin assistant. Mother was glad whatever I did.

I think about Peggy and Sue. They work in the same pool area as I do. Each has her own boss, but our bosses all report to the same Director. Peggy and Sue welcomed me on my first day there, took me out to lunch, showed me the ropes. We've perfected the art of doing as little as possible while looking like we're typing all the time. Typing and emailing and phoning and filing. And organizing the bosses. Technology is great. I hate science, I hate computers—I won't have one at home—but I've learnt how to manipulate them at work so that the boss thinks I work hard when in fact it's the computer. He knows less about the tedious machines than I do, and it's so easy to hoodwink him.

Every month, Peggy and Sue and I go out to a new restaurant for dinner, one that *Toronto Life* recommends. We won't go for anything rated less than three stars. Sometimes we'll go to a show afterwards, something new from Broadway. Every Saturday I go to the library and borrow my week's worth of books. I often borrow books I've read two or four times because it's becoming harder to find new ones that interest me. And I won't buy books. It's not that I don't have the money, but that I want to support Toronto's great library system. Still, cutbacks may force me to buy books. I make a face at the thought. I used to like going to Abelard's or Britnell's, but a Starbucks claimed Britnell's elegant bookstore ages ago, and Abelard's has gone online. I hate the Internet and the endless emails too. I'm not going online to buy books or anything else. And the big chains feel impersonal every time I walk into them, which I haven't for awhile. They're not real bookstores. At least the librarian, when she's there, knows me and knows what I like in books. I smile as I remember last week's conversation when I told her I was turning forty. She'd sympathized and whispered that she'd find me some books about turning forty. At least books remain the same through time: solid, reliable, always there.

Peggy bought an e-reader a month ago, and daily, she tries to have me read it. But ebooks aren't real, aren't solid. They won't last, not like the hard covers I read with their sturdy covers and strong pages. E-readers will change because computers always do, and her ebooks will be gone. Ebooks are a fad, fuelled by those egghead science geeks. I think again about the librarian's promise and pick up my pace in anticipation of my weekly library trip and of those books she'd promised me and of snuggling down Sunday morning after my weekly waffles with a new book. I always begin reading my weekly book borrowings on Sundays. Each day of the week, each day of my life has its own routine—except for tomorrow. At least by Sunday, my fortieth will be a new, fading memory.

"Get ready."

The menacing voice interrupts my thoughts. The hair on my arms and the back of my neck stand to attention. I focus on the people hurrying to work ahead of me, each one alone. One of them must be talking into his Bluetooth, I tell my upright hairs.- I hate this intrusion of technology into our world. I take my iPod touch out, crank the volume up, and keep it in my hand. Forty. I'm going to be forty, and there's nothing I can do about it. I cross another graffiti-strewn alleyway and yearn for my latté.

Suddenly.

Hands grab my shoulders, my arms, my waist. They twist my skirt up. A faint thuck-thuck sounds as my iPod touch clatters to the concrete from my shot-open hand. Shock silences my scream and freezes my arms and legs. The foreign hands drag me down the alleyway. Too late, my vocal chords vibrate, for we're not in the alleyway anymore. We're in a white place where the white walls hum into the space.

I scream.

I thrash.

The white walls wash into the space to vacuum the sound out of my throat.

The hands release me, and I stumble to the luminous floor.

The hands' owners step around me from behind to stand in front of me. I blink and scramble up and see three skinny twenty-something boys with double-espresso-latté-coloured skin smirking at me, their necks sticking up from skin-hugging white suits that cover everything but their heads and chestnut hair. They look identical. Yet as my eyes adjust to this bright place with its strange soughing and electric smell, I see they're not. One has a big nose; one a small one. One has cupid-bow lips; one a straight line. One has long lashes; one has thick brows.

They shove me backward, and a seat edge grabs my legs. I sit down hard. One reaches toward the wall closest to him and plucks out a limp piece of white fabric that hadn't been there before. Air catches in my throat. He throws it at me and tells me to put it on.

I almost drop it but make myself hold on. I look around and cannot see a door. They cackle.

"No escape," says one.

"No door you can find," says another.

They laugh harder. They're right. I see no door, no way out. I examine the limp fabric, and abruptly it's a suit hanging from my hands. I drop it in horror. They bend double, they're laughing so hard. My heart beats rapidly against my ribs. I gulp for air. I can't escape, and I dare not disobey. I pick up the suit with my right forefinger and thumb and eye it warily, trying to control my breathing. It doesn't change; it simply hangs from my finger and thumb. I take a firmer grip on it and nothing happens. I must do what they say. I inspect it and find its feet.

One stops laughing long enough to bark, "Put it on!"

I jerk. I glance up at him and immediately back to the suit. I don't know whether to keep my shoes on or not and then decide it's their stuff, what do I care if the heels of my pumps ruin it. I don't want to take them off. I let the suit fall out of my hand, button up my cardigan, retrieve the suit from the floor, find the legs of it, and insert my feet, right foot first. My shoe gets caught in the stretchy, shiny fabric, and I struggle.

They stop laughing and watch me maliciously.

I try again. Suddenly the right leg of the suit opens up and my foot slides down easily into the foot of the suit. I squeak but duplicate the movement with my left foot in its shoe. I stand up and start to pull the suit up. It's like panty hose, and my skirt's bulk is bigger than the suit. I try to stuff it in because I'm not taking my skirt off. As I stuff one section in to one leg, another section flops back out. The boys crack up, but thankfully the walls absorb the highest pitch of their cackles. I persevere, pushing more skirt into each leg of the suit, trying not to expose the ugly topside of my panty hose. The suit bulges unattractively; lumps and bumps sprout wherever I've been able to shove in my skirt. Finally I have the suit pulled up to my waist, and I'm exhausted. I pause to catch my breath. And I look down at the results of my effort. My skirt in the suit is like a muffin top and feels just as bloated.

The suit morphs.

The lumps and bumps disappear.

My skirt is sucked down into the legs.

I suck in air, suck in air. I scream and scream and scream. I cannot hear myself. I cannot even feel the screams in my throat. But I can't close my mouth or stop exhaling through my vocal chords. I want this awful suit off.

Suddenly I'm sitting down, the wind blown out of me.

One boy growls in to my face, "Finish."

I wipe my face from forehead to chin, stand up, and pull on the arms and shrug into the shoulders of the suit. I reach for the zipper to close the front, but there's no zipper, no buttons, no Velcro. I frown at this puzzle. I hear a choked guffaw and look up. They say nothing; they are too entertained by my perturbation. When I look back down to find some way to close the suit, I see the front edges of the suit moving toward each other, fusing, leaving no seam, making the suit into one fabric. My chest heaves hysterically.

"Watch."

I look up at the boys. They step back, and in sync, their upper eyelids drop slowly, deliberately, stay shut for shorter than a second but longer than a normal blink, then as they open, out of the back of the boys' suits arise hoods that pull over their heads, cover their faces, and fuse with their necklines so that the white fabric becomes one from their feet to their heads. Yet I can see the surfaces and edges of their faces clearly. My heaves turn into quick shallow breaths. One blinks again, that same slow blink. I feel something wispy cover my face. I reach up to touch my cheeks. I don't feel my skin. I feel something soft yet not there, something that prickles and lets my fingers sink into it so that I can feel the edges of my cheekbones. I see clearly, as if nothing is covering me, yet I know I'm as covered as they are. My lungs don't want to work anymore, my heart pounds to get out of its rib cage, and I become dizzy.

"Sit down."

He doesn't have to order me because my swimming senses have sat me down already. I can't breathe, and panic rules. From somewhere rises the thought: I must gain control of my breathing. I reach into my memory back to a friend during university who'd taught me deep breathing. I hear her instructions and obey. My breathing fights me, and I fight it. And as I struggle to gain control, one of the boys blinks that blink again, staring at me much like a cat at a mouse, and a shimmer appears before me and then is gone. They look at each other, laugh out loud, and start dancing. Or at least, I think that's what they're doing. It vaguely reminds me of football players celebrating a goal, no, a touchdown. Knees rising up to chests, arms flailing, heads chucking like chickens out of rhythm. I forget all about my breathing, for their contortions are too weird. This place is too weird. I must be in a dream, caught in a nightmare, thinking too much about my fortieth. I stare hard at the white walls, willing them to disappear and become the soft tangerine walls of my bedroom.

And that's when I notice that the walls don't actually end in corners. They're not round either. School-era geometry floats back into my memory from the past, and I think: maybe this is what the inside of an ellipse looks like. Smooth, never ending, yet beautiful as if it could cut the wind, creating no wave to show it's been there. Seats emerge from the walls here and there. On the other side of the dancing boys, the wall coruscates as if it's about to display something.

The boys stop and leer at me, their grins self-satisfied. They nod at each other, and I feel a faint lurch. And then I have the oddest sensation. I feel like I'm moving yet not moving. I feel like my thoughts are with me then behind me. I feel like every cell, no, every molecule is forming and dissolving and reforming in me. I feel as if the suit is the only thing holding me together. The walls and the boys become semi-transparent, as if every other molecule in them has disappeared. I want to rub my eyes but cannot move. I want to yell for help, even though there's no point, but cannot open my mouth. I want to run, but I'm fixated like a cobra's victim.

My boss is going to be pissed. Peggy and Sue won't have anyone to take to my fortieth birthday lunch.

2

THE HANGAR

I'M prickling. Electrons are spinning in glee, throwing off sparks; the faster they spin, the further apart they're drawn, the farther the sparks jump; each spark provokes the next. Static cling fills me.

Itchy sensations build in my mind to kindle this image. Unpleasant.

A thought animates in my head, stretching itself into my mind. Stretching, stretching.

"Let me off!" I scream in my head.

The scream slows and deepens in tone. Slower, slower, deeper, deeper.

I struggle to suck in air. My lungs are vacuums, devoid of air but not rebalancing with the outside atmosphere because it too is a vacuum. I try to make sense of this strangeness. It's like I have lost half the weight of my ribs, my heart, my lungs, as if the air I inhale is flying through all those little cells in my lungs and straight out my breasts, dragging sparks all the way.

The boys stand, legs wide, watching me through their appearing-disappearing suits.

I stare right back at their blank white faces and scream "I don't want to be here!" But the scream isn't there. Not even in my head. I thought it. I know I thought it. Suddenly there it is: "I don't want to be here!" It's a lengthening deep wail, not a scream. It stretches out and drops into the absorbing white walls.

That's when I notice the walls are coruscating and disappearing with each starry flash. Yet I cannot see anything outside them; I cannot see through them. The only reality is in this cube ... no, this ellipse ... no, this stretchy thing. Its shape is not like I remember it ...

Remember it? How long have I been here? How much time has passed? It seems like many years since the boys grabbed me with their little touchy-feely hands.

Is this a ship? The thought has finally surfaced into my conscious mind, swimming against a tide of time slowed.

The boys deliberately turn toward each other, raise their arms in slow motion, lock them over each other's shoulders, bow their heads till they touch. The ship shifts. The walls coruscate less; they rebound half-way back toward their original curvature; the boys appear less transparent but not yet solid.

The boys raise their heads in real time, drop their arms, and face me again.

They speak, in turn.

"Do you know where you are in time and in space?"

The other two laugh.

"No, she wouldn't know where she is."

"She's a dumb human from the twenty-first century."

"I like the dumb humans from the twenty-first century. They think they're so smart, so tech-savvy, so sophisticated and mature."

"But they make the best screamers."

"She's only screamed once. She isn't as much fun as our usual pick-me-ups."

"Wait. You're too impatient."

"She'll scream and loudly too."

"She tried to scream before her first scream. Didn't you hear?"

"That was no scream, not like that computer engineer guy."

"I understand the problem. She's—what do they call them in their now time?—administrative assistant! She's an administrative assistant, too stupid to know where she is."

"She probably watches so much television, she probably thinks she's in one of those reality shows."

"What's that really stupid one?"

"Punk, something?"

"No. There's another one."

"Well, I don't care. Let's tell her together." The other two join in as he says, "You're not in a reality show, dumb human." The one on the left, my left, leers at me. I can see it even through the whiteness of his skin suit. I say nothing. If they're not human, what are they? They have human shapes. Maybe all aliens are human shaped, the ultimate Nature design. A giggle hiccups into my throat. I swallow it back. Fear and anger replace it, flaming up from my chest. I try automatically to suppress them because my bosses don't take kindly to their employees being angry.

"So you know what this is?"

A kidnapping, you moron, I think. Hey, my thoughts are back in my head when they're supposed to be. And I'm still angry. This is not good. If they see it, they will exact retribution. I swallow carefully.

"We take people to the future."

"And play with them."

"We can time travel to any now time we want to go."

"And whenever we want."

"Because we're the exclusive."

"No one can touch our sires."

"Means no one can touch us."

"Especially a girl."

"Especially you."

"You can't escape us."

"You saw us, you heard us, you could've escaped then before we took you."

"Medieval humans would've."

"They were no fun."

"They were always running and hiding before we got close."

"But you're like all the rest of your now time's dumb humans."

"Too stupid to notice what's going on around you."

"You stepped right into our trap."

"Fun."

The three giggle through their suits, which don't muffle or stifle the sound at all. I loathe them. And instantly shove that emotion down. Terror pops up to replace it.

"So, administrative assistant, we've been watching you,"

"Watching you doing the same thing day after day."

"We wanted to see what it's like to take someone who does the same thing day after day."

"We've only taken the exclusive so far, the what-you-call powerful men."

"Not the antecedents, Guy."

"No, we can't change our future, right?"

"We almost did when we went to the past past."

"That upset the university."

"They tried to eject us."

"Sire stopped them," Guy retorts.

"Guy's Sire accepts."

"He knows boys will be boys."

They giggle in unison.

"He lets us play in your now time."

"He owns stocks so we could."

"The university agreed to agree."

The three chortle.

"We took a few girls you think are powerful," the one next to Guy adds.

The three shudder.

"But we liked taking men that thought they were powerful, rich, and indispensable, the ones who talked about their work to anyone who would listen, who bought tickets to Leafs games but never went, who were considered bright by your dumb human standards. What you call 'hot stuff.'"

"They weren't such hot stuff once we got them in our lab."

Laughter flies out of them, assaulting me, disappearing into those white walls.

I can't help it. I shiver. Yet ... I don't. The shivering is turned back by the suit and chills my core. I wonder: do these suits protect us from whatever is going on, create a barrier between our bodies and the outside world? Their suits let the boys move and talk. This ship has moved without them touching anything, acting on anything. They blink, they nod, and things happen. Can they read my thoughts since the ship can read theirs? I shiver again.

"So we figure a robot like you,"

"Who does your master's bidding,"

"Who never thinks,"

"Should be even more fun."

"But you aren't."

"So far."

I see them pout through their white suits.

We stare at each other in silence for awhile. Is it minutes? Hours? There is no hum, no change in smell. The walls continue to coruscate less and less, and I continue to feel my molecules reforming more than disappearing.

"So listen up, dumb human,"

"If you want to live."

"You have to do what we say."

"Accept?"

They assume I say yes. After all, they have me.

"We're going to get to The Hangar soon."

"The Hangar Master controls the place. He docks the time ships and clocks us in and out."

"We're going to tell him that you're a sick sister."

They lower their heads to examine me as if they can see through the suit my white skirt with its jaunty red roses on it, my plain navy T-shirt, the old red cardigan covered in wooly pills, my plain black pumps with their small heels. Office wear. I feel dirty. They turn to each other.

"We're going to tell him you dressed for blending in to the twenty-first century for a school project you're doing."

"You think that will satisfy him?"

"He isn't in your sire's pocket anymore, Guy."

"Don't worry. It worked last time."

"He'll remember."

"He never forgets."

"She'll convince him."

They turn to me again, and the one they call "Guy" growls at me: "You're going to convince him."

I don't move. They take my assent for granted. And to be honest, I cannot move anyway, not even my lips. I've never felt so terrified before. I had no idea this kind of terror existed. My fight and flight system has decided that to remain frozen is the best way, to obey is the best way. Obedience is natural to me. Not thinking feels more comfortable. I suddenly remember a story Peggy told me of how those who remained frozen on the *Titanic* were the ones who drowned.

I don't feel so good.

I can't fight physiology, my physiology.

I can't fight this ship.

I can't fight them.

Maybe I should comply at ... The Hangar. That's what I do at work anyway: comply.

They start talking again, one after the other.

"We will do all the talking to the Hangar Master."

"Remember, you're too sick to talk."

"You look green anyway."

They laugh and laugh and laugh.

"I've never seen anyone so green before that it shows through the timesuit."

"Maybe she will be fun."

"A sugary section of pie to get her past the Hangar Master."

They give me my instructions; they do that group hug thing again; the ship does that transparent-coruscating thing again; my body fills with static cling again; and then we stop.

The boys raise their hands as one, and the hoods are back off their heads and lying on their backs. So is mine.

I feel dizzy, as if I'd jumped from one reality into another.

The one who blinked first, the one they call "Guy," blinks again, a shimmer appears and disappears before me, and they tell me to stand up.

My legs won't hold me. Guy strides toward me and grabs me, the other two right behind him. The three pull me up. Guy goes before us as the other two adjust my arms over their shoulders; they half-walk, half-drag me through the wall that was to the left of where I was sitting.

I want to upchuck.

"Name?"

The bark that reminds me so much of my boss jerks my head up. A barrel-chested man stands in front of us, legs firmly apart, holding a pen and clipboard on his massive stomach, one hand clutching the top of the board where the clip is, glaring at us.

"Guy Van Der Haguey."

"I mean the ship, wise Guy."

He moves his hand to grab the side of the board and drops hand and board to his side as he leans forward to glare right into Guy's face. I stare at his hand, like a mouse at a snake. That's not a clipboard. It's brown, it's slim, but there's no metal clip at the top. It's not even the same material. It's—

My eyes widen, and I drop my head to hide my startlement.

"*The Rainment*," Guy says.

The Hangar Master lifts his board again, taps it with his pen. "Good. You got the name of the ship you stole right."

"We didn't steal it—"

A glare halts his lie.

Guy continues, "We stole it; we had to steal it. Maggie here was in trouble. She went to the twenty-first century on a field trip for school."

"Girls don't go to school. Try again, wise Guy."

I lift my head slightly in surprise. Girls don't go to school? Where am I? Is this Afghanistan? I surreptitiously look around. But all I can see is the Hangar Master. His bulk fills my entire field of vision.

"They do when Sire says so."

"No, they don't."

"You have me, Hangar Master. She came with me. I had to fit in to the twenty-first century, and girls ...," he halts. The Hangar Master waves away his words as if in shared pain. Guy says, "So I told her to come. It was my field project. But you know girls. They lose stuff, they can't remember anything. She got the twenty-first century clothes right, but she lost her own and couldn't be herself for the trip back. I told her not to lose them."

"Why weren't they left in the ship?"

"You know girls. They do stupid things. I can't explain what they do."

The Hangar Master nods. Guy is bringing him around.

"So then she gets herself sick."

The Master takes a step backward.

"You're supposed to declare a quarantine."

"I meant to. But she's not really sick. She's only time sick. Girls can't handle time travel like us humans. I gave her a chance. But my prof was right. They can't hack our work."

The Hangar Master nods and steps back toward us.

"Take her to medical." He taps the board, which spits out a thin sliver of something that's white and flexible. Boards don't spit out slivers of anything. Fear freezes the scream in my throat. Oh God, get me out of here. I want my boss!

"Put this on her."

Guy takes the rectangular white sliver and slaps it on my chest. A shimmer appears and disappears right before my eyes.

"Take her straight to medical, Guy."

"I will, Hangar Master," Guy smirks.

The Hangar Master turns to the side and sweeps us out of the area with a warning to leave the suits in Rerobing and to go through Disinfecting.

I'm glad the boys are still holding me up and are dragging me out, even if it is further away from home, for my legs are jelly, my mind a frozen slushie, and I'm tasty prey. But as Father always said, "sometimes biding one's time is the best way."

"And don't forget, you have a twenty-four-hour moratorium on The Transporter. Don't think of taking the easy way," the Hangar Master yells after us.

3

3011

ARE we really going to take the vector transport, Guy?" the boy holding me up on the left asks.

"Only girls ride those," sneers the boy on my right.

"And time travellers. Anyone sees us, they'll know when we've been."

The faces of the other two reflect dawning hope at the expected jealousy aimed at them. Guy continues: "Sire explained the consequences if we take The Transporter immediately after using the time ship, travelling as much as we have. Boys, we," he lays emphasis on "we" as he looks over at me, "don't want to experience that. We have no choice but to listen to the Hangar Master."

Their chorus of groans accompany me as they half drag, half walk me through the Hangar. I find the floor fascinating. It's like glass yet has an effervescence that's unlike the sparkles buried in granite; it's like sparkles bubbling underneath the surface of champagne, reacting to our steps.

"Here," the boy on my left snarls. I'm dropped and almost knock my head as it flies backward, and I land with a jolt on a seat that emerges from the white wall of the continuing corridor we're in. They strip off their white suits while I watch immobile. Guy nudges the boy nearest him, and they smirk at me before Guy leans forward into my face and mimes slowly the words: "Take it off." The three liquidate into laughter. Moved into action, I scramble at my suit ineffectually with shaky hands, wondering if it's okay that thing the Hangar Master had Guy slap on me will come off, then not caring if it does. It won't be me affected, I think as I continue to struggle. Finally, my muscles thaw, the suit releases its seams and opens, and I stand to shove it down and off my shoes. But the suit holds on and takes them anyway. I reach down into the legs, into the feet of the suit, and yank my shoes out. I glare at the offending suit; a small sound pulls my head up, and I see the three hanging their suits up on the wall. The wall sucks them in with a whispery slurp. Creep me out. I leave mine on the sparkling floor.

They grab my arms and haul me up. All of a sudden, I want out of this place. I struggle against their grips, keeping myself away from the creepy walls. They laugh. I relax every muscle in my body, and think heavy thoughts. They almost lose their hold but regain it before I can grasp freedom. And then I realize: the whole thing is futile. Where am I going to go? These white walls that suck up clothes and these floors that spark into life underneath my feet are not my world. Literally, not my world.

We continue along our journey in the snaking corridor and stop at a ninety-degree turn. The white wall in front of us loses its hold on its surface molecules. The boys stop, and I bump into Guy, unable to take my eyes off the morphing wall.

"Watch it."

What does he think I'm doing? The molecules spin faster and faster, their energy reaching out to each other, merging into a golden light that expands toward us, bathes us, engulfs, turns red. Guy is just a diminished outline ahead of me.

Suddenly the glow is gone. The corridor is the corridor, and they're dragging me around the ninety-degree corner by my arms. I'm trying to take back my breath as my mind struggles to understand what has just happened. I hear the Hangar Master's words repeat in my head: "Disinfecting" because we already took off our suits. The corridor ends abruptly at a wall, which promptly vaporizes as we approach. I gasp. I pull at my arms to free them. I pilot my legs backward, to no avail. The boys laugh, "Dumb human. It's a door, that thing you walk through every day."

"They all do that."

"It's like they haven't seen a door before."

"They haven't. Not a real one."

"They have those awkward things you have to pull."

"Or push. You can never tell which: pull or push. Some of their builders want you to pull, some to push."

"They can't make up their minds which way a door should swing."

"Dumb humans," they sneer in chorus.

I lean backward, letting my body go limp; they drag me through that ... that unstable wall anyway and into the sun.

My eyes squeeze against the sharp light.

As they adjust, I open my lids bit by bit until I see we're outside in a place so sunny that the light is almost white. The sunlight cuts the shadow of the building like a knife and reveals every vein in the marble monolithic wall that rises across from us, blocking all sight of what lies outside this place, declaring in thick platinum "Toronto 3011." I try to turn around to see the height of the place we left, but the boys are ruthless and yank me forward. They pull me toward an elliptical thing the size of a Nissan car that sits on a smooth white surface that flows from in front of the building into the distance to our left. The thing is white on the bottom, its whiteness a mirror of the white surface it's sitting on, as glossy as ... the road. It's a road, I tell myself. I know roads. But I don't know this thing that sits on what must be a road. It seems to have no top; it's a half egg that floats. I gulp and shut my eyes. When I open them, I see the thing better and realize the top is clear, clearer than glass. I can perceive its outline now, but it's so clear, it's as if it doesn't exist ... I guess this is the ... the transport thing they talked about since we're walking toward it.

"Can't you walk!" the boy on the left barks at me. I don't answer him; I think rag doll thoughts. Score one for me. But my bravery doesn't last long. The car is sliding sideways toward us. None of the boys have keys or fobs; their hands are visible with nothing in them. How is the car moving? Is it, like, alive? I look up at the boy nearest me—his eyes have turned as black as Polaroid sunglasses. I look at the others: their eyes too are black. I forget about being a rag doll as adrenaline surges through me, giving me strength. I break free. I run backward, but as I turn, I see I'm heading to the disappearing, glowing building. I run out of my pumps as I swivel sharply and head in the direction the road flows. My flight doesn't last long. Long hands grab me and hoist me into the air. I kick the air, and laughter rings at me.

"They always do that."

"I don't know why."

"It's not like they haven't seen vector transports moving."

"They call them cars."

"Don't correct me. I know what they call them. It's a dumb human name. I don't use dumb human names."

"You got that right, Guy. Some don't even need keys to open or start their cars."

"But it always happens."

"They freak. Hey, this one's heavy."

The boy on the right stops, drops me, and I land on my knees. Guy grabs my chin and puts his face into mine: "They freak, like you dumb human."

"Aren't you human?" I force through my lips.

"We're not dumb humans, we're real humans," Guy retorts as he lets go of my chin. "Bring her. Time is wasting. I don't want the prof to find her."

The right one grabs my shoes, throws them at me. I stand up and slip my feet into my pumps and follow the two boys who follow Guy to the levitating vector transport, whose side facing us vanishes as Guy reaches it. Both the white part and the clear part vanish, revealing two soft white benches that face each other, one in the front, one in the back, with a generous foot well in the centre, flat, no middle hump. All my adrenaline has flushed away, and I cannot react except in my thoughts. I want to go home. I've seen solid walls that vanish already; it should be old hat. It's not! I want to go home. Tears prickle my eyes, and I blink rapidly, knowing tears will equal greater humiliation. They pick me up and throw me onto the right-side seat, or is that the front seat that faces backward or the back seat that faces frontward? They climb in, Guy sitting in the seat facing me, the boys sitting on either side of me. And the side of the vector transport reappears. Guy does that slow blink thing, and the car settles down before surging forward with a smoothness so seamless it's a moment before I realize the monolithic marble wall is moving backward. I clutch the seat on either side of me and stifle a scream. Guy grins. The car shoots forward without a sound and reaches faster-than-highway speeds. The vivid blue sky and merciless sun scream through the clear top and strike my eyes. I'm dizzy and blinded.

After a while, I let go of the seat and, keeping my head down, pull my red cardigan closer around my chest. I hug myself. I'm in need of warmth. I open my eyes fully as they become accustomed to the sunlight here. I raise my head cautiously. I have to squint, but I can see. I focus my gaze on the landscape in front of us, not daring to turn my head to look out a side window like one usually does in a car.

The road winds between trees, no other vehicle on the road, no other person on the road, on the verge, or in the trees. The trees are so neatly planted, like the gardens in Versailles when I visited with my parents during one summer vacation. Their leaves are the gold of pure gold not green. All one shade of gold, not the various shades of autumn gold or bronze. Every so often, the trees have silver leaves. The trees are so quiet. The boys are so quiet. This thing is so quiet that I can hear atoms hissing time away in my ears. I focus harder on the trees, and I discern a pattern of when the trees with the silver leaves and onyx trunks will appear among the trees with the gold leaves and mahogany trunks. There are no leaves anywhere on the road ahead. Its surface isn't littered or mottled or black or concrete. It's white, like ... like ... I've seen this kind of material before, I'm sure. Ceramic? No, like Limoges china, the set my mother bought during our visit to France. Strange to think of a road being made of Limoges.

The flowing road straightens, and the horizon is a haze of unending trees and road. I turn my eyes away from that mirage and focus on Guy and notice how straight his clothing is. Straight across the shoulders; straight sleeves that end in a sharp horizontal line at the wrists. The fabric hangs crisp yet soft straight down his chest from an elliptical neckline and ends in a sharp horizontal cut. Crisp leggings that don't have one crease or seam encase his legs. I lean over to the side a bit to stare at the side of his legs. He frowns. I straighten up. His leggings have no seams. And neither does his tunic. They look like each are made from one piece of cloth with no discernible flies, buttons, seams, or zippers. I remember how their hoods had sealed to the rest of their white suits in the ship and shiver. I drop my eyes to the floor. His leggings end precisely at his shoes, the edge smooth and straight. His shoes look like normal white loafers, but not as cheesy as what men wear at my office.

His shoes' soft, soft material reminds me of expensive suede but it has that same slightly glowing quality as the vector transport and the road. His clothes are white as well with shadings of grey that emphasize the straight lines. I strain my peripheral vision to see if the boys are dressed the same. They are.

We emerge from the trees and cross a road perpendicular to the one we're on. Now instead of trees on either side of us, there are buildings. White buildings. White buildings rising straight up like vertical rectangles. White buildings of the same height, width, and seemingly depth. White buildings with no windows, no doors, only smooth surfaces with softly rounded corners. White buildings exactly the same distance from each other, exactly across from each other, exactly the same distance from the road. I blink. The road isn't a road like I know it; it ends at the front walls of the buildings. There's no demarcation of road from sidewalk. There are no sidewalks. The road is one smooth, glossy surface of creamy opaque white to the buildings' lucent icy white edges. I watch building after building slide backward by us, refusing to see what my eyes are telling me: their surfaces aren't exactly solid. They bleed into the air around them, and as they bleed they turn from looking like solid ice to icy fog white lit from inside. Lucent with a sci-fi edge. I shudder and turn my gaze inwards, huddling my body into itself.

Our vector transport slows down to city speeds. We're approaching another crossroad, a busy one, full of transports like ours. Yet there are no traffic lights. I brace myself. These are Toronto cars; we're going to get hit. Then I think: I bet medical science can cure injuries in a heartbeat here. I relax. Then I think: but will these boys take me to a hospital? After all, they see me as their personal lab rat. I brace myself again. Our car crosses the intersection without hesitation, deftly sliding in between two oncoming cars in one lane and another two oncoming cars in the other lane. I cannot believe it. I twist around to look at the cars we whizzed through. No, not cars, vector transports. I twist back to face forward again. The boys seem bored and don't react to my astonishment this time. This time.

I relax myself and refocus on the scene outside. I think about how there are no traffic lights and look around actively, moving only my eyeballs. There are no poles or wires, no visible sources of power. The road we were on has become one half of a wider road, like University Avenue with its wide median. The median is like a platform that's arisen out of the road, and it's filled with sculptures. They are chaotic in their materials of grey soapstone and purple granite, in their curving shapes and various heights. Water slithers between them, sparkling from the excruciating sunlight hitting it. People are walking beside them, as well as on the outside edges of the road beside the streaming vector transports. Some ride on Segways, those zippy self-propelled two-wheelers trendy Californians ride, but these have clear handles and white wheels. They are closer to the transports than the pedestrians. The transports remain as equidistant from them as from each other. The people are dressed like the boys. Not one is walking with another or riding Segways together; not one looks at any of the others. Not one notices us, although the clear top of our car extends almost down to seat level, and I stick out in my non-white clothing.

We continue to travel at the same pace, never slowing down at intersections, no matter how busy, yet always remaining at the same distance from the other traffic, whether in front or behind us or crossing us. The more we travel into the city, the more buildings rise up closer to each other, the more cars are on the road, the more people are walking between and alongside the buildings and roads. The road narrows, and I can see that what I thought were men and women are really all men.

I blink.

That can't be.

Where are the women?

I feel conspicuous. Suddenly the CN Tower rises into view. I reflexively turn my head to see it better. It's old and tired-looking in its concrete facade and outdated light show. It looks like a poor cousin at a rich person's banquet.

Guy twists around to look where I'm gawking.

"I don't know why we keep that relic," says one of the boys beside me.

"Sire says it's a link to our past."

"It reminds we of where we've been."

"Who cares about history," Guy states derisively.

"We young don't. But the old generation do."

"They always do. They say we'll be the same. We too won't want to get rid of it."

"Never."

We stop. Yet I don't jerk forward like when Father used to brake the car. The slowing down, the stopping is smooth, oh so smooth. The boys wrench me away from the sight of the familiar as they hustle me through the side of the car and into the building we've stopped at. The people walking close by on the road don't notice because the transport has stopped right at the door. They drag me so quickly through it and the corridors that I cannot register my surroundings. With a resounding sigh of relief, they push me into a room. They slam the door shut.

I jump.

It's the first sound I've heard in this quiet city, other than the boys' voices.

I stare at it. It's a door, a real door in the wall. It even has a handle, but then it's gone, and so is the door. It's another part of the wall. But that's the only way this room resembles the transport and what I saw outside. This room is filled with stuff. There's a blackboard perpendicular to the door wall. It's black with a wooden frame on wooden legs, and there's chalk on its ledge. There are simple dressers with straight handles and ordinary counters and chairs flung around in worn white and dented wood and scratched metal. The old lives here. Just like the university I went to.

4

OOPS

"SO what do we do?"

"The usual?"

"No ... I think—"

The doorway appears, and the door opens. An older man enters with his head down, shrugging into a white lab coat, reading a slim iPad-like tablet in his hand. His coat is not crumpled and out of shape like the ones I saw back in university. It's as seamless as the tunic and fat leggings he wears. The collar is crisp, yet not stiff like a starched collar would be. The requisite pockets seem to emerge out of the fabric like the seats did from the ship's walls. But unlike his clothes, his face is rumpled, especially a rough-cut moustache that dips on either side of his generous lips. He doesn't see me at first because Guy has taken a fast step over to shield me. He bumps into Guy, and his head comes up.

He asks with a displeased frown on his face: "What are you boys doing here?"

"We thought we'd come in to do extra work," one of the boys says.

The older man's eyebrows shoot up as he queries: "Extra? Listen up. I told my daughter she could come here today to service her man's needs, to be nearby whenever and wherever he needs her. I didn't appreciate you confining her to yourselves last time. It is within your rights, I'm aware, and she cannot refuse you. But I'm your prof. If you don't do what I say, I'm going to flunk you this time. Her man is important to my work, and I don't want him discommoded and throwing off my research. The granting agency is already displeased with my research being put back one-quarter because of your poaching. They won't tolerate a second setback. So stay away. Accept?"

Guy and the boys nod. The prof steps forward toward Guy angrily, "Accept?"

Guy takes a step back and almost bumps into me. "Accept," he says.

"Good," and that's when the prof sees me.

"Who. Is. That?" he asks, pointing at me with an enraged finger.

"Who?" Guy asks innocently, trying to hide me. The boys flank him so that I'm even less visible.

"I saw her. That—that girl was not wearing modern clothes. She had a skirt on, for capital's sake. And something long-sleeved. And was that red I saw?"

The boys hesitate, and then as one all three step to the side to reveal me to the prof.

"I don't believe it!" he explodes. "Did we not have this conversation before? Did we not tell you that you couldn't do this sort of thing again? Did we not have all your sires here? Did we not talk to all of them about how you could not keep bringing people from the past here? Did we not agree it was getting more and more dangerous? Did we not get it through your dumb skulls that the more people you brought out of that timeline, the more the statistical probability that you'd pick one to ruin our time, our history, our rights, our very lives?

"You could resurrect the feminist movement of the twentieth century, the one that died through complacency and tolerance of patriarchal cultures! Those very cultures that gave rise to our society today, that showed us how we can oppress while saying because we let girls work, they still have equal rights. Girls agreed with that as much as we did. They helped our antecedents create our society. Our society. Remember? They established girls had their rights. In the name of what they called 'tolerance' and not wanting to as they said 'butt into other people's business' and not seeing their new-to-their-hemisphere sisters as one of them, they let our antecedents insidiously change everyone. They even took on the idea that their bodies were their power. Not their minds."

A chuckle erupts from his belly and interrupts his tirade. The boys and he snort and laugh and clutch their stomachs—until he suddenly stops and resumes. He waggles his finger at them: "Never forget girls did our work for us back then! They helped us put them in the place they belong, beneath us. Only a small segment stayed free. Who were they, Guy? Who saw too late?"

Guy shrugs and yawns.

The prof snaps his fingers under Guy's nose. Guy jumps and eyes those snapping fingers warily. "Access your memory files, Guy!"

"Middle class."

"Middle class. Only middle class girls had freedom, but they didn't share it, did they, Guy?"

Guy shakes his head.

"What happened when they finally understood?"

"They ran," Guy responds sulkily. The prof waits. Guy continues, "They ran west, across the Pacific. To their ancestral land. We should go there next," he ends with a smirk to his boys.

The prof ignores the last and picks up the history lesson: "But it wasn't far enough, was it? Our antecedents had spread; no one could hide from their touch. Do you think they'd do that again once they become educated? Once they learn our history? Learn how oppression became okay? Learn how looking after only their group was their downfall? Be exposed to what was? Did we not agree to stop this? How can you not learn!" he ends on a vocal shot. He pauses only to suck air in through his raggedy moustache. "We have told you and told you that these field trips of yours exposes our population to Parliament-knows-what contaminations, what viruses and prions and ideas. One day we will have an epidemic that our nanos cannot control because of your dumb-boy antics. Aren't you old enough now to stop these hijinks? This cannot be tolerated anymore. Your sires promised this university—promised me—that you would not repeat your mischief again. Are their promises worthless?" He takes a step toward Guy. "Are they to be sneered at?" He steps closer. "Do you feel that because of the no-fail policy that you can do whatever you want and never suffer the consequences?" He is now toe-to-toe with Guy, who is leaning back. It's rather nice seeing Guy afraid. "Your sires put their university stocks on the line," he roars into Guy's face. "They promised that you would not do this again on pain of losing their stocks. And you know what that means, don't you? Don't you!" This question is not rhetorical as he fairly spits it in Guy's face.

Guy opens his mouth, but only a croak ribbids from his throat. I wonder if those nanos have fled him; I wonder what nanos are. They sound like miniature scrubbers whirling around in his cells, cleaning them. Too bad they had not—?

Guy clears his throat and tries again. "It means," he clears his throat once more. "It means that they won't be allowed to participate in university affairs again."

"And?"

The frog still sticks in Guy's throat, and he squeaks, "And ..." He clears his froggy throat fully and speaks in full volume as if reciting some legalese that means nothing in practice. "And it means that we forfeit the no-fail policy. We can be failed."

The second boy speaks, "No, Guy. It means we'd have to change universities. We still can't be failed, but we'd have to start all over again."

The third boy shrugs as if saying, been there.

The prof growls, "Do you think this is no big deal? Your sires' companies rely on their university connections to profit. It would be shameful for them to have to go to the government for equalization payments. A company that can't stand on its own—

"Do you want to bring that kind of shame on your sires?" His voice rises. "On this university?" he shouts. "On me?" he yells right into Guy's nose.

Guy bluffs, "It won't happen."

"You think it won't because it didn't happen last time?"

Guy looks at the other two and silently smirks.

"I saw that. It will this time, Guy. It will this time. Did you get her to medical?"

"No." Guy is back to normal. Somehow he has won. Some things don't change. The privileged boys get away with everything, I think sourly. And what was that about equalization payments? Isn't equalization what the Feds do for the provinces, I ask myself. But now they do that for companies? Seems strange, like companies are governments and are supposed to be equal. Yet here is Guy, getting away with bringing me here. I hope this prof will send me back home, especially as I really need to pee and there was no bathroom in that ship. Good thing I forgot my latté.

The prof does that blink thing and speaks into the air, "Roger. Get down here. I need a medical, stat.... This cannot wait.... The boys did it again."

We all stand in position, and then the door opens out of the wall. Another man in another crisp white lab coat walks in. He asks, "Who do you want me to scan?"

"Her," the prof says as he points at me with a shaking forefinger. I feel filthy.

Roger stares at me as if I have three hooves growing out of my head. "What is she wearing?" he chokes out. "She's so ... so ..."

"Roger, I forgot. You haven't met one of the boys' prizes yet. Luckily, I've caught them before they could get started and fling whatever pathogens she's harbouring into the air and onto all the surfaces. Last time we had to spend the whole day disinfecting every surface and purifying the air in the entire building. The Head was not impressed."

"I see."

"She's from the twenty-first century. It's their favourite time, after they were kicked out of the medieval era, for reasons I cannot fathom. It was a bland century. Get to it, Roger, and stop gawking. She'll submit properly, despite what her garish overdressing may lead you to think, but only because she's out of her element. The faster you get to it, the less trouble we'll have."

That goads Roger forward. He puts his hand into his pocket, pulls it out seemingly empty, and aims his palm forward at me while he does that blink thing at the same time. I blink too, and into focus comes a tiny white hexagonal tattoo affixed to the middle of his palm. A display appears out of thin air to my right. It's not transparent like they show in sci-fi shows. It looks as solid as me.

I scream and jump away from it. Roger screams and jumps away from me. Guy laughs hysterically. The other two join in, the three bending over and slapping their thighs. The prof tuts impatiently, "Roger, get on with it. She won't bite. You," he says pointing at me. "Don't move."

I nod weakly, thankful that at least I didn't wet myself. Close call though. I wrap my arms around my stomach, and Roger looks over to the prof helplessly. The prof barks, "Put your arms to the side." I let go and let them hang. They start to tremble, and my legs start to shake in sympathy. Roger takes a tentative step back toward me, holds his palm back up. He too is shaking. Seeing that, I feel reassured and stop shaking. He doesn't, yet he manages to execute his action. He raises his palm to my eye level and waves his hand from side to side, all the time keeping his palm open and aimed right at me while he watches the display to my right. The display is right beside me, yet I cannot feel the proximity of an object, I hear no sound, no hum, I have no sense of static electricity, I smell nothing. I only see it in my peripheral vision. I don't want to look at it full on.

Roger finishes the scan and says, "She has a cold."

"Governor!" the prof exclaims. "Get her behind the charged curtain now, you dumb humans." The boys hustle me toward the area to my left (right of the door) by making shooing motions toward me. Suddenly they don't want to touch me. I watch them perplexed. Where am I supposed to go?

Guy hisses at me, "Move."

"Where?"

"There, you dumb human!"

"You already got it you know," I say. "You already touched me. And I don't have a cold. I'm fine. Anyway, weren't we disinfected?"

Roger intones, "You received the virus; it is incubating. Disinfection doesn't have your variant in its protocol. We will have to tell them, once we're finished here." He turns to the prof, "We all have to get decontaminated." He blinks and speaks into the air, "Merkle, I need you to bring a virus decontamination unit to Room Two-Twenty-Two. Code red.... Code red, I said.... Why do I have to repeat myself? I expect you here, stat."

We stand in our frozen tableau until the door swings open and a white-haired man walks in, a transparent cart moving by his side. He is wearing red. My jaw drops. The fabric is the same as the boys', the cut is the same. He is even wearing a lab coat, but it and his clothing is all cherry red. A beautiful colour. I'm so relieved to see colour. He walks to the middle of the room, and we shuffle out of his way. The cart lowers itself to the floor, and the man touches the top of the cart. The cart becomes a red cube that stretches higher than the tallest of the men and wider than the cart's original material and shape and the three men standing together. I breathe faster and desperately try to bring it under control. They seem to have forgotten I'm here, and I like that. The surface of the red square expands outward in all directions: to each side, upward, downward, backward, forward. The surface is fuzzy yet solid looking. No one else moves, and so I don't either. As the surface expands closer and closer to me, I have to fight the urge to run. My legs tremble under the strain to stay still. It's in front of me; it's at my nose tip; it's through me. Everything looks red, and I feel ... nothing.

Suddenly the cart is itself again. The man blinks; the cart levitates; and the two leave the room.

Roger turns to Guy, "How long has she been here?"

"We got here during last class."

"Then only this room needs to be done. The decontamination was sufficient. But if we don't get her behind the curtain now, we will have to repeat the procedure. Even so, we will have to let The Head know that the university has been compromised and that we need to scan the entire premises." He turns to the prof, "The boys will have to show us their route, especially what they touched along the way so that we can focus our scans in the rest of this quadrant and measure the spread rate. Why is she not behind the curtain yet?"

Suddenly one of the boys rushes forward, grabs my arm, and drags me with his momentum to an area on the right side of the door, which faces the blackboard. He flings me onto a chair, and I almost fall backward. I windmill my arms trying to regain my balance, and the chair rights itself back onto its front feet. The boy leaps backward, blinks, and a shimmer appears and disappears before my eyes. I stand up and leaning as far forward as I can, I reach my hand out tentatively, fingers outstretched. I feel a wall. It's hard like Sue's granite countertop, yet I see nothing between me and them.

"It's a charged curtain. It will keep us safe from you," the prof intones.

5

THEIR PLAN FOR ME

"ROGER, take the boys and have them show you their route while I stay here with Guy."

I watch Roger carefully to see how he opens the disappearing door with no handle. As he approaches the wall, the door emerges from it and swings open on its own. It must be like those doors for the disabled or automatic ones at Shopper's. I look for the little thingy that usually sits above the door to sense people coming, but the walls around the door are smooth. The door itself is smooth. The highly polished wooden floor near it is smooth as well. The two boys listlessly follow the marching Roger out the door, and it swings shut on them then merges back into the wall.

It's the least puzzling and frightful thing in this whole day.

Morning.

Whatever.

Sunlight is pouring into the room from somewhere, though I haven't seen any windows. I look up. No skylights either. Aside from these anomalies, this place feels the most familiar to me.

There's wood; real furniture; walls that don't ooze their surfaces into the air. Nothing too weird.

I return my gaze to eye level to stare through the invisible wall.

The prof and Guy are facing each other.

The prof is angry.

Guy is visibly controlling his face, trying not to look afraid.

The prof's back is to the door.

They are in profile to me.

I stare at them staring at each other.

The silence continues.

Chaucer's words snap into my brain from my English Lit past: "He was a verray parfit gentil knyght." Guy is the antithesis of Chaucer's description of the knight in *The Canterbury Tales*. And then I wonder: how can I understand this errant knight's language? I'd had to spend months and years learning to understand Chaucer's English, which was less distant from my time than Guy's time is. Guy's English should be as obscure to me as Chaucer's was when I first began reading him in university. I had thought verray was very. It wasn't: it was truly. Truly, truly—

Bang, the door opens, interrupts my thoughts, and hits the bench behind it. Roger plows through with the boys following looking slightly sick.

Roger barks, "We have to get Merkle back to decontaminate the entire route. I don't trust these boys when they say they rushed her here and didn't touch anything. I had them show me the route and followed them. They claimed they touched nothing, even now they claim it, but I saw them touch the walls, the tables in the foyer, chairs careless students left wherever they had been sitting. Merkle's going to have to decontaminate the entire outside, front foyer, and hall up to and past this door to be safe. Luckily, this hall is not trafficked after first class begins. We don't have to worry about secondary contamination

...," Roger pauses and eyes Guy. A slow smile backlights his face. He adds, "I think we should infect them and let them fight it off on their own."

"You can't do that. Sire won't let you," Guy squeals. In front of these men, he's nothing but a jellyfish. They can see it, can't they?

"You've said that before. You know we can't."

"There, see," Guy retorts, relief flooding his face.

"Accidents happen," Roger retorts back. Guy opens his mouth. Closes it. Roger waits for him to say something. We wait. Roger blinks, speaks into the air, "Merkle we need the hall decontaminated. Here are the parameters ... You have them? ... Good. Let us know when you're done."

I was wrong. Weirdness is in this room too. Roger sent him nothing. How could Merkle see parameters? I drag my hands down my face. I don't care anymore. I'm tired. I want to nap. I want to hide. I don't want to be here. I even want to be back in the office with my boss treating me like an idiot; I so don't want to be here in this awful time.

The prof says, "After Merkle decontaminates, we'll have to confer with the Time History Professor."

"Yes," Roger replies.

They all stand in their positions. I slowly fall onto a bench angled against the side wall, pull my feet and legs up onto it as quietly as I can, put my head on my crooked arm, curl into a ball, and watch.

Suddenly, the prof and Roger nod. The prof blinks and speaks to no one. "Professor Neutron, we have a problem.... Yes. The same as before.... I appreciate that." He focusses on Roger, "He's coming." Roger nods, and they all continue to remain in position.

The door swings open, and in walks another man with chestnut hair, cappuccino skin, white tunic and leggings like them all, but instead of a white lab coat, he's wearing a very light, greyish-blue one. If all their clothing and walls were not so white or grey-white, you couldn't even tell it was blue. It's a relief, again, to see colour even faint colour.

The new prof glowers at the old prof, "Who'd they bring this time?" The old prof nods at me, and the new one strides over and halts all of a sudden. He glares at me. I stare back, tiredly. He whips around and bellows, "How long has she been behind the charged curtain?"

"Since Roger got here and after Merkle decontaminated," the old prof replies.

"Very well. Do you know who she is?"

No one answers.

"Guy? You did do your background diligence?"

"We watched her. I know where she works. She's a nobody. We chose an unimportant dumb human this time. I—"

"What century. Your usual?"

"The twenty-first century. I like it there," Guy replies defensively. His whole body swells and his back lengthens. "She's what they call an admin assistant. The dumbest of those dumb humans."

"To whom?"

Guy's body shrinks back into itself, "I don't know," he mumbles.

"You know the company of course."

Guy looks at the other two boys, who look away. "I ..." Suddenly, Guy expands his chest like a belligerent peacock. "I don't remember," he pronounces.

The new prof says incredulously, "You don't remember?!" It's like Guy had said "I don't know how to pee," the new prof sounds so astonished. I move my head into a better position to watch.

"We didn't take notes on that."

"We? Don't you mean 'you' Guy? Those boys do what you want."

"I—I didn't take notes on that."

"What about your nanos? How can your memory fail?" The new prof narrows his eyes, "Did you look at the company sign? Its name?" Guy looks down, suddenly finding a crack in the wooden floor interesting, his belligerence deflating out of him. The new prof snorts, saying, "Sloppy work. We don't know if she's part of a company that matters or one of the thousands that had no lasting effect, now do we?"

"No. But—"

"No 'buts,' Guy. No 'buts.' I won't have sloppy work done by I students. Where was this company located?"

"Toronto."

"I know that it's Toronto. That's where you always go, Guy. You're too afraid to move in Space, only Time," the new prof roars. "Where?"

"Queen and ...," Guy mumbles the last part.

"Are you kidding me? You got her from that part of town and you don't take note of the company? Dumb human!" The new prof's roar has gone from loud to deafening. I try not to move to protect my ears. They may not be noticing me, but I don't want to take the chance. Guy's whole body is leaning backward by this time, but his feet remain planted. Not so the other two boys. Somehow they're as far away from Guy and the profs as they could be.

The new prof notices. "Get back here."

The two boys take a step toward him. He continues to glower at them. They creep back to stand beside but slightly behind Guy.

"So. We don't know who she is."

"Her name is Time."

"Time? Is this a joke?"

"No. No joke. Only her parents' joke."

I choke, open my mouth, then prudently snap it shut as Guy leers at me and the new prof turns his head to examine me like my old first-year psychology prof did when looking at his rats and deciding on their names. He liked to name them according to their fate, giggling that they were too unevolved to take on the fatality of their names, that he didn't need to worry about their names skewing his results. I never took psychology again. Stuck to English. The profs were nicer and not weird.

"Time," the new prof repeats my name. "What's your last name?" I don't answer. He harrumphs, and his eyes scan the air above him back and forth, back and forth. "There is no record of a female with the first name of Time in this space location other than birth, a late marriage (I get married?), and a death. She doesn't have children and is an only child. This is good." The prof lowers his eyes back to Guy, "Again, you are lucky, Guy. We can do with her what we've done with the others."

Guy grins broadly. The other two boys look at each other with great relief.

"This time, make sure it's done within one class span. You'll have to take The Transporter."

Their grins disappear. Guy says, "We can't do that. Not enough time has passed since our trip in *The Rainment*."

"We can't have anyone seeing you. This will be the last time you take someone from that century, Guy. There will be no going back. I am revoking your nano time badge."

"You can't do that! I'll talk to Sire."

"I can. And I will. I have absolute say in the matter. I am the Time History Professor, and one of the few powers I have over everyone else is control over the nano time badges. Upon your return, I will be deactivating it."

"What if she does something?" Guy asks with slight desperation.

"What is she going to do?" the new prof looks over derisively at me. "She has no bearing on the future, on our history. You said yourself that you chose someone who was unimportant."

"She may try to get back home."

"Her?" The new prof's contempt could not be more obvious. "A girl? A girl subservient even in her now time? Someone like her—how will she get home? No, you are looking for excuses."

The old prof interrupts, "He may have a point. Some of these dumb humans have spunk and persistence. Sometimes they do unexpected things, especially the girls. They had more power back then though they hadn't minded giving it back under the illusion of sex is power." They all turn their heads to inspect me. I try to look stupid and innocent and cowed. Not hard.

"Has anyone gotten home before?"

"One time, this man tried. We went back and fixed it," Guy answers.

"A man?"

They turn their heads away from me and contemplate each other. The new prof says to Guy, "You may keep your nano time badge. But I will restrict it to the time period you will take her back to." He speaks to the old prof, "Prepare *The Rainment*. We need to get her out of here. Now."

The Time History Professor storms out, the door opening up barely in time to let him through.

"What are you going to do with me?" I croak. No one hears me. I clear my throat and ask the question louder.

The prof says, "You don't need to know."

Guy cackles, "We're taking you to—"

"Enough!" The prof admonishes Guy. "Do you have the timeline?"

"The timeline is programmed into I's nano time badge."

"Good. We'll download it into *The Rainment*." The old prof examines Guy with dawning admiration and says, "You took a different ship last time, one that you had to program in a new timeline with each trip. Smart taking one where it's one input, and you're done. Always stealing the newest and best of the Time History Professor's ships, aren't you? I'm astonished he didn't call you on that. But boys will be boys. And we were once your age."

All three boys relax visibly.

He adds, "We will need to borrow four timesuits."

"Will they protect us in The Transporter?" one of the boys asks.

"You know the suits have nothing to do with The Transporter. No suit can protect you. Did you fall asleep in your space physics class again?"

"No. I ... I was just confirming."

The prof snorts, "Hoping more like."

"Nothing's going to protect us. But it's going to be harder on her with her old physiology," Guy ends on a chortle.

"Make no mistake, Guy. It's going to be hard on all of you. Your particles have not repropagated yet to a full complement. Take this as a lesson. And remember once the Time History Professor's orders are carried out with you using The Transporter, it will happen again. Precedence is everything."

"I'll talk to Sire. He won't let we use The Transporter."

"The Time History Professor already sent him a message. Did you not see it? Has your sire contacted you?"

"If he knows, he'll stop it."

The prof looks skeptical. "We must stop wasting time and prepare *The Rainment.*" He pauses a moment, "And if it's any consolation, I will see you receive immediate particle support on your return. We will speed up your nanos to stabilize your molecules and return you to a normal count."

Guy looks at the other boys, one at a time. In sync, they all three look toward the old prof and nod.

The prof leads, and the three boys follow him out the door. I bleat after them, "What about me? I have to go to the bathroom!"

6

BIKINI'S TIME MACHINE

THE door opens cautiously. A head peeks around, one with shiny black hair done up in swirls and twirls, white braids and ringlets hanging down both sides of her face. She scans the room and scuttles in, shutting the door behind her manually, quickly, quietly. She whips over to one of the dressers on the far side from me, rummages through it, pulls out something, and as she turns and jogs over to me, places it on her side and activates it. She's bathed in red, like that disinfecting beam. But what I can't take my eyes off is her dress or rather her undress. She's wearing a white bikini, the kind female beach volleyball players wear, except the fabric has a mutable quality to it as if it could change from opaque to transparent on a whim. The bottom band of the bra part of the bikini is royal blue. The upper band of the bottom is the same blue. A flush overcomes my face, even my body. I sidle my eyes away from her.

She presses the wall switch and walks through the blue-shimmering charged curtain right up to me. I try not to look, but with her this close to me it's difficult. My eyes, against my will, look into her face. Her eyes are the same royal blue colour as the bands on her bikini. Her skin is flawless. Her lashes a perfect thickness of white, as are her eyebrows, each hair tipped perfectly in the same shiny black as her hair. Her lips are a sultry bow, and her teeth enticingly show off their white through her slightly parted lips.

She pulls my frozen body up to a standing position and pushes me over to the chair. She presses my temples, and I rear back, pulling at whatever she stuck on.

She grabs my hands and snarls, "I don't have time to indulge your fear. Leave it on, else you won't learn. You must learn if you're going to get home." She flings my hands down, presses harder on my temples, whips around, and strides to the board. My mouth hangs open, and I desperately want to snatch off whatever she stuck on me. But I dare not. Suddenly lights are flashing in my eyes, not enough to obscure my vision, but enough to startle and alarm. At the same time as the lights begin, sounds thrum through my bones in a pattern that gets faster and faster in tandem with the lights.

She picks up a piece of chalk and begins writing on the chalkboard. I cannot pay attention because my bladder is aching and paining and about to let go. She turns around to look at me. I am now bouncing up and down, legs crossed.

She frowns, "What's the matter with you?"

"Don't you people have bathrooms?"

"What?"

"You know. Bathrooms. I have to pee!"

"Oh. Well, use the elimination vessel."

"The what?!" I yell, jiggling up and down faster and faster. God, doesn't anyone speak English here?

She gestures vaguely behind me. I turn around and scan the back wall. There's a counter with a number of things on it. What the hell is she talking about? I seriously consider peeing on the floor, but then they probably wouldn't give me a change of clothes, especially as they find my skirt so offensive, although I think the roses are jaunty. I think these thoughts, trying to distract myself as I look for a portable toilet. I hear a huff behind me and turn to find her pointing straight through me. She's pointing at a hexagonal red petri dish-like thing, sitting in a vessel that's glowing faintly ultraviolet. I shuffle over there legs crossed and look at it. No way. It's the size of my palm, way too small.

"Put it over where your bladder is. Hurry up." I pick it up gingerly, and the light in its vessel turns off. I stare at it. "Hurry up," she barks at my back again. I immediately place it over where my bladder should be. Relief. I'm so astonished, I drop it. My bladder has gone from great urgency to being empty, feeling nothing, not even residual pain from holding it in so long.

"Why do you habitants always do that?"

I wince at the contempt in her voice and squat down to retrieve it. As I'm about to touch it, I suddenly think about what's in it. I evince an ewww. A great sigh comes from behind me. "It's not in there." I pick it up and replace it in its supporting vessel. The light comes back on as it softly settles into place.

I swivel to face her, open my mouth to ask how, but her impatient look silences me. She turns back to the board, and as she writes, she instructs: "Listen. They're not going to take you home. They don't dare. You may change their timeline, and they can't have that. But we—we girls—"

She doesn't look like a girl. Her skin is flawless, like a young woman who's left the teen-acne years behind but has not yet begun to age. Still, an older age shows through her eyes, her expression, her bearing. Her bone structure is not that of someone my age, and the flatness of her stomach makes me envious of my twenties, long gone now.

"How old are you?" I blurt out to this girl in a bikini. Bikini girl, I giggle internally, slightly hysterically.

"Sixty. You need to listen." She continues with her instructions while, all hysteria gone, my mind grapples with how a sixty-year old, never mind forty, looks this young; not even Botoxed, plasticated, exercised, well-fed celebrities or the rich American women who visit the Directors at my work look twenty years old like bikini girl does. I narrow my eyes and lean forward to scrutinize her face closely. Her face doesn't have that fake look of women who want to look eternally young either.

"You can't be," I exclaim. "You're older than me."

She sighs, "Look, you must stop focussing on me—"

"I can't help it."

She turns fully around so that I can see her full frontal, she spreads her arms wide, and says, "Look at me then. This is why I want you to go home, why you need to go home so we won't be treated like this—look like this."

"So you can look older like me? You don't want to look older. Everyone wants to look younger. If my girlfriends could see you, heck if any pop star could see you, they'd be so envious. You are what we want to be. Why would you want to give that up? Why'd you want to be old looking? Men don't like their girlfriends or wives to look old. No one likes looking at women with wrinkles or grey hair. Men would never marry someone who looks older and wiser than them. Anyway what difference would it make to you me going home? And why are you here if you're on the way to a beach?"

"I'm not on my way to a beach. This is how we dress. This is how girls dress."

"Girls? Girls are too young to dress like that all the time," I retort horrified.

She stares at me both puzzled and as if I'm too stupid to be tolerated.

"Well," I swallow, "It's true."

"What do you call yourself?"

"Time."

She blinks at me. She stares at me.

I say defensively, "That's what my parents called me."

"Oh. My name is Bikini."

"Oh," I hesitate then have to ask, "Is that because you're wearing a bikini?"

"No! Did you not hear me? We all do; we girls all wear bikinis."

"What do women wear?"

"Who?" A frown mars her perfect face.

"Women, you know, people like me, my gender."

"Gender?"

"Sex." Her puzzlement grows, so I try to elaborate more, "You know, men and women, women and men."

"You mean, men and girls. What are women?"

"Grown-up girls."

Her face undergoes a radical change from bewilderment to realization to fury. "This is why you must listen. See what we have lost. We are not grown-up. We are never allowed to grow up. We must remain perfect. We are kept perfect and innocent and knowledge exempt. We receive trouble if we do not show up for our monthly body maintenance. We are all monitored, all the time, men and girls, for our health, but only us girls must be monitored and fixed up cosmetically. We must be available for our men, service their every needs, no matter where they are. And when they do not need us, we must stay out of view. We have our own travelways that run underground. We are not allowed to use the roads, roads are for the grown-ups, not for us. They do not educate us beyond what we need to know to service our men. We are given to a boy when we are both young so that our education may be tailored to his needs as he grows into a man. I was given to a boy who came from an old, very ancient family, who do not believe in this ... this ... this inequality, and so they educated me in secret. They taught me everything I wanted to learn. My passion is time travel even though my man is not interested. But as long as I also learn what I need to know for him, then he is satisfied with me knowing physics and philosophy. I have read his family's ancient texts in the original language. It is difficult because they thought so differently from the way we do. I have learnt of a time when girls ... I mean, what did you call them?"

"Women."

"Yes, women. They were equal to men. It was many millennia ago."

I frown as I recall the sign I saw at The Hangar, "I am thousands of years in the future?"

"No, you are one thousand years ahead. It's 3011. The ones who came before me told me it's 2011. But your time didn't have equality either not like the time I learnt about. I don't know much about your now time, but I can tell by the way your men and girls react to me when I try to teach them like I am you that you're not equal. Maybe that's why the boys like 2011: you pretend to be equal but the seeds for 3011 were planted then."

"Well, you're wrong. We are equal."

She just stares at me with utter contempt, "Do not argue. The boys will not be all day, and I must teach you. But I see I can't teach you until you accept. I want to be like them, the girls from the distant past, like the ones like me who were warriors, who led armies, who led nations, who studied alongside the men, who were not seen as freaks or unusual for doing any of that. We want that. We girls. And only you can bring that to us."

"Me?" I squeak. "I'm an admin assistant. I'm nobody."

"See, you call yourself a woman, but how are you any different from me? You're more clothed, maybe you are more educated, but you are just as powerless. At least my powerlessness was imposed upon me. Now listen!"

"I am listening! But ... why do they call those three 'boys'? They look like boys, act immature, but they are in university and can do sophisticated things."

"They're called 'boys' because they are. They're not grown-ups yet. Guy is twenty-seven; the other two are twenty-six. They do everything he wants them to. Now listen!"

My mind reels. How old do these people get? When do they become adults? Grown-ups? Who uses "grown-ups" to talk about adults except children or adults talking about children? I struggle to focus on her, to listen, but I still don't get it. It's all gibberish.

She picks up a chalkboard brush and vigorously cleans the board. She begins her drawings again. "See here. You need to go back in time. They will take you back partway using reverse velocities. They will reverse their trip with you until they reach a time between your now time and our now time. But reversing velocities is too complicated for you to build a ship that can do that in the now time they're taking you to. You will need to build a backward time machine. It is simple."

I choke. Her back straightens more, if possible. Her spine is glaring at me. I gulp and say, "Okay."

"See, it is simple if you will only pay attention. You must change the particle density so that it becomes negative and when you move forward in space, you will move backward in time. To do that, you must find an energy source that is compact yet emits great power, like your atom bomb. But you will not be splitting the atom. Instead your energy source will create particles on one side of it and annihilate particles on the other side. And, as well, any particles that spontaneously appear in the negative field, it will shift to the positive field until there are two-thirds less particles in the negative than the positive.

"So. Your source will create two fields, one that has more particles in it, and the other that has less. You will locate yourself on that side of it in a ship. You will locate yourself on the negative-particle-field-creating side of the source. The time they will take you to has the source. I have found out that all the people they take there end up at the same place, and there is a girl there whose mother will have the energy source you need.

You will need to work with that girl. The time they will take you to has the materials that will withstand the stresses. Find someone who can get their hands on ceramonanocarbon tubes. I think that girl's mother will know how to. Only those tubes will work. They have recently invented those tubes in that time. That's why they are not as easily available as now. But I cannot give them to you to take back with you. Work with the girl. She will help you. The ceramonanocarbon tubes can be stimulated to deploy themselves into the shape of an egg, like the ship you came in. You will want a ship the same shape as the one you came in. Then on one side of the ship, you will locate the energy source. It will need to be bolted on but able to be ejected off the ship when the time comes. That source must have only one outlet; through that outlet it will stream out the fields in front of you. You will need to aim that source toward your slice of now time, the time from which you came. This is the location for your time and space." She jots quickly a series of numbers and symbols, her chalk making rapping sounds on the board. "To reach your now time, space-time must curve negatively. That is what the negative particle field is for, to curve space-time negatively. When you enter that field, your ship will need to protect you from that field and keep the particle density inside around you normal. The ceramonanocarbon tubes will help, but your ship will also need to create a shield of neutrinos that will take you through all matter and space on the way back to your now time." She stops speaking and sketches out a diagram of a neutrino-creating machine. She jabs at it, "Look at it. Memorize it."

"But ... but I'm not a physicist. I'm not an engineer. I'm an English major who assists a cranky boss with his administrivia, and he isn't a physicist either."

She clucks her tongue, looks unhopeful, but with a deep sigh perseveres. The fight has left her, yet still she teaches. "Memorize it." She sticks her finger on the diagram again and continues: "The energy source must cleave off your ship once you are in a safe time, near a star. Your sun will effect the job. You cannot afford to have one of the boys find the source and turn it off before the fields are established. That's why it must stay with the ship until the energy source has established the fields. It will take a little bit of time in that now time to establish the fields, and while it is doing that your ship will need to get off earth in that time and head to the sun. Once the fields are established, they will remain for the trip long enough for you to get back to your now time. You will not need the source to be with you then. You will dump it in the sun and go back home."

"Huh?"

Anger and her impatience with me lends her voice an edge as she continues, "Unfortunately, all this space-time, particle-density change, will not be good for you. It would be better if you had the suit. But I cannot send it back in time with you. They'll take it; they never forget to have their subjects strip it off. But the ship will protect you if you build it like I say." She scratches out a diagram, anger sharpening her chalking on the board, as she grinds out, "Although you are in the same space as you were, you must leave this space in order to return to it only so that you can secure the energy source and destroy it. If you didn't have to do that, you could stay in the same space and merely move in time. Here is the programming." She writes so quickly a series of letters and numbers that I can barely see her hand move. "This," she points to one of the equations with her middle finger as she holds onto the chalk, "is the location of your sun. You will drop the energy source in there. This," she points to another line of equations, "is the path of your negative particle field that you will travel in to the sun and back to Toronto into your now time. Scan I equations. Memorize them."

I stare at them but have no idea what I'm looking at. My eyes glaze over. Her shout and the sudden increase in light wattage from the thingy on my temples make me jump. "Look!" She stabs the board with a dull threatening sound. "Memorize!"

I gulp and walk closer until I bump my nose into the charged curtain, "Ow." I rub my nose.

"Memorize! You must memorize." Does she choke on a sob? "The others, they looked but they didn't do anything. You are my last hope. You are our last hope. They are shutting the boys down. I peeked into their communications. They don't know I have learnt how to break through their individual habitant walls. They would never suspect I could anyway."

"Being a girl."

"A girl cannot know this stuff. If you do not help us, if you do not get home and change your time, we will remain like this!" she gestures to herself in despair. Bikini girl's bikini seems to be going transparent. I hastily look away.

I creep my eyes back to the board. I look obediently at each letter, each number, each line, each symbol, line by line from the top of the board, left to right, to the bottom of the board. When I look back at her, her bikini is half-transparent. I blush. She looks down at herself despondently. Suddenly, she inhales as she looks sharply toward the door. She grabs the eraser brush, energetically wipes the chalkboard clean, tosses the brush and chalk onto the ledge, and leaps over to me. She rips off whatever she'd stuck on my temples, making my skin feel like it's been scraped off, leaps back through the charged curtain, bangs the control on the wall so that the charged curtain returns to invisibility, scurries to a far corner, peeling off her red-field-creating device and tossing it into the open drawer, shutting the drawer, on her way past it to her hiding place. She tucks herself in behind another dresser. I'm amazed at her flexibility. Just before she disappears, bikini girl puts a finger to her lips, then waves at me to look away.

I look away.

7

BACKWARD THROUGH TO THE FUTURE

THE door swings open, and the prof strides in with the three boys following, each clutching a suit to their chest. They look unhappy.

"We'll activate The Transporter here, now. I can't risk her being seen outside this room."

"We can smuggle her out as easy as we smuggled her in," Guy pleads.

"You were lucky."

"But—"

"The discussion is over Guy. Your sire agreed with the Time History Professor and I too. Activate it."

Guy nods to the other two; they pull on their suits while the prof walks over to me and presses the wall. The charged curtain shimmers blue. The prof tosses a suit through the curtain toward me and presses the wall again. The charged curtain shimmers away, invisible to my eyes.

I struggle into the suit as before. When I have it on and glance back up, there's a small square platform floating over the floor in the middle of the room. It's white, of course.

Guy says, "I'll go first." It's the first brave act I've seen him do.

The prof barks, "Did you put in the suit co-ordinates as well?"

"The suit and my clothes," Guy replies. He vacuums air deep into his lungs and blows it out his mouth. He still looks afraid. He blinks, and the back of his suit becomes a hood, which pulls over his face and merges with the front of his suit. He steps onto the platform. The sides of the platform ooze out into the air, rise up like wisps of fog on all four sides of Guy, and enclose him at the top. A flat square of mist, parallel to the surface of the platform, drops down from the top, and slowly moves through Guy. It reaches the platform and disappears. There's a pause. It's like the room is holding its breath.

Guy disappears.

The wispy sides of the platform that had been enclosing Guy vanish down into the platform's base. The platform looks like a normal floating flat object, with slightly blurry white edges, again.

The other two boys follow Guy, although the prof had to push the first one on to the platform. A glare is sufficient for the last boy to step onto his fate. He vanishes in an instant too.

It's my turn.

The prof says, "I am going to push this into your quarantine area. I will then seal your suit for you, and you will step onto the platform. Is that clear? I will not tolerate rebellion. There's nowhere for you to go. You can't get past the charged curtain. So do what I say."

I nod. I will myself not to look into the corner where bikini girl is hiding. The prof walks over to the wall, and the charged curtain appears and shimmers blue. The prof blinks, and the platform moves itself through the curtain until it is right in front of me. It stops. The prof blinks again, and I feel the suit create a hood that covers my head and face and neck. I no longer feel fear, I am so numb. But neither can I move.

The prof yells, "Step on it!"

I swallow and think strong forward thoughts. Think to my legs: move. Instruct my arms: swing. Nothing happens. I stare at this platform that makes Guy afraid and disappears people. It doesn't look anything like *Star Trek's* transporter. It's not fancy with lights and telltale sounds. I remember watching the show with Father who was a Trekker. I was not. And when I hit my teens I stopped watching that geeky show even though no one would know I did if I had. But my classmates' thoughts about it, about sci-fi and nerdiness, were enough for me to stop. Sadness flows through me as I recall those close times with Father, times when we joked about what we'd do if we could have a transporter, times I tossed away because I didn't want to be one of them, an egghead. I sigh. That transporter was fun. This one is silent and simple. It is evil.

The prof strides over to a dresser near the corner. My heart speeds up; I hold my breath. He yanks open a drawer, rummages around in it, and with a muffled shout of triumph, brings out the small round device bikini girl had used. Like her, he slaps it onto his chest. He swivels round to walk my way as he presses the middle of the round thing. It glows red. He's encased in his own personal red-charged curtain. He walks through the curtain separating me from him, walks right up to me, grabs my arm, and shoves me onto the platform. He pulls me around to face him. He lets go, and I sway. The instant he removes his hand, he blinks. The platform I'm standing on changes from feeling solid to like I'm standing on mushy ground. I sink into it like one sinks into Spring-soaked earth, then it grips my feet. Yet though I feel the grip only around my feet, my entire body cannot move. I'm held completely still. The platform's misty edges rise up all around me. I'm enclosed in a wispy fog, a frightening fog. Against my will, I aim my eyeballs up and wait. And wait. That square of mist drops down into my view and descends, slowly, oh so slowly, toward me.

"Eyes forward!"

My eyes drop to face the prof. He glares into me, and I'm hooked. That scanning square passes before my vision, temporarily blinding me. I blink rapidly. My vision is restored. Otherwise I feel nothing, sense nothing, smell nothing, hear nothing, taste nothing. It's like what I see doesn't exist.

And then it doesn't.

And I'm in the ship.

Guy says morosely, "You're here. Let's go."

The boys don't bother to make me sit. We all stand as the ship lurches, and then we're moving yet not moving. My thoughts are with me yet ahead of me. And that's when I realize I feel different. It is that same weird feeling of my molecules appearing and disappearing. But I also feel like only part of me arrived in the ship, as if part of me is being put together, being created, even as we are moving backward through time, while the other part is somewhere else. I don't know where. I wonder how their Transporter works. I wonder what the prof meant about repropagated. I'm looking forward to going home. But I worry: will I arrive in one piece, literally in one piece? Only this suit is holding me together, I suddenly realize, even before we left the future it was holding me together through The Transporter.

"Um, how did we get here?"

"The Transporter contacts our information, updates it with its scan of our 3-D copy, destroys our 3-D copy, and recreates it. Here."

"What?"

"We are all copies. Our 2-D originals are found on the surface of the universe. As the universe expands, it has more room to create more 2-D objects on its surface, which it then makes 3-D copies of so that we can interact with each other.

We've learnt to read the 2-D originals, back them up, and move the copies around the universe."

"Plato."

"Who?"

"Plato is the ancient Greek philosopher who said that everything we see is just a copy, and there is only one perfect original. So every chair is a copy of one original perfect chair that's stored up there, somewhere in the sky."

"Plato didn't know about time travel. He didn't know you can't make a copy from an imperfect original that hasn't repropagated fully after time travel, that The Transporter updated its info from an incomplete 3-D copy. That's what you are after we brought you here: incomplete. If you hadn't gotten us found out right away, you would have had a chance. We have nanos who will heal us and put us back together because they have a permanent copy of our entire lives and can reconstruct us from our stored history. You don't. We will be whole again. You won't."

I gasp at him blaming me. It's so typical that the one who does the dirty work blames his victim, but I shut my mouth. I don't like the look on Guy's face.

Guy says in a low tone, menacingly, "We are taking you to a safe time—for us. We can't have you go home and tell people about the future or be able to change the future by living your own life. We're going to take you somewhere between your now time and our now time. It's a bad time. A nasty time." Through the fabric I can see Guy's lips stretch into a grin. "We picked it because dumb humans can't do anything to change our time when they're in the nasty time. We thought of that, I and the boys. We did. Not the profs, not our sires. We did because they didn't find out about our projects until the third one when that dumb human tried to get home. But he's the only one who did try. And he failed. In the nasty time, you won't have any friends. You won't have work. They still use money, and if you don't work, you can't survive. It's worse in the nasty time than in your now time if you don't work. And I know you won't work because work isn't like it is in your now time. It'll be so different you won't be able to function; you'll be fired or quit before you even start. That's why it's the best time to dump you dumb humans when we're done with you." Guy stops speaking. I shiver as I look at the three boys staring at me with their white blank faces, the only sound the molecules disappearing and reappearing in me, bursting like little flashes so faint you think they're only in your mind.

Guy growls, startling me, "We never got to do anything with you. The prof ruined our plans. And the Time History Professor did what he said he would, he restricted our nano time badges. He did, he restricted I and the boys. I!" Guy sounds aggrieved. "Sire won't help," he says incredulously. "Sire always helps. He never lets I down. But he didn't like you. He wanted to get rid of you fast. He wouldn't give the boys and I any time to carry out our plans with you. He has before. I don't accept! What's a little time? But Sire wouldn't budge. The prof didn't have to convince him, like he could anyway. Sire had already decided. He meant it when he said no more. He meant it! And to prove it he made I, his own son, take The Transporter. Because of you, we can't have any more fun. Because of you, our integrity is threatened. I don't like losing even one molecule of Iself." I can almost see his white suit flush with anger. He growls lower, making the hairs on my neck vibrate, "We're going to keep an eye on you. You don't die like the others did, you try to get home, we're going to find out, and we're going to come back and make you stop. Accept, dumb human?"

"Die?" I squeak.

"Die. No one lives in the nasty time." Like hyenas, the boys cachinnate. All my hairs stand on end as their laughter assaults me. Thankfully, the walls vanquish the horrid sounds so that they can't bounce off and echo into me.

The ship slows down. We regain solidity.

"Out."

"What?"

"Wait. She has to take her suit off first."

"Take it off."

I grapple with the fabric on my head. It won't let me grasp it, not even a millimetre of it. I snort and snuffle in my futility. Suddenly, the hood is off my face, and the front seam of the suit becomes visible and splits open. I grab the edges and pull it off, struggling with the arms as they cling to my cardigan. I finally roll it off my arms. I push and pull it down off my body, my hips, my legs. I use my feet and hands to yank it off my shoes. One shoe goes flying to the opposite wall. I run to grab it before the boys hurl me out with only one shoe on. I'm just in time, for as I bend over and put my fingers on either side of the shoe upper and tighten my grip, a rush of air flings me head-forward through the wall, and I land on concrete chest first. My shoe flies out of my hand, but it hits the curb in front of me and stops. I reach my right arm forward, clutch the shoe in my hand, and collapse in that position.

Through the air, Guy's voice follows me, "Don't forget, we'll find you if you try to get home. We'll let you live here in peace if you don't try to get home." Their cackles, their voices mockingly shouting "peace" clobber my ears.

They're gone.

Slowly, I pull my shoe toward me, turn myself over to sit up, and pull on my battered pump. I don't move for awhile; my body is bruised, my ego is shattered, and I have strange pains that buzz and fizzle in every organ, every blood vessel, every cell of me. It feels like my body is in an agony of wondering where half of it went, buzzing around looking for its missing pieces. It's like tiny tickles everywhere.

After awhile, the pain of the bruises lessens, and I start becoming used to the strange tickling pain. I realize I cannot sit here forever, and no one is going to rescue me. I stand up, brush down my skirt whose white is now splotched with dirt, and look around.

I shiver and pull my cardigan down. I yank down its sleeves to try and cover my hands. But the sleeves aren't long enough.

Clouds rumble the sky. The asphalt under my feet is crumbling. A concrete pole leans dangerously, a wire swinging from its top, its angled base breaking open the concrete ground. There is no one around. A wind picks up and blows my skirt against my legs. I'm standing on the road. A road that looks like a road. I step backward and up onto the sidewalk that looks like a sidewalk, its surface cracked, mottled with gum patches, and streaked with tar, like the one at home in my neighbourhood.

The building across from me is grey. But it's not grey concrete or grey brick. It's like grey glass that has been covered in grey grains of sand. It's all one surface from about the second storey up. At street level, the grey glass is clear. But all the rooms I can see through the glass are empty.

What time is it?

I look at my watch. The second hand isn't moving. I shake it. I take it off and fiddle with the button on the side. I watch it for awhile. Nothing moves under its glass. My watch refuses to work.

Is it my fortieth today? Is tomorrow today? Am I older? The date on my watch is still the date it was this morning—or was it yesterday?—when the boys took me.

I start walking, and as I walk along the sidewalk, past a couple of more lone poles, past the grey building, toward a distant road, the silence of the street is swallowed up in a growing crescendo of footsteps that comes from ahead of me.

8

2411

THE nasty time, they'd called it. So far it looks like the grey time. The sidewalk I'm on is bordered by a worn road on one side, a barrier on the other. The barrier is old, made of concrete bricks, and is a metre taller than me. A spiky rail is jammed into its top, the black paint almost all flaked off, revealing the flat grey of its zinc undercoat. I cannot see or hear anything on the other side. I sidle up close to it, hugging it as I approach the end of this street and another building facing me like the one opposite to me. The footsteps are soft but like the constant buzz of the Gardiner Expressway. I can hear people and strange whines, but I cannot see anything. I arrive at the end of the street or rather a ninety-degree turn in the street. Plastering myself to the barrier wall, I peek around. This part of the street is a block long, if that, before it bumps into a busy intersection. From my perspective, the building facing me seems to crawl along its entire length. I scout the cross street and the intersection as best I can from my vantage point. It helps that it's so cloudy; there is no sun to blind my vision.

The cross street is quite different from this empty one with its grey buildings. Its buildings soar like Christmas trees, wide at the bottom, narrow at the top. They're white at the top. I groan. I've come to hate white. I look down disparagingly at my white skirt splotched with its red roses and road dust. Maybe the dirt makes it better. I stop procrastinating and examine the scene ahead of me again. This time I notice that the buildings are different colours on their bottom two-thirds. The one kitty-corner to the street I'm on is sandy on the bottom; the one across the intersection and on my right is slate grey on the bottom. They don't have windows. Instead the top third is an opaque white that almost glows gently. The bottom two-thirds bares its insides through semi-transparent glass. Well, I think it's glass. It looks like glass, but it has faint traces of that glowing look of the future. I cock my head, for there's something else odd about the glass. I scan the building from the top to as far down as I can see. And then it hits me: the glass is not rectangular. There are no edges, no breaks, no changes in angle. Each floor is a crossbar of matte white or sand or slate grey that sits behind the glass, yet the glass or whatever it is, is one smooth waterfall from top to bottom. Only its transparency changes; the opaqueness becoming less opaque as it flows halfway down the white until by the time it flows into the coloured part, it's transparent. The corner edges of the buildings are made of the same material as the crossbars. It's like a geometric pattern of trapezoids, sitting behind a perfectly smooth waterfall, that become smaller and smaller as they go up the building.

I crane my neck, until my vertebrae pop, to scan the top. A faint crown of green rises above the glassy exterior. And growing taller than that green is a veritable forest of trees. Well, again, not trees. They look like trees with leaves and branches and trunks. But there's something odd about them too. I narrow my eyes.

They remind me of the magical decorations in the Winter Garden Theatre on Yonge Street across from the Eaton Centre.

I'd been to that theatre soon after it had reopened. Father had dragged me there, insisting I see history. I thought it'd be boring. The play was, but the theatre was stunning. I couldn't stop gawking at the painted trees and golden, rust, and green leaves hanging from the ceiling. Sitting in the new plush seat felt like being in the best artificial garden ever made.

Now I see its superior.

A breeze blows my skirt against my legs, and the leaves way up high rustle enough for me to see them move. And when they move, I see that their uppers are chanterelle gold and oxblood red and ocean green while their bottoms are deepest forest green. The breeze falls away; the leaves stop rustling. They show off their green sides to us below.

I drop my eyes back down and rub the back of my neck. Again, I feel like I'm missing something. I turn to look at the concrete landscape behind me, then back to the street in front of me. I turn again. And again. Poles. On that modern street ahead, there are no poles. No poles to carry the wires for electricity, and no poles to support streetcar lines. There are no hydro lines. No bus stop signs. No street signs at any of the corners of the intersection. I marvel at the detritus-free air above the people. Only trees rise high from the ground and take up space above human level. Tall leafy trees. They reach to the cloudy sky at each corner of the buildings. They're identical to the ones on top, but here so close to the ground, their multicoloured uppers are visible; their trunks are a brown so dark and smooth, they're like obsidian rock. They soak in the dead light of this cloudy day. They look imposing as they rise well above the hordes of people walking at street level.

And I mean hordes.

The people are a blur of sandy beige and igneous grey and soil brown and murky green. There are so many; I can barely distinguish individuals. As my eyes adjust to the chaos at street level, I'm glad to see there are at least women. But once again my red cardigan and white skirt with its red roses will make me stand out.

I scuttle closer, trying to blend in to the barrier.

And that's when I realize not only will the colours of my clothing be noticeable, the length of my skirt will also make me stand out.

I track one woman as she weaves in and out of the crowds. Her hair is cropped short and matches the colour of her skin. Her left side is to me as she crosses my line of vision from right to left. The left sleeve, the one I can see, of her top is short, and the fabric hugs her arm and side. It has a smooth look to it, fluid even, and it moves easily with her movements. I see no seams, but as she turns to look over her left shoulder, I see a sash or some sort of easy-falling fabric that drapes over her left shoulder and down her torso, front and back. It's clipped by some means at her hip but parts itself below. I can see her entire leg from hip down to feet. It's embarrassing, yet I cannot stop staring at this exposure. I wrench my gaze down to find her feet, which are encased in shoes. Well, I think they are; it's hard to tell because the colour is the same as her flesh: cappuccino.

Most people are that colour, some a little lighter, some a little darker. I haven't seen uniformity in skin colour like this in Toronto before, except in 3011.

I've lost the woman in my distraction. I scan the crowd again and lock onto another one; she is walking from my left to my right, and her right side is visible to me. She too has cropped, coffee-coloured hair. Her top has a low scoop neck and short sleeves like the other woman's. I'm relieved to glimpse a row of fabric-coloured buttons marching down her middle. Well, only about three or four buttons, for the top is short. I think I've seen something similar. I wrench at my memory. I have it! It was a sari top on a visiting manager from India. But the fabric of the visiting manager's top was wrinkled, and though tight, not as beautifully form-hugging as this one. And a little longer too, I think. This woman's sash is clipped at her hip on the right side, but it doesn't end there it drapes like a fat-pleated skirt and falls to mid-thigh, hiding the upper part of her leg. The only difference between her clothes and the first woman is the colour. The first woman was dressed in variations of sandy beige; this woman is in variations of green.

She stops walking and turns to look down my street. I can see then that the sash has a wide waistband that interrupts the pleats above and below and is like a loose skirt in front, with about half her left leg exposed vertically. I flatten myself against the wall and stay as still as possible. She shrugs and walks off into the crowd. I resume my examination of this alien society.

The men are more clothed. Typical. They even wear caps that expose only their front hairline, that fallback in a short floppy point, and that curve round behind their heads to end at their necks. Hair cascades down from underneath: long tendrils curl to their waists. They wear above-the-knee-long tunics where the left side crosses the right to create a V-neck. Three-quarter length trumpet-like sleeves end above the wrists. A sash nips the tunic in at the waist. Their pants look like narrow pyjama pants, except the fabric isn't loose or baggy, and they sport a shaded stripe where seams normally would be. They follow the contours of their legs to mid-calf, moving easily with their long strides yet not sagging from use. I look at pants after pants and see: no baggy knees. Their tunics would hide their saggy bottoms, but I don't think they have them. This fabric is ... weird,... and I'd love to wear it. Again no seams. Visible ones anyway. Those stripes must be hiding them. I check out their feet: they're wearing boots, supple boots the colours of their pants that rise up underneath the hems of their pants. The colours of their clothing and their caps is like the women's: boring. All the men also seem to have coffee-coloured hair and cappuccino-coloured skin.

I look down at myself and wonder: how will I ever blend in?

I go back to scouting the road ahead. And that's when I notice all the dogs. All sorts of breeds, but mostly golden retrievers. They're trotting through the crowds, tails wagging, apparently on their own, and they all wear doggie rucksacks, like service dogs do. I blink and rub my eyes. I open them wide and see: many, many dogs travelling along by themselves as if they all have a destination and know them. A gap opens in the crowds of streaming people and dogs. At the foot of the buildings are wide beds of flowers and bushes, a vibrant contrast to the people. The plants garishly flaunt their reds and purples and blues with green filling in each cranny. Thin streams of water spout into the air and fall back down into the lush plant life.

The gap fills in as new hordes of people arrive.

I edge closer.

And closer.

Until I'm at the end of the concrete-block barrier, right on the edge of the streaming people—who don't notice me. I edge my foot forward, and something grips it. I look down: the cracked, rough concrete has given way to a smooth, glossy northern Ontario granite pink that slightly reflects the cloudy light. I step on it fully with one foot and pull it back. The gloss is not slippery; instead it grips and provides spring. Between the feet of the passing people, my eyes roam to find the roadside edge. There is no edge. My heart thuds against my ribs. I want a road with a sidewalk like I'm on, I scream inside my head. Shaking my head jerkily, I stop my internal screaming and lean around the wall. The most astounding sight greets my eyes: an enormous garden that sits slightly elevated above the street. The barrier is hiding bushes and vegetables and flowers and bees and butterflies and squirrels from the view of the grey street I was dumped on. Taking a breath, I scoot up a mini hill and in behind a bush bursting with little white flowers. I peek through its leafy branches at this new street I'm on. I have no idea where to go, what direction to take. And so I continue to investigate the lay of this time.

Being closer and a little higher, I can see there are actually two streams of people, each stream on each side of the street. The road is a continuation of the sidewalks: the same material on the same level. No tar streaks or gum patches. The entire granite pink surface is clean. A steady stream of cars—at least I think they're cars, maybe they're vector transports—move in both directions down this road. Like the ones in the future, they're equidistant from each other; they move at the same speed; they have no wheels. The cars are elevated and seem to glide over a cushion of air. I would kill to see wheels and hear their annoying hum. And then the horrible thought hits me: Am I still in 3011 but another part of it? Did they fool me?

A woman stops right on the other side of the bush I'm hiding behind. No, it can't be that future. There was not one woman in sight there, except for bikini girl. And she was strange and indoors. There are lots of women walking along the sidewalks or whatever the sidewalks-part of the road is called.

The woman moves on.

My legs fold under me as I collapse on the ground. I watch the traffic go by. The cars here are shades of ice. Blue ice, white ice, greyish ice. They look like bugs with their large curving tops and tiny bumps front and rear. Their roofs are not clear like where I had been, and they sport a wide stripe of matte black curving up and over them front to back. The windows are smaller, oval, and all the same size: front, back, and sides. I catch only flashes of heads. I watch for awhile until my eyes adjust to the cars' speed and I can see inside them better. I blink. No, I'm not hallucinating. Every car has only one person inside but not at the wheel. There are no steering wheels. And every person's head is accompanied by a doggie head. While the human heads are in every position imaginable—looking straight ahead, bowed over something in their lap, watching the passing scenery—the doggie heads are all regally erect, like Afghan hounds, their blonde-streaked brown hair flowing down. No, that one that just passed by, with its tall pointed ears and short-haired amber coat, reminded me of something else ... something old. Egypt! Did they resurrect Egyptian dogs here? It wouldn't surprise me with all the DNA work they're doing in my time. In this nasty time, as Guy called it, there sure are a lot of dogs, even more than in my neighbourhood, and I hadn't thought that was possible. Sue used to say she'd prefer to live where I do, not in her cat-dominated neighbourhood. I countered that barking dogs interrupt sleep. And she said cat people let their cats wander around outside preying on birds and not catching the rats and pooping in her petunia beds. She had a point.

Despite there being so many people and dogs on the sidewalks, not one strays onto the part where the cars travel, neither the humans nor the dogs. They're chaotic in their numbers yet regimented in where they move. One of the icy blue cars stops at a gap in the gardens in front of one of the buildings, and the most amazing thing happens: the sea of people heading to my left stops in an even line from the car to the building's front door while about a metre away in a parallel line, the sea of people heading to my right stops in an even line. It's like a walkway from the car to the building has opened up in the people. An Egyptian-type dog appears on the walk on the opposite side of the car from me, wearing one of those rucksacks the colour of burnished mahogany. He stops, turns his head back and forth to survey the paused people watching the action at the car. He nods. Nods! A man's head appears; I can tell it's a man because he's wearing one of those pointed caps, except his point is long, his cap taller, and as he walks toward the building, I see that his hair is thicker, straighter in lush waves rather than ringlets and longer than any other man's I've seen. The dog moves in behind him, his head swivelling constantly left and right as they walk through the garden. The thin leaves of tall ferns brush the man's shoulders but don't reach down to the dog's level. They're in the building, the empty car is driving off, and the sea of people rushes into the empty walkway space. Soon, it is again as it was.

I hear a rustle behind me. A woman is bending over to snip a ragged branch of a bush, tie-dyed in colours of burnt maple leaves and summer greens, and a grey squirrel beside her is industriously digging into the giving soil. The woman is totally covered in white. From her head to her feet falls folds and folds of white fabric. Her head is down, and I imagine her face is covered in white too. It's like a burka or that other kind of disguise that is popping up more and more on Toronto streets. Those ones are black. This one is white. She cannot see me. And she also seems to be oblivious to the raccoon waddling up to her rear while the grey squirrel shoots his head up, freezes, then bounces a hasty retreat, his bushy tail flicking his irritation. But she will see me first as soon as she stands up. I straighten up cautiously and take a step away from the barrier, keeping the bush between me and her. I don't want her to hear me. I take another step and another as I keep a close eye on her until I'm far enough away that I feel safe enough to walk normally while staying in the bushes.

This enormous garden ends, and a line of buildings begin on this side of the street. Each building is fronted by its own garden. I scoot between their gardens when I get to gaps.

I walk for awhile along this long, long block.

I don't recognize any of the buildings. They're all the same as those white and sand buildings I first saw. They're all semi-transparent; all variations on those two colours. There are no brick buildings, no marble buildings, no stone ones. They're all set back behind wide beds of flowers and fountains and bushes at pavement level from the granite-like road surface.

There is something else missing in this city, aside from the familiar buildings and hydro poles.

Billboards!

Neon signs!

There are none.

How blessedly peaceful to the eyes. All this greenery and plant life and no glaring ads.

I start to like this nasty time.

I come to a new street, turn a corner, see the CN Tower, and my heart leaps in relief.

Finally, a familiar landmark. I am in Toronto. I am in my city. I am home.

In my relief to see the soaring Tower, I stop noticing my surroundings. I stop being careful, and I step fully out into the middle of the crowd, which slows down and parts around me.

"Who that?"

"What that, you mean?"

"Why she covered?"

"Check her finger."

"She have no ring. She not married. Not acceptable."

Spittle lands on my cardigan. My head flies left and right as I look for the source of the voices. All I see are hostile faces. Spit lands on my skirt, followed by catcalls. I try not to panic. But there are so many people, so many, I cannot figure out which way to turn, I cannot figure out to whom the voices belong.

"Get her."

I've heard that before. I run.

I weave through the crowd and bump into people. I thread my way toward the road. I pop out from the edge of the crowd, gain better thrust, and run faster toward the cars.

I smack into a wall.

An invisible wall.

I try to push through the clear air and get nowhere, achieve nothing but pain.

Oh God, another one of those charged curtains.

I look over my shoulder and see three males crashing through the people toward me.

I veer back into the crowd and head to one of the building gardens. It'll be easier to run on the dirt and weave between the neat vegetable rows. I'll just have to avoid the gardeners in their white burkas and their baskets full of fresh produce or cut flowers, or the gardeners bent over weeding the friable soil by hand, or that raccoon suddenly rising on his hind legs, baring his vicious teeth at me and growling threats. I hastily leap to the side of the garden opposite him. Once past the beast, I dive back to the side farthest away from what passes for a sidewalk. I finally get to my target, and I run faster. I can't help it; I have to twist my head around to look, and I fly into a white-clad back. She falls face-first into the soil, my hands balancing my weight on her back. I stumble back to my feet in time to avoid being caught, my legs spurred on by terror. The males chasing me can run faster too in these lovingly-tended gardens. There are three of them. Why three? Why always three? I stick to the vegetable strip, which becomes rows of bobbing flowers, which becomes rows of small pine trees like baby Christmas trees. I aim always for the CN Tower, yet I turn the corners every time I come to an intersection, not wanting to run into another one of those invisible walls, and the CN Tower is lost to me. How can anyone know where they are?

"I have!" A hand brushes my back, and I dart into the crowd. The hand falls off. I see the CN Tower again. In my relief, without thinking, I run directly toward an intersection. I slam into a person, and we're across the intersection. I don't have time to think about what has just happened. I keep running. I cross another intersection in the same way, glued to a stranger. I see buildings ahead of me that I recognize. Old buildings. Brick ones. With stone collonnades and tall glass windows. Old-fashioned light standards line the street in front of them. I know this place. It's Marché. I'm on Yonge Street, heading south. My heart sings.

The people are thinner down this part of Yonge Street. Suddenly, I feel hot breath on my neck. A hand grabs my arm.

I'm approaching a door. I wrench my arm out and fling myself through the door. A real door. One with a knob, one I know how to open.

I flee into the interior, the door smashing against a door stop on the wall. And almost trip over my feet as I try to slow myself down before hitting the side of a wall bookcase. It's dark inside. I regain my balance, wondering where those guys are. I turn around to look through the open door. They're standing outside, shifting from foot to foot, glaring at me. One takes a step forward; the taller one next to him grabs him and shakes his head at him.

He shouts, "We catch another time." They walk off in the direction we came from.

Where am I? What kind of place did I run into that even those guys fear it?

The door swings noiselessly shut on this murky room.

9

THE ATTIC

I contemplate the creepy door. I don't want to go back out there. I don't like sticking out, and the denizens don't like seeing someone startingly different either. I don't want to stay in here. It's gloomy, unknown, and I'm shut in.

I force myself to move my frozen body. My eyes begin to adjust, and I examine where I am. Out of the gloom appear book shelves on the near wall, the wall opposite, and the end wall. One of those library ladders stands waiting for someone in the middle of the end wall. There's an L-shaped counter to the left of the door, its top made of thick beaten-up dark wood. Maybe stained oak, like the shelves and the wide-plank floor. On the far left wall halfway down the space, a stairway rises into darkness. Tables sit higgledy-piggledy in the middle of the floor, their accompanying battered wooden chairs askew.

I'm in a bookstore.

I relax.

Bookstores are comfortable, safe places. I begin to scan the books nearest me, below my eye level.

Faint clicks emanating from behind me, from inside the murkiest of the gloom, send all my nerves on end and shoot my head up, eyes narrowed, darting around, hunting for what caused the sound. I see nothing. Then out of my peripheral vision, I sense a lighter colour break out of the recesses of this space and fly toward me.

A golden Lab skitters to a halt in front of me, growling. A low, back-in-the-throat growl. I stand petrified, desperately trying not to look into its eyes, willing my heart to slow its thudding, my limbs to halt their quivering. They say dogs sense fear, and when they do, they will be more aggressive. I stare at its soft ears, its soft, gentle, unthreatening ears, while its nose vibrates centimetres from my stomach. I try not to imagine what it's be like to be eviscerated by a dog.

After awhile, the growls recede.

Cautiously, I lower my eyes from its ears to its snout. It immediately bends down to commence sniffing me. It sniffs my black pumps. Its brow furrows, and it sticks its nose right against the toe of my pump and snuffles up whatever scents are plastered on it. It sneezes, its nose hitting the floor, its legs splaying out. It shakes its head and sniffs my other foot in its pump. It sneezes again, its entire body convulsing, gooey droplets littering the floor and the coating of dust on my shoe. I'm too overwhelmed to be grossed out at dog spit on my shoe. It shakes its whole body and recommences sniffing.

The golden Lab inspects the rest of my shoes and feet, making its slow, sniffing way up my legs, round the rim of my skirt, up the back of my skirt. I can't help it, I jump away from its feather-ticklish nose. It is undeterred. It glues its nose against my butt and slowly detects its way up to my waist. When done, it trots round to my front, raises its head, and sniffs the airspace in front of me, inhaling whatever scents I'm giving off.

It's not enough.

It raises itself up on its hind legs. Balancing easily on them, its forelegs up, its paws hanging down, it begins sniffing me at shoulder level. When it gets to my face, it looks into my eyes, and I swear, it smiles. It lowers itself back down and, jutting its head to my side, barks once.

"Thank you, Atticus," a soft voice replies from somewhere in the back. I squint my eyes. From behind the stairs, a man slouches toward me. A soft, slightly dumpy man in a blue-grey checked shirt, open in the front to reveal a black, rumpled T-shirt. Faded jeans hang from his waist, the belt barely holding them up. He's wearing clothes I know! I can feel my mouth widening, the muscles stiff from non-use. But as he rounds the last table in his zig-zagging route toward me, I see his shoes. They are like those the others in this time wear, not anything like twenty-first-century sneakers. My grin stops in its tracks, and I become wary. He stops in front of me, Atticus between me and him, Atticus facing me as well. I examine this dumpy man as he examines me. I slowly become aware that underneath that soft fat lies dangerous strength. Its aura reaches out to me. I don't ever recall feeling a person's aura before, and it frightens me. I focus on the superficial. His light brown hair is cut short, like a blurred brush cut. His nose is straight and a decent size. His lips are thin and unexpressive. His skin is the colour of my morning café latté, no whip, soya milk, half-sweet when stirred. He wears round spectacles. They reflect me and the closed front door. I cannot see his eyes.

It's unnerving.

We stand, all three of us, in silence.

He sighs. His entire body slumps, and he shoves his hands into his jeans pockets.

"Another one, Atticus."

The dog seems to nod. Do dogs nod? Dogs don't nod. Maybe in this time they do. No, dogs do not nod!

We stand, all three of us, them in comfortable silence, me trying not to freak out and becoming really tired of being so afraid and so confused for so long.

"Hello. That's what twenty-first century people say, isn't it? Hello?"

I croak.

I clear my throat and try again. I whisper, "Yes."

He waits.

I say, "Hello."

"My name is Space. It's my name because Thrall don't own property, but I do. I have my own space."

He waits.

"Um," I say. "My name is Time."

His blonde-white eyebrows shoot up from behind his spectacles.

This reaction, I'm familiar with. "No, it's true. My parents named me 'Time' because I took so long to be conceived, and then I was two weeks late. They said it was about time, and the name stuck."

He nods. The dog chuckles. Chuckles? My mouth hangs open as I stare at this golden Lab that chuckled. Dogs don't chuckle. I know dogs don't chuckle. They just don't! My breath quickens until I can't catch it. The man admonishes Atticus, leaps to the counter, reaches over it, grabs a paper bag, and hands it to me, "Here, blow into this."

I grab it and breathe in and out into the bag.

"Slower. Breathe in, breathe out. Atticus won't hurt you. I won't hurt you. You're safe here."

I take the bag away from my mouth and exclaim, "He chuckled. Dogs don't chuckle!" I end on a squeak.

"It'll become clear. Let's have some tea."

Tea? My head spins. Space grabs my arm. Atticus starts to trot toward the back but the man, no Space, halts him by saying, "Atticus." Atticus turns to look at him, and Space shakes his head. Space guides me gently to the nearest table. He tells me to sit while he goes to make some tea. I sit. I scrape my chair shakily closer, plunk my elbows on the scarred table top, and lean my head in my hands. Atticus waddles over to me and sits too. He leans over until his head is brushing my lap. I stay perfectly still, but after awhile my muscles shake with the effort, and the warmth of his head against my leg is comforting. I relax.

"Here we are. Tea."

I lift my head. Space sets down a tray in front of me on which sits a rose-festooned china teapot, two teacups, one with a little chip in the rim, a strainer atop one, a creamer and sugar bowl, two spoons, and a plate of Cadbury's chocolate biscuits. Tears sprout at this familiar scene from home. This is so English, and though I'm Canadian, Cadbury's is one of my favourite biscuits, and the old-style tea set is like something out of a cosy English mystery book. I wipe my eyes on my sleeve, and Space affects not to notice as he pours the tea through the strainer into the cup. He removes the strainer from the top of the cup and places it on top of the second cup with the chip. He hands the first cup to me and pours himself a cup. He sits down and passes me the plate of biscuits. I take one, put it on my saucer, and pour milk and sugar, lots and lots of sugar, into my tea. I pick up one of the spoons and stir and stir the milky liquid until Space places a soft hand on top of mine to still it. In all this time, Atticus hasn't moved.

"Eat your biscuit. You'll feel better. Help yourself to as many as you like."

I gingerly pick up the biscuit and nibble on its edges. It is a Cadbury's biscuit, just like the ones I buy at Loblaws at Christmas. I devour it. And help myself to two more. I do feel better after I've eaten the three and drunk my tea.

We sit back, and Space asks, "Do you know where you are?"

I shake my head.

"I know how you got here. Dumpees arrive at my doorstep, and they all tell the same story. I'm unsure how they find their way to The Attic. That's the name of this once bookstore," he gestures around to encompass the store. "We never see more than one dumpee at a time. A new one arrives soon after the old one—

"Atticus ... Atticus is my ... dog. Atticus and I searched for where dumpees are dropped and discovered it's in one of the few spaces in town that's empty. It's a block Torontonians avoid because the two largest Wealth families have fought over its ownership for centuries ever since one architected on a cemetery and the other objected. We don't believe in ghosts; nevertheless habitants avoid the area and use that as a cover story. None want to be seen as taking one side over the other by walking on to that land, the Wealth or Thrall. Over the years, it's become deserted. Those future-century boys I've heard about somehow discovered it and found it a convenient place to dump their victims unseen."

Space bends his head, takes off his glasses, rubs the lenses on his shirt, puts them back on, lifts his blank eyes back to me, and resumes his tale: "The dumpees have a hard time here. I try to help them. And I'll try to help you. But this is not your now time. Do you know what year you're in?"

I shake my head. "No, I mean, they said it was the nasty time."

Space's thin eyebrows rise above his spectacles, and then he slowly nods, "I hadn't heard that before. But ... it fits. 2411 is a nasty time. That's the year you've come to. The twenty-first century, your now time, is a nicer place. You will find it hard to fit in here, particularly since you're female. Girls ... in our now time, girls have it harder than men. You will find out our now time too alien for your sensibilities. But it's necessary to fit in. Unless you can find a job, it's difficult to have a chance to fit in."

I nod shakily.

"I will help you. Atticus will keep an eye on you."

I quaver, "Those ... those ... boys, the ones out there chasing me. They wouldn't come in. Um—"

"No. None dare come in here. They know that Atticus is here. They know that The Attic won't let them come in without unpleasant consequences. One of them tried to follow the first dumpee into The Attic. He has not been the same since. He sweeps the street, goes home, eats, sleeps, and repeats. He speaks to no one, and no one speaks to him. The rest learnt the lesson and stay away. As long as you remain in The Attic you will be safe."

We sit awhile while I digest this. How will I live in this gloomy place, day after day? A memory flashes into my mind, one of Peggy and Sue and me in our local Chinese restaurant, laughing over the office manager Dirk and his secretary Liz thinking no one knew of their affair while we all gossiped on their daily hookups. My heart pangs me.

Space's even voice interrupts my thoughts scattering away from this reality. "You will have to go out. Atticus will watch over you. We will teach you. But it's up to you to learn." I can tell from his voice that he doesn't expect me to learn. Something he said earlier, or didn't say, comes back. "What were you going to say when you said one arrives when another one, what?"

Atticus shifts his head and looks up at Space. Space doesn't say anything for awhile, his face unreadable. Atticus puts his head back down, this time fully on my lap. The weight of his golden head squishes my legs, his heat burns them. But I dare not move him, and I watch Space for an answer. It isn't going to be good.

"Die."

"Die?" I ask bewildered.

"Dumpees die in this now time. Somehow those boys know when a dumpee dies because soon after one does, a new one arrives. The last one died not long before you turned up."

"Oh," I swallow. I don't want to die. I was just going to work, like I always do, thinking about my fortieth birthday, when all this happened. It must be a dream. This can't be real. I rub my hands hard over my face, up and down, up and down. I dig my fingers into my forehead and under my cheekbones and rub deeply. I drop my hands and snap open my eyes. Space and Atticus are watching me.

It's real. A cry burbles up, and I grit my teeth till they hurt. Suddenly, I want to turn forty. It sounds like the sweetest age. I wonder if I have yet, or if it's still the same day. I haven't seen night or stars or the moon, only sunlight or cloud light.

"What day is it?"

Space reaches across the table and pats my hand; Atticus lifts his head up and pads toward the staircase. He stops and sits his butt on the first step.

"Can you read?" Space asks me.

10

APPEARANCES

WHAT a strange question. I blink rapidly. He's waiting. I say, "Yes, of course I can read."

Space nods, "I keep forgetting. Your time is not our time." He stands up and walks toward the stairs. I watch him go and wonder whether I should follow. I turn my head away from him and look out the streaked front window. The idea of dying doesn't appeal. Maybe if I go back to that place, maybe the boys will come back and say it was all a joke and they'll take me home, then maybe all of this will go away.

"It won't go away. Your safest place is here."

I jump. Do they mind read in this place? But he's right. I'm being delusional. The boys are not the joking kind. They are just mean.

Space is standing next to Atticus, and the two are watching me. Fear shrinks me into the back of the chair. I don't want him to be right. I want to go home. I turn away from the sight of the two of them, my vision blurring, hoping they'll be gone, this place will be gone, I'll be in my office.

Something taps against the window. I rub my eyes to clear my vision. Tap. Tap. Tap. It's like a metronome; its annoying regularity is a welcome distraction and subsumes my fear as I search the window for the source. I don't find it, but I escape from this space, this time, by minutely inspecting the street. The building on the other side of Yonge is not one of the old ones, the ones I'm familiar with like the one I'm in. It's wide, wider than the view afforded by the window, and set well back behind a garden of hostas and clematis and flaming bushes and dainty birches. Its sand-coloured edifice rises Zamboni-iced-smooth up out of sight; through its transparency, I see many people moving around. They are in hues of earth: browns, sands, muted blue-green seas. No reds or bright yellows or Sue's favourite colour: peacock blue. I sigh, a full-body draining sigh. I'm not in the twentieth century. And I stand up.

I force my head away from the window and force my body to follow my head, my legs to walk toward Space and Atticus and that staircase up to another unknown.

Atticus stays seated on his step while Space starts up the stairs. After I pass Atticus by, I hear his paws click one step at a time behind me as I make my slow way up. At the top, a balcony over the main store floor shoots off at right angles to my right. A hallway marches ahead of us with a shut door on the right and a shut door at the end. Space walks toward the door at the end, and I follow.

He opens it, and light floods the hallway. I blink against the sudden onslaught. When my eyes adjust, Space is standing near a club chair in the middle of the room, waiting for me. I take a few steps in and stop. It's a room of bookcases that cover the walls floor to ceiling, starting from my right and going round all the way up to a tall window across and a bit to my left and past it too. Just to my right, on the wall perpendicular to the door, is a bookcase. On my left, along the door wall and along the adjacent wall, is a bookcase. And on the wall facing me is one.

The bookcases are jammed with books, old and tattered books, standing up vertically or piled haphazardly horizontally. Some are paperbacks, the mass kind I read for escapism. They look like they'd fall apart as soon as one touched them. Some are trade paperback size, and again look too fragile to last. The sturdier ones are bound in leather or hard covers, the kind textbook publishers used or did use in the twentieth century. I haven't seen so many books jammed in so little space in years except in an independent bookstore I used to frequent in my university days.

I finally stop ogling the books and notice the rest of the room. The tall window on the opposite wall ends right next to the wall to my left and its bookcase. Its thick glass is streaked, and compared to the transparent edifice I was just looking at, seems to be full of impurities and ripples. Through it I see a fire escape balcony and a lovely view of the endless grey sky. A couch sits perpendicular to the window, a wing chair sits on its far side with little room between it and the window wall bookcase, and a heavy, padded chair—a club chair in worn brown ... leather?—sits in front of the couch almost touching the bookcase to my right. A small table stands next to the club chair on its right-hand side. Three books lie on it, each with a worn bookmark sticking out.

Space says, "This is my library." Atticus plods over to Space's fat chair, settles down on the floor next to it with a deep sigh, and curls up into a ball. He readjusts his nose into his tail a few times, not opening his eyes while burying his nose in the crook between tail and butt until he's comfortable.

Space settles down into his chair, its seat sighing in response. He looks up at me rooted in place standing near the door, and jumps up again. He disappears through the door and returns carrying a Barcelona chair. A modern, expensive chair, it seems at first to me. Space drops it next to the couch, facing the wing chair, and it rocks back and forth before calming down. The seat is white leather. I peer at it properly. Worn, cracked white leather with buttons missing their white. The chrome is chipped and mottled. The seat droops, and it finally dawns on me why: it's centuries old.

A commotion draws my gaze to the window. Boys are crowding through it, and I sag back.

Space holds out a hand to me, saying, "It's fine. They're my group."

Though it had seemed like a whole passel of boys was entering, there are really only two. Behind them come two girls. They are all dressed like the people I saw outside, except that the materials of one of the boy's clothing is finer. The tunic is perfect in its fluidity with not a kink to be seen when viewed close up. The fabric has a soft sheen. The pants have no stripes and no seams and do not crease when he falls down onto the couch. He is sitting nearest to me. Next to him, on the arm of the couch one of the girls sits. Another girl sits between him and the second boy, who sits furthest away from me on the couch.

"What up?" asks the first boy.

Space gestures toward me. They all turn their heads in sync and for the first time see me. Their eyes go wide. The boys scan me up and down; contempt sneers their faces. The girls barely glance up, being intent on their nails, blowing and buffing them on their sashes.

"Another?"

"We must take them in," Space answers evenly.

"Won't fit. Look at her hair!" I grasp a tendril of my long hair and check it out. It's titian. I always liked the colour, Nancy Drew colour I thought.

"We must take her in."

"Why?"

"Hospitality is the cornerstone of civilization."

"Old. Ancient. Irrelevant."

"Why do you come then?"

The boy shifts uncomfortably. "H'long?"

"We hope for a longer time," Space answers.

The boy shrugs, and both boys become fixed as they stare into space in front of them, almost like they're seeing something I cannot. I frown, perplexed.

Space's voice recalls me to him. "Time, these are," and as he points to each, starting with the first boy near me, going to the second boy, then the girl nearest me, and finally the girl sitting in between the two boys, he tells me their names: "Byane, Michael, Brittayne, Marie." He claps his hands; the shot of sound jerks everyone's heads to him. He says, nodding at me, "This is Time."

The boys don't say a thing and return to their forward stares; the girls join them in that strange posture. Space doesn't seem to be bothered by their staring or expect acknowledgements. I continue to stand and watch them staring into space.

Space says, "They're consuming."

I look at him blankly.

"We have birth chips in our heads," he points to a spot behind his left ear. "They grow tendrils into our lobes, one of which becomes a control chip in the temple. They mature as we mature. Birth chips facilitate our interaction with green earth, our environment, and each other. We can remain private, allow others to share in our private experiences, or interact with the public environment. The latter is when we're on the streets. Then we all see the same habitat." He nods to them, "Right now, they're in their private environments, being shown games or contests for things that interest them that they might want to participate in."

Byane tosses his head toward Michael. Space says, "Byane is sharing his game and thoughts with Michael." He smacks his hands together hard. We humans all jump to pay attention to him; Atticus stuffs his nose into his butt further.

"It's time to read."

The boys sigh and relax into the back of the couch, locking their gaze onto Space. The girls resume examining their nails. Space glares at them. Brittayne glances up and sees his glare. She drops her hands into her lap and shifts herself into a more comfortable position on the chair arm.

A clatter outside makes my heart pop out of my chest. The others seem oblivious. A bag flies through the window and thumps onto the floor. A girl clambers over the sill, getting her trailing leg caught on the outside of the window. She grouses under her breath, hauls herself forward, seemingly uncaring about her trailing caught foot. It releases suddenly, and she hops forward two hops and falls down into a push-up stance. She scrambles up, grabbing her bag at the same time, and slouches to the wing chair. She flops into it, letting the bag fall onto the floor next to it on its window side. She glares at me.

That's because I'm staring open-mouthed at her, giving her a good view of my tonsils.

She doesn't look at all like the other girls and women I've seen. She has black hair so thick and long, it hides much of the top of her face and buries her head and neck in silky waves down to her shoulders. Her skin is white, not the pink-skinned fairness of Europeans, but white edged with the palest of burnished brown. She's neither dressed in a burka nor a revealing sari-top-toga. She wears layers of scoop-necked grey knit tops that hang loosely from her shoulders, the outermost dark grey one having sleeves shorter than the innermost blue-grey one. Her skirt reminds me of Catholic girls' school uniforms, being a plaid of grey and deep, deep blue with thin white stripes. It's not as short as the sash-width-skirts of the girls in this century and ends mid-thigh. Her legs are encased in thick charcoal tights, and she wears shoes that look more like the boys' ones than the girls'. I can barely see her eyes through her hair and thick lashes, but I can feel their intensity. I look away and blush.

"Time, this is Hope. Hope, Time."

She grunts. I mutter hello to the bookcase.

Space waits until we're all looking at him, sorts through the books on his side table, takes the middle one, and opens it to the bookmark.

"We'll continue with Plato. Byane, what are we reading?"

"Phaedo."

"Michael, why?"

"Dunno."

Space sighs. "Plato was an influencing Roman philosopher of the sixth century before the fall of Rome."

"Um," I raise my hand halfway. "Um, Plato was Greek and born before the fall of Athens."

Space furrows his brow slightly and says, "I think you have that wrong."

"No," I draw out the word. "I don't. Plato is Greek, an Athenian. Why do you think he's Roman?"

Byane snorts, "Rome greatest."

I stare at him. Rome was great, but it's a matter of opinion if the greatest. I say so. Byane sits up to rain contempt upon me. Space raises his hand and says, "We will not argue with a guest." He drops the book on his lap and claps again, for the two girls and Michael have returned to that staring to space thing. Meanwhile, Hope has drawn up her knees and rested her chin on them to watch the show. Space says, "We will continue. Plato was an influencing philosopher—"

"Old," Michael grumbles. Hope scowls at him. Space continues without acknowledging either, "Plato believed in thought, not in scientific experiments. He believed in conducting an experiment in his mind by thinking through it. Though frowned upon as not legitimate, especially after the scientific method had been established, we can learn from thought experimentation. Plato excelled at it." Space brings the book up to his nose and begins to read out loud from behind it. I feel like I'm watching my old classmate in grade twelve, the one who never got beyond a grade five level in reading, when our flinty teacher made him read out loud to the class.

"Simmias and Socrates are in a dialogue." Space brings the book back down to his lap and asks, "Who is Simmias?"

Byane answers, "Simmias disciple of Philolaus. Socrates took him to him."

Space nods, brings the book back up to his nose, clears his throat, and reads: "Also I believe that the earth is very vast, and that we who dwell in the region extending from the river Phasis to the Pillars of Heracles inhabit a small portion only about the sea, like ants or frogs about a marsh, and that there are other inhabitants of many other like places ..."

Space reads slowly, so slowly it's like each word is an hypnotic drop of water falling suspensefully from a leaky faucet. I cannot tell if it's because he has trouble reading—although he pronounced the Greek words correctly and he speaks well otherwise—or if his hearers have trouble following. Hope's eyes are upon him so intently, it's as if she is sucking the words out of his mouth before he even forms them. Byane is watching him carefully. Michael is frowning hard in concentration. I can feel his effort sucking the energy out of the room. The two girls are identical in their stances: heads down, playing with their sashes, sneaking glances at each other and smiling, shifting every so often, probably to wake themselves up.

"... for everywhere on the face of the earth there are hollows of various forms and sizes, into which the water and the mist and the lower air collect. But the true earth is pure and situated in the pure heaven—there are the stars also; and it is the heaven which is commonly spoken of by us as the ether, and of which our own earth is the sediment gathering in the hollows beneath. But we who live in these hollows are deceived into the notion that we are dwelling above on the surface of the earth; which is just as if a creature who was at the bottom of the sea were to fancy that he was on the surface of the water, and that the sea was the heaven through which he saw the sun and the other stars, he having never come to the surface by reason of his feebleness and sluggishness, and having never lifted up his head and seen, nor ever heard from one who had seen, how much purer and fairer the world above is than his own. And such is exactly our case: for we are dwelling ..."

My body grows lethargic. I need to sit down. I fold into the old Barcelona chair. My head sags. It drops lower, lower, lower until my chin rests on my chest and my eyelids close against this world.

11

HISTORY

A sharp voice snaps me into the present. I refuse to open my eyes though.

"You're wrong."

"You're Thrall. You know nothing."

"Am not. I'm middle class like Space," says a derisory female voice.

"Phhfft. Dying off."

"Why d'you come here?"

"Don't be impertinent."

"Look at you, using a big word, eh?"

Silence. Tension. I can feel the weight pressing down on my chest even with my eyes closed. I slit them open. Hope's eyes are tightening; if looks could kill, Byane would be dead. He's smirking. The two girls are copying him. Michael is doing that staring-ahead-of-him thing again. Space is rubbing his eyes. What did I miss?

Space slips his spectacles back on, adjusting both arms to stall for time. The book he was reading from is splayed on his lap. One page is crumpled as if the book had been laid upside down quickly, angrily.

Byane reaches his hand into his tunic and retrieves a piece of paper. It's folded in four and wrinkled.

Hope exclaims, "CEO, Byane! You're ruining it, folding it like that, eh. How many d'you go through?"

Michael starts, touches his temple, and looks over at Byane.

Byane shrugs, "They update weekly. Got newest upgrade beginning of week."

Hope says contemptuously, "They're not real upgrades. They just make you think that, eh. Waste!"

"You want."

Hope says, "Waste! What d'you do with the old ones?"

Byane looks at her as if she's a hopeless case, "In recycler."

"Give em to one of the Thrall!" Hope exclaims.

Byane looks at her as if she's sprouted two heads. He says, "Jealous. Middle class can't afford."

"Can so. I'm middle class!"

My head hurts from all this short-hand speech. Byane snorts while Michael grumbles sotto voce, "Being Wealth nice." At normal voice, he says, "Can't pay upgrade till next pay cycle." The girl next to Michael moves away from him and closer to Byane. Byane doesn't notice, but Michael does. He grabs at her arm to retrieve her, and she obeys.

Byane's reply is to unfold the paper and smooth it with his left hand while holding it with his right. He stops and grabs the top with both hands. He pinches the top right corner.

Suddenly a book is on his lap, open. And a bookmark is hanging out midway through the book.

I yell. I scramble out of my chair. I run round behind it, as if it can hide me. I peek over the top of it, my breathing rapid, my heart tearing along like hell is after it. Everyone stares at me, jaws hanging, eyes wide with surprise. Even Atticus untucks his nose from his butt and blinks confusedly at me.

A book appearing—a solid book with real pages and a hard cover, not some hologram like in the movies—out of that folded piece of paper is too much. I can't bear it. I want to go home.

Space sighs, lays aside his book—his real book, not a create-out-of-thin-air-magic book—heaves himself up, steps over Atticus, walks over to me, grips my shoulders, pulls me upright, puts his face so close that his nose touches mine, and stares deep into my eyes, his spectacles revealing a shadow-gram of his eyes. I feel a calmness emanate from him that seeps into me, my head, my mind, my emotions. I take a deep breath and exhale slowly. I expand my diaphragm again, and again I exhale. I enter a rhythm of deep breathing, and my heart slows down. My legs strengthen and hold me up. Space leans away, watches me for a moment through those show-nothing spectacles, nods, and drops his hands.

After a few moments, we're all seated again, although I'm trembling from returning fear and tension. I sit on the edge of my seat, afraid to relax back into it.

Byane says, "Enough Plato. Real history. I read. Thrall reading drinks."

"Not Thrall. I'm middle class," Hope growls, but no one pays any attention to her except for me, for whom these terms are puzzling. Are there no middle class? Who are Thrall? It's a strange word; it sounds bug-like and reminds me of being enthralled. But the only thing they're enthralled with is the space in their own heads, unseen by others.

My thoughts screech to a halt; Byane's horrible reading has suddenly penetrated my thoughts and yanked me back into this reality. He stops and starts; he stumbles over words; he moves his head from side to side as he tracks the words across and down the page, or whatever that part of the fiendish book is called. Is he dyslexic?

They all look up at me.

Oops, did I say that out loud?

Space says, "By the time we reach twelve, none of us have cognitive issues. We assess infants for every disease and mutation and epigenetic change, and our doctors make corrections to every not-normal cell. Dyslexia is obsolete except in the very young."

"Oh," I reply. But ... "Why is he reading like that?"

"Is reading. Real reading, type men need," Byane replies contemptuously.

"No, it isn't. Anyway, Space doesn't read like that."

"Space different. Old."

Michael mutters, "Antique."

I can feel my brow furrowing. I reach my hand up to rub the wrinkles away. I massage my eyes. "No!" I exclaim, "Space reads really slowly, but he reads like everybody reads."

"Not so," Byane retorts, as if that should be the end of it.

"Yes, they do!" I yell back so loudly, even he shuts up.

Byane throws his book at me.

I rear back, and it bounces off my hands, my lap, and onto the floor. The bookmark stays in place.

Byane sneers, "Try read." He looks over at Michael. The two guffaw, holding their stomachs as they laugh and laugh. The girls titter behind their hands. I think one says, "Real girls no read." The other snickers, "Mabbe she like Hope." Hope yells at them to shut up. They ignore her. Space shakes his head sorrowfully. With a loud sigh that ruffles his lips, Atticus raises himself up on his forelegs, struggles his hind legs up, gives a mighty yawn, then pads leisurely two or four steps over to me, gently picks up the book with his soft mouth, stretches his head over my legs, and opens his jaws. It falls onto my lap, opening up to the bookmarked page. I look at it with fear and loathing. Atticus ignores me as he goes back to his spot and his snoozing.

Space says, "It won't bite." He pauses and continues, "That's the old euphemism?"

"Yes," I reply.

"It won't bite," he repeats.

I reach out a tentative finger and touch it. I immediately retract my cherished appendage and contemplate what I'd felt. It had felt like a page, a real book page, although a little smoother perhaps. I reach my finger out again; I let it rest on the page to tell me what it senses. It's solid. I push my finger against it like one does to turn a page. It moves like paper, although like stiff paper. It doesn't feel as if it's made of nothing or of hologram particles or light. Its surface is smooth, like pebbles burnished by waves but smoother. I slide my finger over to the edge. There is no edge, at least no feeling of edge. There is paper, or pretend paper, and then there is the sense of paper, and then there is none. I touch the edge on its edge. My finger feels like it's sinking into nothing and then it encounters resistance like a magnet repelling another magnet. But the edge isn't sharp. No paper cuts.

I retract my finger and contemplate again this pretend book. Guffaws erupt from the couch, but I ignore them. A huge sigh precedes a demand, "Open book!"

"It is open."

"Know what I mean!"

I suck in a deep breath and pick up the book. The hardback is not rough, like the uncovered hardbacks of textbooks, but it is hard. I turn it over to inspect the cover closer. It looks real. Weird.

"Um, what do you want me to do with this?"

"Me? What 'me'?" Byane asks.

"She means 'I'," Space explains.

"Why she not say? Read!" Byane exclaims with impatience.

And so I do. For several minutes I read, my mind zeroing in on the text until all I see are the words, comfortable, familiar words and sentences and paragraphs I understand. When I look up from my reading, except for Space's, their faces register variations of shock. The boys are frowning. The girls are frozen, gaping at me, disbelieving what they hear, and Hope looks smug.

"What?" I ask.

Space says, "None of the other dumpees read. Unlike you, they refused to touch one of our books. And when they finally spoke, they spoke only I when I was in the room. Some of the men said they didn't want to waste their time reading but to get on with getting home; some of the girls refused to speak to anyone, even me. They had been terrified into silence. You are the first twenty-first-century habitant we've heard read a book out loud."

"Oh." Thinking of nothing else to say and liking the soothing feeling of reading out loud, I recommence reading to the little group: "The survivors on the island had to pass many tests to be allowed to stay on the island. Losers had to return to States society empty-handed. These tests involved feats of stamina or dexterity. They braved overheating, dehydration, semi-starvation. Food and immunity were the winner's reward." I interrupt myself, "Hey, I love *Survivor*. Did you see the first one? What a jerk that first winner was. Me and Peggy couldn't believe what he did with his money. We thought it hilarious. Everyone knows the IRS gets you in the end." The smile on my face melts in the face of perplexed stares. "Um, this is about *Survivor*, right?"

"It's your history, eh. You should know," Hope retorts.

"History?"

"CEO! History is how you lived, eh? In your now time, leaders made the decisions. They chose who to send to remote earth, to get away from States society. Losers had to return, but winners got money to leave Thrall. They became part of the original Wealth. Right?" she turns to direct her question at Space.

I say, "Thrall? Who's Thrall?"

"Thrall!" Byane rolls his eyes at my ignorance.

"I don't know Thrall. There is no Thrall. I should know. I lived back then—now! I mean Now! I know my own time! It was *American* society, not States society. Who calls it that?! And what's with leaving off apostrophes! It's the possessive form! Don't your writers know that! And what are you talking about 'hand picked to have the chance to get away'? It was a show!"

Glares are my reply. Space nods at me. I sigh, my rage washing out of me as quickly as it had rushed in, and go back to reading, "Similarly, groups were picked to rejoin mainstream States society by losing weight. More and more Statians," I stop on that strange word. "Statians? What are Statians? You mean Americans, right? They're Americans! Whoever heard of Statians?!"

Space's sigh halts my tirade. I click my mouth shut, search the page for where I left off and continue: "More and more Statians were kicked out of middle class by gaining too much weight because they reflected what the middle class really were: wasteful. Because of the old-fashioned ways of growing as much food as possible and of creating meals, Statians and Canadians gained weight. These methods were designed to make sure habitants put on fat. In pioneering generations, this was a good thing because the winters were harsh and technology for creating food to eat and keeping habitants warm was primitive. In the twenty-first century, technology was still primitive but it had progressed enough for habitants to no longer need layers of fat to protect themselves against the cold. This applied to most Statians and Canadians. They had not yet learned to make meals the modern way and still used energy-wasting methods that harmed the planet while their emphasis on growing animals as plants and instead of plants and on monoculture ravished the air and land and drained their water. Their punishment for being what they called "environmentally unfriendly," what we know as "green earth unfriendly," was to gain weight. Their environmental movement was still in its infancy, the middle class were still in control with their energy-wasting and green earth unfriendly methods, and the Wealth had not ascended yet. As a result, Statians and Canadians had not yet discovered the optimal method of creating food as we do today.

"They did try to reduce the load on green earth by forcing obese habitants who ate too much into the periphery. Highly-lauded leaders devised a program to go one step better and reduce the burden of the obese on green earth. Although these leaders still used methods bad for our green earth, they were less bad than the ones the obese used.

"Their pickees had to go through a rigorous screening process that they, the leaders, had created in order to decide who joined the group each year. It was a select group. At the beginning of the program, the group was divided into two groups because competition between habitants makes winners. Internal competition was insufficient. Even in the twenty-first century, States and Canadian leaders knew that the Wealth could only be created from habitants who had not only survived competitions but won them as well. The winners left at an acceptable weight and became part of a select group of Statians and Canadians who eventually became the Wealth of today." I stop reading. I can't go on. Are they writing about *The Biggest Loser*? Seriously? And what is this about obese habitants—I mean, people!—and the environment or green earth or whatever. What are they talking about? "This is history?" I blurt out.

"I tell; girl doesn't listen," Byane replies.

I eyeball the page I had just read. It looks like text; it looks like paper. But they aren't. And those words aren't history. They're made up, like this book is.

I say with finality, "It isn't."

"What is it?" Hope asks.

"It's television."

They look at each other, shrug their shoulders, and look back at me.

"Television? You know the goggle box, the boob tube, the time waster? The thing that sucks the hours out of your day? The thing we can't live without? Everyone has one." No clue sparks in their eyes. I might as well be talking about records to the iPod generation. Television has been in my life since as long as I can remember. It keeps me company while I make dinner or do the laundry. It's something to talk about with Peggy and Sue because the news is so depressing and who wants to be depressed? No one watches the news. Television is better. Besides, it's fun to gossip about the latest shows, better than to get down about what our government or some big corp is doing to us. That's what's great about television: we all love to watch the same things. Reality shows are part of everyone's lives. I mean, who doesn't watch reality TV? I suddenly remember: tonight—or was it last night?—is *America's Got Talent*. I can't believe I'm missing *America's Got Talent*! Sue is rooting for that girl with the dimpled cheeks and sweet voice. I think she's too cutesy to be believed. Peggy and I are rooting for the threesome clog hoppers. We'd go to Vegas anytime to see them.

A bump on my knee brings my focus back into Space's library. Satisfied he has my attention, Atticus fluffs down at my feet, but instead of putting his nose in his tail, he keeps his head up and his eyes on me. I clear my throat. "Um ... does Apple exist anymore?"

"The fruit Space insists we eat?"

"No, you know. Apple."

Again with the shrugs.

Hope says, "You were telling us what ... what that word you used is."

I squint at her until I remember. "Televison?"

They don't reply with words just with gazes that bore into me.

"Um ... well ... it's ... uh ... a box on which you watch shows—"

"Shows?" Hope asks.

I search my mind. "Like plays."

"Plays?" Michael asks.

Hope says to Michael, "The plegans for The Holiday. What the Wealth—"

Plegans? I mouth silently.

"What the Wealth give Thrall—," Michael interrupts.

"I'm not Thrall!" Hope retorts.

"—for laughter at habitants pretending on hoverform?" Michael asks.

"Even so," Hope replies sourly. "Plegans."

"People play in boxes?" Michael asks.

"No!" I yell.

"Where?"

"I don't know. Some set or other. But the cable company sends the shows into our boxes."

Hope says dismissively, "You don't know much, d'you?"

"I know more than you. I know this," I slap the pretend book, "isn't history. I know reality shows aren't history. I know we don't have Thrall or Wealth, or whatever you people are. And *The Biggest Loser* wasn't about the environment either. It was a pun. The winners lost the most weight. Get it? You lose, you win? It's fun; it's just fun. And it's fun to root for your favourite team or loser. Everyone watches them. I mean, everyone but those who take themselves seriously, who think they're the elite. And who cares about them?" A giggle erupts into my tirade, to my surprise. I'm losing it, but I finish: "Who watches The History Channel but losers, real losers not punny losers? History is boring. It's so boring, even you future people have to make it up."

They have nothing to reply to that.

12

THE FIVE Ws

I'M sitting at a round wood table that has seen better days in an ordinary kitchen atop Space's building. We're inside the mansard roof and facing backward. I can see the CN Tower, or a slice of it anyway, enough for me almost to feel like I'm at home. In Space's lair, time points backward.

Space places on the table in front of me a heaping plate of French toast, drowned in maple syrup, dotted with red, blue, and golden berries. The plate is followed by a cloth napkin and a mismatched stainless steel fork and knife. I pick the knife up and turn it over and over again. It looks like mine.

"They're from the twentieth century. I collect from that era and the twenty-first century," he says as he places above my plate a glass of water and a cup of coffee whose steam rises lazily into the perfectly conditioned air.

"Oh."

He sits down across from me with his own heaping plate, and Atticus plunks himself down between our feet under the table. We eat in silence awhile, the only sounds Atticus's snuffling as he searches for errant crumbs and our chewing of the delicious egg-soaked bread. I'm so hungry.

"Who are you?" Space startles me as he swallows the last of his first slice of French toast.

I choke on a largish piece of French toast, force it down my gullet, cough, sip a long draught from the glass of water, then swallow too-hot coffee, gasp, and clutch the table as I catch my breath.

Space waits until I'm sitting upright again and asks, "Who are you?"

"I'm an admin assistant."

Space pauses in his slicing of his next slice of French toast and cocks his head at me.

"Um, I have two friends, Peggy and Sue. My boss is a jerk."

He finishes slicing, forks the cut-off portion, and pushes it through a pool of maple syrup in a figure eight. The maple syrup drips as he raises the portion up toward his mouth. And then he halts his motion and simply looks at me.

"I, uh, well, um, I live alone."

Atticus blows air out his nose onto my foot. What do they want me to say? That I have no man, I have no other friends, I have no family since my parents died. So I say that.

Space chews his portion thoughtfully. Atticus plonks his head on the foot he blew on. The weight of it mashes my poor foot into the floor, but I dare not shift it out from under his heavy jaw.

"In our now time, we define 'who' by our jobs as well." He doesn't sound impressed by that. "What are you?" he asks.

I'm chasing berries round my plate with my fork when he asks me that. I drop my fork in surprise, and it hurtles off my plate. I lunge for it, and it bounces off my hand, lands on my skirt, stickies it with syrup, eludes my snapping hand, slides off my skirt, until finally I catch it as it's tumbling to the floor. I put it back on my plate as if nothing has happened and repeat after him: "What am I?"

"What are you?"

"I'm, well, I'm a ... an admin assistant."

"An admin assistant?"

"Yes."

He says, "Mmm ...," as he methodically cuts the last section of French toast slice number two into two. He plunges his fork into it, scoots it through the thin film of maple syrup left on his plate until the plate is clean, puts it in his mouth, and chews the whole thing slowly. After he swallows, he asks, "Where are you?"

"Uh, here, of course."

His spectacles flash as he shakes his head impatiently. He waves his fork as he asserts, "I'm not talking geographically. Your answer would be this is Toronto, just as you were from Toronto."

"What are you asking? Where else would I be?"

"Where are you in your life?"

"Where?" What a strange question. I'm where I've always been: in my parents' house or at work with side trips to see Broadway shows or a Christmas-release movie with Peggy and Sue. And then I remember: I'm turning forty. Or maybe I am forty already. I say that.

"You don't know?" he asks.

"It's a silly question," I reply, stepping around the forty question and going back to his original "where" question.

"There are no silly or stupid or obvious questions. Only dumb answers." He pours more maple syrup onto his plate from a faded Santa Claus jug and proceeds to dig into his third slice of French toast. Atticus's head becomes heavier; he begins to snore, his exhalations a soft flutter of air on my bare leg. It tickles, and I try not to jump.

"How are you?"

"Well, that's obvious," I retort. "I'm not good. I'm in a place I don't want to be. I mean, a time I don't want to be in. I'm in Toronto but it's not Toronto. The CN Tower," I say pointing through the window with my knife, "is the only Toronto thing here. And well, this place. Your place, I mean. It looks normal too."

"The Attic."

"What?"

"It's called 'The Attic.'"

"Oh. Well, it's not my home or my attic or anything to do with my life. I was minding my own business. I wasn't harming anyone. I wasn't sticking my nose into anyone's life, certainly not my friends' lives, I wouldn't be so disrespectful. I wasn't interfering or involving myself where I don't belong. I kept to my own business, and let people mind theirs. And then these ... these ...," I sputter crumbs and berries I'm so outraged. I wipe my mouth with my sleeve.

"Your napkin is on the right hand of your plate."

"What are you, my mother?"

"Your host. I hope my guests are not barbarians."

I drop my knife and fork onto my plate with a clatter, snatch up the napkin, scrub my mouth and cheeks and chin, throw it onto the table. "Those jerks. Why'd they take me? I'm nobody. I'm not important. I can't do anything. I don't make any trouble. I put up with my boss's trivial requests, even him telling me how to do my job. Why'd they think I mattered enough to play with? Why'd she think that?"

"She?"

"Bikini girl!"

"Bikini, who?"

"Well, her name is Bikini. She said," I say emphasizing "said," drawing it out, "that I had to change things, that her name isn't 'Bikini' because she was wearing one. Why was she wearing beach clothes at the office, or lab, or wherever they took me?

She made me watch while she drew all these equations and numbers on a blackboard. She said," I say drawing out the last word with sarcasm drooling from my vowels, "that she wasn't allowed to learn. Since when are girls not allowed to learn?" I scoff, disbelieving that Brittayne and Marie can't read. "Bikini girl says she learnt because of her boyfriend. But no normal girl wants to learn that stuff, equations and math and stuff anyway. Only eggheads want to. And who wants to be labelled an egghead? No guy is going to want to go out with a girl smarter than him. Yet she said," I say sarcastically, "that she has one, has had a boyfriend since birth. She didn't look Indian. Anyway, what I wouldn't give to have a man since birth. It must be nice to be married. Sure, I've been on lots of dates, but as soon as you talk children or marriage, they run away, like mommy is after them or something or they have to, you know, take responsibility for more than their own lousy selves. Men always get their way. They talk about 'the wife' as if she's in command, but if a man really wants something, he knows how to seduce to get it. So I don't believe her. She's probably miffed that she's gone into physics because her boyfriend told her it would be fun, and she's getting back at him by wearing a bikini. And then she has the nerve to say that I," I say drawing out the pronoun, "have to learn this stuff so that I can save her. Like who does she think she is? Why is she asking me to help her? Doesn't she know people don't like others interfering in their business. She should help herself like a real adult. I don't go around expecting people to do stuff for me. I mind my own business, and others mind theirs. Who does she think I am anyway? I'm an admin assistant, not a physics major. I never liked science. I can't do math. I mean, it's not feminine to do math or want to. The scientists say so; they say male brains are meant for math. Maybe English lit doesn't get you a job, but it sure is better to study than math," I say drawing out the short "a" in math. "And anyway, I can't make a difference to anyone. I type. I file. I organize my boss's schedule. How's that going to change the world, or her? How am I going to help bikini girl? She's in the future! I want to be back in my present. I want to go home, and I want to go home now!"

Space has sat quietly all this time, his forearms resting on the table, his hands clasped. He nods when I halt breathlessly, sits back up, and slices off another section of his French toast. He masticates it slowly as he watches me through his impenetrable spectacles. I hack off a section of French toast, slash it through my pool of syrup, slap on some berries, and stuff the whole thing in my mouth. It bulges my cheeks, and I have trouble getting purchase on it with my teeth. Tears start from my eyes, and Atticus lifts his head, heaves his body up with a scrabbling of paws on wooden floorboards, scrambles close to me, and lays his solid head on my lap, against my stomach. He waggles his eyebrows up at me. He pauses, and then he raises his entire body so that his front paws are on my lap. He methodically licks the tears off my cheeks.

I'm not a dog person. I'm not a cat person. Mother and Father never had animals because they felt I couldn't take care of them, and they didn't want the burden at their age. And whenever some high school friend's dog licked me at one of their high school parties, I found it slobbery, gross, and itchy. But Atticus's tongue is not slobbery or rough; his spit and tongue are like body-wash foam on the softest cloth.

I fling my arms around his neck and cry into his fur.

When my sobs ease, Atticus finishes licking the last of my tears, pulls himself gently from my arms, and lowers himself back down to his haunches. He sits beside me, keeping an eye on me. I draw my hands across my clean cheekbones and exhale noisily.

"How am I? I'm screwed."

Space sighs, deeply sighs, as if he's heard the same thing a million times before and is deeply disappointed.

I use my knife like a glaive, like an old-fashioned blade, on the last slice of my French toast. But my anger is weary and sad, and I use my fork less violently. We eat together in the quiet room, me with brows knit so hard they hurt, him unchanging. He cuts the air with another question, "Why are you?"

Space is relentless. I grouse, "I think that's obvious."

He shakes his head, "I ask because you will need to reach inside yourself to survive in this now time. Many have come before you. They died because they wouldn't think about these questions. I haven't heard of Bikini before. One man did talk about some girl who wanted him to change the world. But he dismissed her as being demanding and impossible. His sole concern was to get home. All the dumpees' concern was to get home. They were unhappy. It is not surprising they couldn't adapt here. But they couldn't get themselves home either. Did Bikini say she had asked the others?"

I search my memory, "I think so."

He nods, "Yet they said nothing to I about meeting her. They must've thought like you: what she was asking was impossible. They didn't want to provide what she asked of them, and so they must've dismissed her from their minds by the time we first met. They didn't mention her and her equations when I asked them the same questions I've asked you. I wonder why you have remembered?" He places his fork and knife on his plate together, adjusts them to be in a perfect straight line aimed at me, and looks up at me.

I shrug.

"You alone have said her name. Like you, the man thought her demand impossible, and like you, the man thought he couldn't do it. But he also wouldn't do it. Would you though if you thought you could?"

That's a ridiculous question. Of course, I can't. I tell him that.

"The others died by their own hands because in the end they thought they couldn't either: they couldn't get home. Some tried on their own until they gave up; some waited for I to get them home. Neither method worked. Adaptation was ... difficult. They couldn't conceive of adapting so wedded were they to getting home. I don't want to lose another dumpee. Habitants from whenever now times are valuable. You say you want to get home, but ... how will you get yourself home?"

I shrug.

"What were the equations that Bikini drew?"

"It was a time machine."

Space's fair eyebrows rise into his hairline, and his spectacles drop enough for me to see a sliver of his ice blue eyes. He quickly recovers and pushes the spectacles back up his nose.

He says, "Fascinating. She showed you how to get home."

"I can't do it. Why does she think I can get myself home? That's what engineers are for or physicists or whoever. They're the ones who build these things. Why is she asking me to do it? I couldn't build a time machine if my life depended on it. I couldn't even build a toaster. You could build one, I bet."

"I can't build a toaster."

I stab at the last blueberry on my plate. It rolls away from me, ahead of my angry prongs.

13

TORONTO

I'M in Space's library, fingering my way through his books in their bookcases, one book I'd thought interesting already in hand. Space is sitting in his chair, reading. Atticus is sitting at the door, his eyes on both of us. He seems to be waiting.

A knapsack flies through the window. And Hope scrambles in behind it. I drop the book in my hand, *thuck*. "Do you always scare people like that?" I shout at her. I pick up the book, smooth out its pages. She doesn't answer; she flops in the wing chair instead, right leg over one of the arms.

Space says to his book, "It's not group time."

"Know."

Space slaps his book shut and looks over at her.

"Tutor sick," she says.

Space narrows his eyes. "Maybe you can show Time the town."

Hope looks derisively over at me and starts swinging her right leg, back and forth, back and forth. I stand there, uneasy.

I'd like to go shopping, get out of these clothes. They're starting to feel past their best-wear date.

Space says, "Take her shopping. The female dumpees liked to shop."

Hope's only answer is a snort. Atticus pads over to her and stops to stare right in her eyes. I'd find that unnerving. She merely sighs deeply and grumbles an "Oh, all right."

She flings her right leg off the chair arm and bounces up. She heads for the window, kicking her knapsack into the far bookcase as she passes it.

Space says curtly, "Not that way."

"Not front door."

"Not? Who are you?"

Hope huffs, "We can't exit The Attic front door. We'll be visible, eh."

"Atticus will accompany you."

"Assure I?" It's the first time I've seen Hope brighten.

With Atticus leading the way and Hope behind him, we walk through the door, troop down the stairs into the unlit first floor, and stop at the front door. Atticus sniffs round it; he takes an extra long whiff near the sill of the door. He nods. I swear the dog nodded! Hope sees nothing odd about this and yanks open the door. Atticus waits for me to follow her out, and we head north with him bringing up the rear, a very close rear.

We reach Wellington and I walk into an invisible wall while Hope appears across the street with the rest of the crowd. Atticus barks "Stop." I swing my head down at him in shock. Dogs don't talk. I must've misheard. Suddenly my hand is being grabbed, and I resist.

Hope tells me curtly, "Hold I hand."

"Why?"

"Take it," she commands as she grabs my hand tightly and pulls me forward. We're on the other side of the street and walking, Atticus trotting slightly beside me, slightly behind me, his head keeping constant touch with my right leg. I breathe hysterically; I can't even scream.

Hope barks, "Why can't you breathe? Hey, don't stop."

I stop, and the two of them can't budge me. "What—what—what—" I take a deep breath. "What just happened?"

"You never seen a neutrino bridge?"

"A—a—what?"

"A neutrino bridge. Neutrino bridges are for crossing streets without interrupting the Wealth, eh. In their vehicles, eh." She hauls me forward, and I stumble behind. Atticus steadies me. My nerves calm down, although I face the next intersection with dread. The crowd swells, yet Hope doesn't let go of my hand, and Atticus doesn't lose touch with my leg. She steers us to the garden side of the sidewalk into a cacophonic stream of people hurrying in both directions, away from the two sedate streams of people, one flowing north, one south, that fill the strip between us and the road. She speeds up. I feel hemmed in. I feel like I can't breathe. But I don't want to say anything; I'm already drawing stares with my splotched white skirt and dirtied red cardigan. Some look down at my feet and point. Some pucker their lips, suck in their cheeks as if they're about to shoot out their spit at me. Atticus fluffs and grows. Alarm at Atticus puffs out their cheeks and lends wings to their feet taking them away from us.

I want to go home! I desperately want to go home. I clamp my free right hand over my mouth, for I can feel a scream rising, pummelling my throat to be heard.

Hope looks over at me: "What's wrong with you?"

I carefully take my hand off my mouth, and the scream doesn't come. I say, "I don't like this place. All these people. So many people. Where'd they all come from? And you and Atticus are hemming me in. I'm not used to holding hands and a dog walking at my leg. I just want to go home, go shopping, do something familiar, be in my own place. This doesn't even look like Yonge Street, except back there where Space lives."

"Yonge Street?" Hope wrinkles her brow. "What's Yonge Street?"

"This street we're on," I reply impatiently.

"Not so, Yonge. This is ...," she pauses to scan the air, "Pecksniff Street."

"Pecksniff?"

"That's its name."

"Pecksniff ... Pecksniff ... that name sounds familiar."

"It should, eh. He's the tenth biggest Wealth."

"I don't know the Wealth, so that can't be it."

"Everybody knows the Wealth. They've existed since your now time."

"Well, I don't. They didn't exist in my day. I mean, they're not around! Who are they anyway?"

Hope sighs. "The Wealth are our power, eh. They run Toronto, and all the big cities in Canada, and own the land. They earned it through planting millions of trees in the boreal forest. It gave them right to use Thrall mental energies to drive their knowledge power into developing ecologies—"

"Ecologies?"

"Ecologies are ...," she sketches in the air. I have no idea what she's talking about. She huffs then continues while I struggle to follow: "Ecologies are the most important habitats on the planet. Without ecologies, we'd have no growth. With no growth, we'd have no Wealth, eh. You want to go shopping or not?" She pulls me forward faster, and I trip on the grippy, pink sidewalk-road. I see the granite-like surface rising toward me, fling out my free arm to rebalance myself, and straighten up.

Hope says, "You're so clumsy. Don't you twenty-first century habitants know how to walk?"

"Yes, we know how to walk. But we don't walk so far or fast. Why are we walking? Why not take the subway to Bloor?"

Hope rolls her eyes, and even Atticus seems to chuckle.

I lean back to stop her as we approach what I guess to be King. Crowds cover the sidewalk space. The pyramids of this century are set back farther than the stone and glass skyscrapers I know. They look alternately translucent dull and glowing in the shifting light while water tinkles in the wide gardens at their bases. The surface under my feet is matte, all Canadian rock-like sparkle and colour gone under the clouds that roll in from the west toward us. I lunge to my left blindly toward where I think the subway is, dragging her with me, dodging people, desperately needing to see something familiar. I almost run into the back of the corrugated concrete TTC subway entrance. I let go of her hand and grab the concrete. Stains and cracks mar the three-sided entrance wall. The steel pole is pitted, and the nicotine yellow of the old glass sign, the one that was being replaced in slower and slower TTC time, back in the twenty-first century, obscures its inner light. Strangely for this time, dirt subsumes the TTC icon. People flow around the subway entrance wall, around me, and continue along King, but a few make a U-turn to aim themselves down the subway entrance steps and an equal number aim themselves up the steps, shoulder-to-shoulder, unmoving. I lean over the wall and gape downward. The mass moves a step.

I don't like walking this much, but the subway looks worse. I straighten and turn to Hope, my jaw hanging open. She grins, a "told-ya" grin.

"Why ... why is King station so crowded?"

"King?"

I wave my hand at the subway entrance, "You know, King."

Hope looks up at the old sign and says, "Quilp."

"Quilp?" I twist to look at the sign and see only the familiar TTC name and icon. "No, King."

"Quilp. He's old Wealth, eh. Old from your now time. Quilp ecology owns only factory left in Toronto. They build EM glass sides for our architecture."

"Oh." I stare up at the building across the street and notice again how the glass flows and kind of glows. I finally look at her again and ask again, "So, uh, why is it so crowded?"

"The subway is old. It runs but arrives in the time it takes to walk three blocks. Then it leaves in the time it takes to walk four. Waiting means crowded."

"All of it is this crowded?" I wave disbelievingly toward the subway steps.

"Wall-to-wall habitants. Barriers edge platforms, eh, and subway doors line up to barrier gaps. Old gates in the gaps open when the subway stops to let habitants on and off. But habitants get feet caught between subway and platform in gaps. Sometimes they fall onto the tracks when gates don't close with subway doors. More waiting," Hope ends with an impatient roll of her eyes.

"But ... but ... aren't there more lines?"

Hope crinkles her brow in memory. She drawls, "Mom said they used to talk about architecting new subway lines, but every election, politicians deleted old plans, architected new ones. In one section of now time, politicians architected lines on far-away roads and forgot the main city. Every election raised fares more than inflation. Mom said that's when Thrall started walking, cause they couldn't afford it, and middle class moved into cars—when middle class had cars." She shakes her head, "Hard to believe middle class had cars. But Mom said it's true. Leaders declared subways passé and built more lines on roads. Streetcars run on the lines on roads. More habitants stopped using slow and crowded lines on roads, and land Wealth didn't like them for raising new architecture. Mom said it became a downward spiral of not enough capacity at too high a fare.

"When the Wealth got strong, they subsidized fares to keep subways running to get their Thrall to ecology knowledge creation centres. But they didn't see why they should pay for more subways when they didn't need them. The Wealth don't use subways or streetcars. They allow only themselves to have cars. That way never too many cars, so cars never stop till they reach their end point. The Wealth are not interested in how long it takes Thrall to walk to work. Mom angers when she tells this part of the story, and she tells the story every September when school starts," Hope rolls her eyes. "She hisses when she relates how the Wealth said if Thrall don't like slow commutes, Thrall can work closer to home. Only the Wealth need fast travel." Hope shrugs, "It's always been this way, eh."

I stare at her. I finally manage to speak: "Uh," I stop, I'm so afraid to ask, but I must know. I take in a breath and ask, "How many subway lines are there?"

"Easy," Hope replies. "YUS, BD, and Sheppard."

I blink at her. She shrugs back. I mentally parse out the acronyms: Yonge-University-Spadina (the one U-loop line going north and south), Bloor-Danforth (the straight-line one that goes east-west), and Sheppard (the stump). I stammer, "Three?"

She nods.

"We don't need 'em. We walk. Bigger streets have streetcars and bicycles. They're in their own lanes with streetcars next to the sidewalks for habitants to get on directly from their space, and bicycles between the streetcars and the Wealth lanes. Follow I."

We squeeze through the people to the charged curtain at the edge of the sidewalk area. Cars are streaming in both directions along the middle, but the lane next to us is empty. I lean my forehead against the curtain and turn it to stare down the street to my left. Way down I see a round light moving toward us. Hope grabs my head and turns it to the right. On the opposite side, streetcars are lined up nose-to-tail, like they do on Queen during rush hour, except these ones are in the far right lane, hugging the sidewalk area. They're really sleek, low to the ground, like the ones they're introducing in a few years. Or I guess that was centuries ago now. These ones' sides are streaked with rain grime; the lights sputter on and off sickly yellow; inside, standing bodies are jammed chest to back to shoulder right up to the windows. I wipe my eyes and look again. Yes, there seem to be no seats in these streetcars.

"Where do the disabled sit?"

"The ... disabled?"

"Yes, people who have trouble walking or standing."

"Everybody walk or stand."

I rip my eyes away from the first Red Rocket as with a whine it, the streetcar, starts down the street, and I gawk at her. "Everyone can walk?"

She frowns at me, "Why not? Special nanos grow new legs or repair spine if someone stupid enough to break it."

I marvel at the health care here. I wish we had that. I return my gaze to the street as the second Red Rocket pulls up to the corner. Bicycles are packed in the lane next to the Red Rockets and move jerkily, chaotically, and every now and then one veers into the invisible wall next to the car lane and almost ricochets into the other bikes. Some wobble against the Red Rocket's unforgiving side. Meanwhile, nothing disrupts the even current of cars east and west. I frown: "The bicycles are on only one side."

She shrugs, "It's the way it is, eh. They need to keep lanes for the Wealth." She grabs my hand, pulls me away from the charged curtain, back to the intersection, and suddenly we're on the north side of King.

I twist back to take a final look at King as we walk north. I ask her, "Those bikes going east. How do people go west? Is that the same for streetcars?"

"Mom said Red Rockets never changed their routes from old. But bike routes change every election. Newest Mayor said one way west on," she pauses to look back up at the corner of the intersection, "Gradgrind, and east on the next street, then west, then ... the bike lanes used to be two-way."

"Two way? In that one lane?"

She shrugs, "Better."

We drop into sync with the crowd and walk in silence for blocks. I think we're near Queen, but there's no Eaton Centre. I ask, "Where's the Eaton Centre?"

"The what? Oh, Carker Centre. Over there." She flaps her hand to her left, past the garden. I look up at the building that she's waving to. It's like the others, in that it's completely clear with trees at the corners and crowning it up top, but it's sandy beige from top to bottom. And instead of people working inside, it's filled with people walking and shopping in stores. It rises only three stories and has a dome ceiling, like the old Eaton Centre. I stop to peer through its transparent walls, and I grin when my eyes land on the Canada geese, those familiar, flying geese. "Let's go in here."

"Not so."

"No? Why not? I need new clothes."

"Not so, I decided. We're going somewhere else first. Clothes can wait. Besides," she looks me up and down, "You won't like those clothes. What is it with twenty-first century habitants that you like artificial colours?" She tugs my hand, but I let gravity keep me put as I stare into the stores. I don't like the colours: endless greens and browns, but shopping is shopping. Hope leans forward and drags me, while Atticus pushes me along. I sigh and turn my feet to once again walk north. And I spy those thugs who tried to attack me. I breathe in sharply.

"What is it?"

I point. Hope follows my finger and says, "Atticus." Atticus moves up forward and growls. The boys see him, gesture at me with strange "we'll get you later" configurations of fingers and arms, and take off. We continue walking again. We cross street after street as we climb steadily upward. My legs grow weary, and I whine, "Where are we?"

Hope pauses as she scans the air, "Pecksniff."

It takes me a moment to remember Pecksniff is Yonge. I knew we were on Yonge, I think sourly. But why didn't she know? I ask, "Don't you know the name of the street?"

"It changes."

"What do you mean, it changes?"

"The Wealth are awarded street names, but they pay for it, eh. Whoever's ecology garners highest profit is awarded name on the street. Only Quilp and Barnacle names are permanent on streets or subway stops or architecture."

I'm speechless. We walk until I manage to blurt out, "How do you know what the streets are called? How do you find your way around? What about tourists?"

"Street names are updated."

I scan the area and see no signage. No ads, no numbers on the buildings, no street names. I even check every corner when we reach the next intersection.

"I don't see any names. I don't even see any signage. How do you get around?"

Hope taps her temple. I'm puzzled. They memorize them? They just know? We reach another intersection, and as we go to cross—I'm now crossing these neutrino bridges as blasé as everyone else—I look down the street at the cars streaming toward us and away from us and see something familiar. I squint. "Is this Bloor Street?" I ask Hope.

"Fagin," she replies.

"Well, it looks like Bloor. Let's go shopping here. It has great stores."

"Not so. Thrall and middle class not allowed on Fagin."

"What do you mean, we're not allowed? It's a public place."

"It's for the Wealth, eh. They want Fagin free of neutrino bridges or separated sidewalks from Pecksniff to Barnacle Avenue for their elder Wealth. The old subway stops on this stretch are closed, eh. Some Thrall use them for their weddings. We're going to Forest Hill."

I have no breath left to reply or energy to think for the rest of our walk. My legs ache, and I'm puffing as we climb the hills. We reach an elevated park, and Hope leads us up a set of stairs to it, where she drops my hand. It's blessedly quiet along here, the only people are the women in burkas bending over shrubs, snipping roses, pulling weeds, like I'd seen when I'd arrived. I follow Hope as she walks along the path down its middle. Atticus brings up the rear. We walk down another set of stairs back to street level and into another park. Trees, real trees, the kind I'm familiar with reach up tall, dominating this park. We walk through tall grasses, following a beaten path. We're the only ones on it. We crest a steep hill, and in the distance are houses. They attract me as we draw closer, and I don't notice that Hope has stopped until I bump nose-first into an invisible wall. I'm beginning to hate these charged curtains.

14

THE WOMEN

HOPE grabs my arm, Atticus my skirt, and they drag me away from the charged curtain as I'm trying to wipe the pain from my face, my eyes shut tight in protest. This one hurt. It not only felt like an invisible wall, it felt like an electrical fence too. Nerve endings are popping and zipping across my cheeks, through my temples, and over my nose. And now these two are practically pulling me off my feet. What's their problem?

I shriek, "Hold on a minute!" desperately trying to hold onto my face, to stop the pain zig-zagging everywhere.

Hope hisses, "Not so. We have to hide now!"

"Why?" I force my lids open, perplexed at seeing no threat. "Don't be stupid!"

Their urgency finally penetrating my facial pain, I acquiesce. We duck and hide in a bush. It's as tall as I am, dense, with branches rising up and folding and twisting back to the ground. There are three bushes growing together, and Atticus somehow brushes out our footprints in the soft soil around them as he follows us in, for when I peep through the leaves, I notice they're gone. With one hand, Hope pulls me deeper into the middle of the bush we'd crawled into, while with the other she reaches under her hair. Atticus pushes in behind me. We hunker down and stop moving.

A voice sounds on the other side of the bush, in the same direction as where I'd bumped into the charged curtain: "Alarm here, sir."

I hear beeps: rhythmic, steady beeps. Atticus sighs silently, ruffling my hair, tickling my skin. Hope puts a hand over my nose as I inhale sharply. I almost choke, but I get the message. I reach up to remove her hand, and she does so slowly. The air around us no longer smells of freshly turned soil, leaves, and dusty branches. Instead all scent seems to be vanishing into the ground beneath us.

"Have the scent?"

"Did, sir, but it's ... it's gone. Sorry, sir."

"Chip signatures?"

"No, sir."

"Bla! We'll do it old way. Goggles on. Use eyes men."

Footsteps fan out, and Atticus sighs again. This time it feels like the molecules around us are slowing down; it almost reminds me of the time ship. The warmth on the edges of my body is being frozen and turned into an impenetrable layer of cold plastic. It is the weirdest sensation, especially as I should be cold, but I'm not. Footsteps thump closer to us; we hold our breath. The footsteps stop at our bush; the outermost branches sway, and the leaves rustle. I have never been so still in all my life.

The footsteps march away. But neither Hope nor Atticus relax, and I follow their lead. We hear the footsteps and voices of the men recede. But still they don't move, and so I don't either.

We wait.

It's quiet again.

We wait.

I become restless.

They seem to be fully focussed on something.

I mouth Hope a question: "Can we move?" My legs are so cramped. First all that walking, and now this awkward squatting.

She reaches slowly up to her temple, taps it in a pattern while closing her eyes. She stops, opens her eyes, and then Atticus heaves himself up and leads us out of the bush. We all shake ourselves. Atticus is the best shaker of us all. The leaves and dirt fly off his golden coat; when he's done, it's as if he never lay down in a bush. I end up picking leaves off of my pilly cardigan for the rest of the day. For now, Hope brushes them all out of my hair, and I return the favour. Her thick hair hangs on to them worse than mine does.

She whispers, "This way."

"Aren't they gone?" I whisper back.

"Mabbe."

We walk down the hill a little ways, walk east, across its steepness, following its meandering contours. My calves scream resentment. Hope and Atticus do little leaps and trot along like it's no big deal. I grit my teeth and limp after them, failing to keep up. Atticus nudges Hope, who stops and turns. Her exasperation writes itself all over her hand-on-her-hip stance as she waits for me. Atticus sits down and cleans his chest as I catch up. He stops, tongue in mid-lick, as soon as I reach them. He stands up, and we're off again. This time Hope and Atticus walk on either side of me, trying to jostle me along. My pained legs and aching hips and sore lower back refuse to obey, and they finally give up and saunter at my pace.

We turn back up the hill and encounter a decorative black metal fence. Hope grabs my hand, and Atticus glues himself to my leg. They drag me down to the ground beside the fence. But I raise myself up slightly to get a good peek of the lush garden on the other side of it, a garden with airy shrubs abutting the black bars, magnificent blue-green hostas in front of the shrubs, and rioting daisies of golds and reds in front of those. The daisies edge a path. Paths of small stones meander and spider out to the middle where sculpted bushes and trees hold court. Disneyesque nineteeth-century park benches of blond wood and gleaming ebony metal sit in front of them. Two long groves of leafy trees march away from us, on either side of the sculpted garden, with paths separating them from the sculpted garden. It's a strange mixture of artifice and natural. On the paths women promenade with Afghan hounds. I blink. No, not all Afghan hounds. Some are that shape that reminds me of something. I wrack my brain, and almost yell "Ah-ha!" when I remember, except Hope clamps her hand over my mouth, pulls my head and body toward her, and puts her finger up to her lips as she frowns a "Shhh" at me. I nod. She pulls her hand away. I excitedly lean in and whisper in her ear, "They're Egyptian dogs, like the Pharoahs had."

She whispers back in my ear, "They cloned them from old DNA. Now shhh."

We watch through the shrubs, through their thin branches and sparse dancing leaves. The women walk and preen to each other. There's not a man to be seen. Some are followed by those women in white burkas holding on to the hands of matching children, one boy and one girl, always. Some of the women, who are enveloped in billowing white upside-down sacks, push carriages that look like the most perfect caricatures of nineteenth-century baby carriages, with whirls of metal and beautiful hoods pulled up to shade the babies from the sun, except that they float and don't make a crunching sound on the pea stones.

That's when it hits me.

We're under cloudy skies; they're in the sun.

I twist my head slowly, so as not to engender attention, to look up at the sky. Right above the fence, the clouds stop. I can see the line of an invisible barrier.

"Uh, what's up with that?" I whisper as I point with just my finger.

Hope looks up, "It's the weather curtain."

"The what?"

"The Wealth control the weather. They gained the right by replanting the boreal to counter greenhouse gas storms."

"Greenhouse gas storms?"

"Our now time has mostly cloudy weather. The clouds build on each other cyclically until they clash and release their water. Then they restart building. In between the rains, the clouds move air masses faster and faster. It's difficult to control for entire region, eh. Toronto region encompasses Lake Ontario East to Lake Erie West to Lake Huron South. The Wealth architected weather domes to protect themselves and their land homes from the storms. But then they got tired of all the clouds. Sci Wealth say cloudy weather changes our mood and physiology. They programmed nanos for Thrall and middle class to counter it. But the Wealth want to see sun like historians say you had in your now time. They changed weather domes into weather curtains to keep clouds away from their space, except on cloudlight times when we have the nice kind of rain—"

"The nice kind of rain?"

"The kind that waters our plants but doesn't blow down our trees."

"Oh."

"Can I continue?"

"Oh sorry. Yes."

"Changing curtain permeability allows rain to move over their space, and when their gardeners say they don't need any more, and ...," she looks sideways at me, pauses, then plunges on, "When the Wealth have had enough reality, they change curtain, push back clouds. The clouds bunch up around curtain periphery at first, and we get more rain than normal in that space. Until the weather curtain, all received half sun, half cloud, eh." She shrugs, "That's why they have sun, and we don't."

I have nothing to say. I go back to watching the women. There's something odd about them. I squint my eyes, I push my head forward duck-like. It's not their clothing. The style of their clothes is the same: a short shirt and a low-slung sash that reveals one leg up to the hip. The fabric is softer though and glows. And their clothing is worse than what the girls wear—their sash ends just below their bottoms—but I've almost gotten inured to seeing half-naked women on the streets. And we twenty-first century Canadians think some women look half-naked on our streets! I'll never see what we call scantily-clad women as that ever again. If I ever get home again. A pang smites my chest, and I swallow a lump. I bat back tears and take hold of my breathing. I will not cry. I focus furiously on the women.

All emotions of home vanish as I realize: their shirts are transparent.

It is not the sharp, shiny transparency of high fashion in my time; it's like milky glass. Their sashes aren't transparent, yet somehow I feel like I can see their entire bodies, that nothing is hidden.

Hope blurts in my ear, "Their clothing is designed to show what they are."

I turn my appalled, puzzled face to hers.

She sighs, turns around, and slumps down on the ground, leaning her back against the fence, completely hidden from the women by their self-absorption and the thicker, lower part of the bushes. I copy her. Atticus curls up on my other side to catch a quick snooze. She says, "I don't know why I'm whispering. They won't see us, eh. I come here with Atticus and talk to him in a normal voice, and they never see us."

"You want to be like them?"

"Not so!" she replies in a horrified voice. She looks up at me. "I don't."

"Then why come here?"

"I want to remind myself of what I will become if I stop being vigilant."

"What do you mean?"

"I'm middle class, eh. The Wealth can't touch us. Laws forbid the Wealth to take old middle class land or force middle class girls to receive Wealth or Thrall education or make us like Thrall girls. Middle class don't become Thrall; we become the Wealth. Every conversion dwindles our numbers. I know all the middle class in Toronto. Mom said that used to be not so," Hope pauses.

"What do you mean, 'their education'?"

"Wealth girls attend own girls' schools," Hope stops. "How do schools work where you are?"

"Well, there are public schools and private ones. Boys and girls attend them together. There are some girls-only private schools. Same for boys. Some religious schools that are also gender segregated. And, oh yeah, there's this new Africentric school. But the province sets the curriculum, and we're all supposed to learn at least the three "R"s: reading, writing, and arithmetic. I don't know if it happens or not. It does in the public schools, though some do it better than others."

Hope furrows her brow in thought. She pulls absent-mindedly at the blades of grass beside her outstretched right leg. She says, "In our now time, there are schools for Thrall girls and schools for Thrall boys. Same for the Wealth, eh. Educators also divide habitants into race and religion. So if a habitant is considered Indian, a girl, and Thrall, you learn at

Thrall school for Indian girls. Same for African, German, English, Welsh, Original, Karen..."

"But that doesn't make sense. You all look the same. Well, except for you. Your skin is lighter, but your hair is darker."

"I family ancestors never intermingled. We're pure Parsis. I look same as my great-grandmother. Nanos cure inbreeding problems. But everybody else is mixed, eh. Africans with Chinese, Chinese with Europeans, Indians with Originals. Only DNA reveals most dominant race. We're all in the habitant base, eh, so they know how much each of our ancestors donated to our genes. To keep multiculturalism going, they decide what our culture is from which racial gene predominates. That determines Thrall and Wealth schooling. Not so middle class. We educate our children in our own mixed schools, boys and girls, every race together. Up until university."

"Oh. But. That ... uh, does that mean, your race is determined by genetic typing?"

"Even so."

"Your race is?"

"Parsi. Parsi genetic typing is written on our faces, they say. They don't DNA type us. Also Mom and Dad and all our relatives refuse it. And all Parsis are professionals; we know how to skew the results. They stopped trying."

"Oh. What are Par—But ... so ... um, how much race of one kind does anyone have?"

"Everybody has every race in their DNA. Only delicate, precise DNA testing reveals which tick more a habitant has of one kind over others."

"Does it work?"

"Parsis know every culture. Thrall and the Wealth know own culture. Thrall only learn of cultures and races not their own if make friends from other cultures. The Wealth learn ones their family ecologies do business with. If you're a girl though, it doesn't make much diff."

"Why not?"

"Thrall girls learn the basics, what they need to know to serve customers and serve the boys in their lives."

"Like cooking and stuff?"

"Cooking? Not so. No one cooks except Dad and Space. Dad tried to teach I. I learnt, but no one cooks! Nutrition printers are more ecological ... though they taste ...," she sticks out her tongue.

I decide not to follow up on that. My brain is overwhelmed with too much information, and I still don't understand this whole Thrall and Wealth thing. I ask, "So what do they learn?"

Hope cocks one eyebrow and drops the other at me, "You know." She won't elaborate. I twist my head to watch through the bushes the women walk along their paths. Hope joins me. Atticus keeps snoozing.

"Wealth girls have to know more than Thrall because they help their men make money. They learn to read and write and do math like boys; they learn business principles and how to change the law in their favour like boys; but they don't attend university. They attend finishing school. It teaches them persuasion skills to bend husbands' rivals for benefit of their husbands. It teaches them how to keep perfect and show what they can offer when called upon."

I turn and rise up on my knees to stare better at these walking monuments of perfection. And that's when it hits me: they look almost as flawless as bikini girl. There is an artificiality that's reminiscent of all those Hollywood actresses above forty, with their skins that have none of the bloom of nature left and have a slight unwell swelling. But their bodies move and their skin has a glow that Botoxed and plasticated women in my time don't have.

Hope says, "Protons."

"What?" I frown at her.

"Wealth girls undergo regular proton replacement therapy in their skin. They haven't discovered yet how to do it in their deep muscles safely, but sci Wealth are working on it. The Wealth who flourish more get therapy in their collagen and shallow muscle layers."

"What?"

Hope sighs with impatience, "They have their protons replaced, the particles in every atom that makes up their skin. You have heard of atoms, eh?"

"Yes."

"They swap out old protons for new ones to rejuvenate their skin at the atomic level. It keeps them perfect. When they show their bodies to any voyeur, they show level of their prosperity and reflected power from husbands. Only wealthiest Wealth afford full body, collagen, and shallow muscle proton regeneration. Lesser Wealth afford full body but not collagen and shallow muscles. And bottom Wealth afford only faces. Their husbands too acquire a visual reminder end of every cloudlight of how their ecologies are flourishing. It incentivizes them to compete harder, eh. Rivals know how a man is doing when they talk to their wives at night, eh. Rivals' wives report on proton replacement levels they see during cloudlightly promenades in this space."

Hope drops her head and her hand to her lap. She picks at her skirt. I flop into a sitting knee position and ask, nodding at the women in white burkas, "What about them?"

"Who?"

"The women in white burkas."

"They're married."

"What do you mean?"

"You know married, eh?"

"Yes, but ..."

Hope blows air out. She twists around to look through the fence again. We both follow one of the burka women as she pushes a carriage behind the Wealth woman, girl, whatever, as she walks along the perimeter path, then turns to go down the path between the grove of trees and the sculpted garden. The Wealth woman sits on a bench beside another Wealth wife. The woman in white stops and pushes the carriage into a little layby next to a tree sculpted like Mercury, behind and to the side of the bench.

"Once a Thrall marries, she cannot work in public anymore, in the stores I mean. Thrall need as much money as everybody can earn, but it's dishonourable for married Thrall to be seen by men not their husbands. They can work in the gardens, because most men work in architecture and plants obscure them from view, and they can be nannies to Wealth children. Some are allowed to work in girls' schools; it depends on how strict their segment of the Thrall community is. White is easier to see."

"Easier to see?"

"To identify and follow."

"Oh."

"Our birth chips let habitant base and Wealth enforcement patrol monitor us."

"Wealth enforcement patrol?"

"Wealth enforcement patrol."

I scowl in thought, and then my brow lightens. "Oh, you mean those men looking for us?"

Hope nods.

"Okay, Wealth enforcement patrol. But they didn't find us."

Hope smiles, triumphant sneakiness widening it. "Parsis know how to turn off our chips so they can't track us, eh? We don't do it often so that they don't know we can. And Atticus, well, Mom programmed him for Space to give him special abilities to hide us in other ways."

I don't follow that up either. I don't want to know how one programs a dog.

Hope continues, "But everybody wants to know by looking, who the married women are, and white tells. They're fully covered too. No one can see through their clothes."

I examine Hope's clothes and ask, "Why are you dressed that way?"

"I don't want habitants seeing my body! I have respect for Iself!"

"But you're so different."

Hope glowers at me, "Even so?"

"Don't you hate sticking out?"

"I hate being treated like a habitant more. I hate having men decide what I should wear and what I should learn, and I hate girls trying to make I do it too."

"You didn't go to girls' schools like the Thrall—"

"I told you, not Thrall."

I raise my hands in surrender, "I'm sorry."

"Mom educated I. She's a mechanical space engineer. Dad educated I too. Parsis educate their own even after we begin school. That way we girls become women. Parsi girls are also allowed to attend university because of some grandfather clause from before parents' time. As long as they let I be, that's all I care about, eh. That's where I'm at now: university. But though they let I attend because they have to, they try to keep I down, especially in philosophy and literature. Theology is illegal for everybody. They don't want Thrall men to learn any of that either, but Thrall never go to university, and there are less middle class girls in university. So they think it's safe to teach everybody philosophy and literature in the classes because everybody is Wealth men. Then I tried to take one. They don't want I in those classes. They have to let me enroll, but ... I don't know how they keep I away ... it's like they've designated certain boys to prevent I from reaching one of those classes, even to audit it.

"Space is an old friend and started a group to teach curious Thrall and I philosophy and literature and theology. Space is taking a chance teaching theology, but Dad says it's important. Byane heard of it and showed up one cloudlight. He says the philosophy and literature they teach in university is green-earth-related only. He told Space he's bored and wants more than what will prosper him. He wants his mind prospered too. Space believed him. Space let him stay. Byane also said he wants true friendships, not the shifting loyalties of the Wealth." Hope snorts at this. Then: "The Wealth cannot be friends. They see everybody as rivals, eh. They play games with each other, and they consider needing other human beings, especially when times are tough, to be weak. Thrall have friendships and community but don't rally around to support each other when times are even tougher because they're all weak. We Parsis rally and have friendships, but Thrall, they're all at the bottom, eh. They're all maintained in their places equally, girls at the bottom of the bottom. What you don't know, you don't miss, eh? But they resent any looking like getting better and attack weaker before the Wealth can, to prove loyalty, eh.

"But Space is teaching them what they're missing by reading the Classics, and Byane has begun bringing his history books. Michael and the girls prefer their interactive books when they're not in game rooms, so Space is teaching them how to read and enjoy Byane's text books. But I guess they're all wrong," she ends on a grousing note.

A tiny umbrella of white fluff floats into my open mouth, and I begin choking. Hope bangs my back. Atticus sits up, worried. The Wealth women on the path and the benches don't notice. The woman in the white burka guarding the carriage catches the sound. I can't tell what she's thinking; even her body language is hidden from me. I try to stop choking, to hide, but I fail. She returns her head to its former position, to look blankly into space as before. With a final wallop from Hope, the fluff flies out. I drop to my hands and knees, gasping in relief.

15

SHOPPING

WE'RE back at the Eaton Centre, Canker Centre, Carker Centre, whatever. Hope is ahead of me. Atticus walks beside me with two saddle bags on. I have no idea where they came from, and I don't want to ask. The outside ground floor wall on Queen is not a wall; it shimmers. My head is swimming. I have barely taken in all that Hope had told me at the garden, and I can barely take this in or the tumult of people ahead, behind, around me, all looking at me with knife-like contempt but not acting on it like before.

We enter.

There are no stores like I'm used to, with their branded signage and variations of heart-pounding beats spilling through their doorways. There are no info signs or info kiosks. Instead, uniform square spaces like boxes sit on each side of the central aisle with their outside and aisle side walls transparent while walls between the boxes—stores—are white. Clothes mannequins or shoe displays or unfamiliar objects dot the inside sparsely. Trees grounded by lush grasses march down the centre of the mall, while vines sway down from the ceilings over the trees, tickling our heads where they dangle and dance into the aisles unabashedly. People stuff the aisles. It's like Christmas Eve, it's so thick with shoppers. Hope silently leads me to one of the clothing stores. Lifelike mannequins model the sash and shirt combos I've grown accustomed to seeing. Not a lot of imagination here; there isn't much difference between one model and the next except for colour and the width of the pleat in the draping. I can get dull green, murky green, hosta blue-green, soil brown, tree brown, cacao brown, sandy beige, reddish sand, or grey sandstone. I desultorily finger one of the sashes. The cloth is so silky; its fluid texture stimulates my nerve endings, and I feel my heart beat faster. A rush hits my brain, and I feel a pleasurable warmth invade my body and spread down. I drop the sash and look at it in horror as it falls back into position. Cloth is cloth. It's not supposed to give me an ... an ... "What is this?" I demand of Hope, staring at her horrified.

Hope laughs mirthlessly. "Touch that one," she points to a soil brown sash a metre away. I hesitate until she presses me on. I walk over, Hope and Atticus on my tail, and gingerly take it between the tips of my forefinger and thumb.

Hope sibilates, "Grab it."

I look at her as if to ask if she's sure. She nods vigorously. I grab it. Immediately, I feel a surge of energy, an urge to work, a feeling that I have to move and move now. I let go and step away.

I hiss at her, "What is this place?"

"Clothing store," she replies.

"But ... but ... these are ... these are ... like possessed!"

Hope throws back her head and laughs so loudly others stop their own sash fondling and glare at her. She claps her hand over her mouth and grins at me around it. "Clothing makes habitant." Her shoulders shake, up and down, up and down, until finally she gets her mirth under control.

I see nothing funny. I carp, "Are any of these safe to try on?"

"Try neutral suit."

"Which one is that?"

She points to a sandy beige shirt that is overlaid with a sandy beige sash. I frown at it and say, "I thought you said suit."

"It is a suit," she retorts.

"That's not a suit." I gesture to my cardigan and sorry-looking skirt. "This is not a suit either, but it's closer to a jacket over a shirt and a neat skirt, which is a suit."

"There's nothing else. You want to fit in or not?"

I notice at that point that everyone is staring at us, no, at me, pointing at me, and talking behind their hands. Some look disapproving. One man is weaving his way toward us with an unhappy expression on his face. He looks me up and down as he stops in front of me and says, "The married room next door."

Hope says, "She's not married."

"What she wearing? That not suitable for a single girl."

"That's why we're here."

He rakes her up and down and sniffs, "Not suitable either. But one says nothing to Parsis. They wear what they want." Hope grins at him. He ignores her easy freedom and asks, "Is she one too?"

"Not so."

"Good. I dress her. The beautiful cinnamon and cacao brown shirt will look good with that ... that hair colour." He takes a lock of my hair to study it, "I recommend a hair dasher. He will make her a girl."

I blurt out as I grab my hair and pull it back from him, "I like my hair."

He frowns then relents, "Clothes first."

Hope says, "She wants neutral suit."

The furrow lines between his eyes deepen, "Not so."

"Even so."

They stare icily at each other. Hope won't budge, and he finally acquiesces. He bows and leads us to the sandy-beige mannequin. A beam lashes out from it, and I jump. He tsks and tells me to stand still like a good girl. I stand still. The beam scans me, and a spot on the white wall to our right flashes. He leads us to that spot, and that's when I notice almost invisible lines of doors all along the wall that separates this store from the next. He presses the wall next to the door, the spot stops flashing, and the door slides open. A suit in my size is hanging inside the mirrored cubicle waiting for me. I enter but don't know how to close the door. Hope reaches in and slaps the wall next to the door and retreats sharply as the door shuts.

It's so quiet. I see myself—lots and lots of myselves. There's something wrong with my reflected selves. I shiver, stop trying to figure out what's wrong, and eyeball the shirt and sash hanging, waiting. With a sigh, I strip down to my underwear and pull on the shirt. I stand for a moment, scanning myself internally for changes. None. Relief floods me. I button up the shirt. It fits snugly, yet not tightly. But my bra straps show. I make a face to my mirrored image, sigh, and experimentally move my arms. No restriction. I can't even feel the cloth. I focus on my image again to check that I have something on. Though I'm loathe to admit it, I rather like the feel of the shirt. I eyeball the sash. I move my head to check its sides; I reach out a finger to pull it away from the wall and check its back. I'm not sure how to put it on. I slip it off the hanger and let it dangle from my hand as I check it from the top angle. Maybe I should just put it on. So I do. It easily slides over the shirt and drapes into place. There's a clasp on the left, and it snaps closed at my touch. I lift my head and gasp when I see myself in the mirror. I'm fully dressed, with my underwear showing here and there, yet so naked. I can't go out in public like this! I try to pull the sides of the sash closed over my left leg, but the fluid, soft material won't be pulled into that position.

It's like it has a mind of its own.

Heart thudding, I yank it off, rip at the shirt, the buttons popping open, and haul on my dirty T-shirt, its texture now rough in comparison to these twenty-fifth century clothes, but so comfortingly covering. I haul on my skirt, shove my arms into my cardigan so fast, one hand gets caught in the sleeve. I don't care. I push my feet into my pumps as I keep tugging at the errant sleeve, pausing only to slap the wall. The door slides open, and I stumble out. "Let's go." I practically run out of the store and weave through the crowds, backtracking from where we came, pushing and shoving until I'm outside, still surrounded by crowds but at least breathing fresh air, fresher than anything I've ever tasted. Hope bumps into me as I stop abruptly to catch my breath. Atticus had kept up with me.

Hope says, "You didn't like it."

I give her a dirty look.

She pats Atticus, and his saddle bags disappear.

"Stop doing that!" I shout.

She looks at me perplexed, "Doing what?"

"That!" I point a shaking finger at Atticus's bare back.

She glances at him then at me, still confused.

"Making things appear and disappear! Don't do that!"

She rolls her eyes.

"I want to go home!" And to my horror, tears spurt out, and I'm bawling into my hands. I feel her grab my sleeve, the one that still hasn't allowed my hand to go all the way through it, and drag me until a wall has my back. Atticus's gentle body leans on my left leg. Hope lets go of my sleeve, but I can sense her standing near me. I wail and blubber and snuffle, and they wait. My sobs quieten. Hiccups take over.

Hic. Hic. Hic.

I can't stop.

And because I can't stop, keening rises from my throat again.

Hope shoves something round and small between my right hand and the eye its covering. She closes my hand around it and commands, "Suck it." I palm it into my mouth. I suck. The hiccups stop. The sobs stop. I wipe my eyes and wet cheeks with the back of my hands. Atticus rises up on his hind legs and puts his paws on my shoulders, and I rear back. His head reaches forward, and he methodically cleans my face. His spit is still not like any dog spit I've felt or smelled before. When he's done, he lowers himself, and my face is as fresh feeling as if I'd scrubbed it with my facial cleanser.

Hope says, "I'll get you clothes."

We walk for blocks and blocks, through gardens and in crowds until we get to a people-free neighbourhood, to a house, a normal-looking large Toronto house. As we approach the house, I hear it unlock, and we enter.

It's blessedly quiet. Hope tells me to wait there in the hall, and she disappears up the stairs. When she returns, she's carrying an armful of clothes. She leads me to the back and into a small room with a curtain covering the window.

She tosses them onto an overstuffed chair and says, "Put these on." She leaves, taking Atticus with her, and closes the door like one does in my time: shuts it until the latch clicks into place.

I tiredly strip off my clothes again, and struggle into the new ones. The texture is as soft as the naked shirt was, the drape as fluid as the sash's. But this shirt covers me to my waist. And there's a sweater that goes over top that glides on easily. No tugging to pull it over the long shirt sleeves. The skirt is a familiar tartan. It's been a long time since I wore a kilt though this one is not as scratchy as a normal kilt. I sniff as tears threaten again, and I drag my new sleeve across my nose and down my cheeks. I flop down on the chair and hang my head, as I contemplate my bare legs.

"You done?" comes Hope's voice through the door.

I nod and then grate out, "Yes." I clear my throat and repeat myself louder.

Hope bangs open the door and slams it closed after Atticus enters. He's back to his normal size. "Here are shoes." She drops them at my feet. "You didn't put on your legs."

"I will. I'm so tired."

"You need to get dressed before Mom and Dad arrive home."

"Okay. Who are they?"

"Mom and Dad?"

I nod. Energy flickers in me, and I pull the stockings out from underneath my butt as I ask her, "Tell me about them."

She drops to the floor to sit cross-legged and starts picking at the carpet. Atticus stands by the door, on guard. I inspect the stockings as I wait. They're like those expensive Dim-Ups Peggy sometimes buys when she has a hot date but with no visible upper band to hold them to my legs. Hope's voice interrupts my inspection: "Mom is a mechanical space engineer. She designs and builds machines that create their own energy. I'm not supposed to tell anybody she can create machines that can supply power from no power input. But you're not anybody. You're nobody. You don't count."

I grimace, "Thanks."

Hope doesn't notice and keeps picking at the carpet as she continues: "Her prototype doesn't need lubricants. In our now time, all engines use solar or movement power and need leaf-oil-based lubricants to make their parts move, else they seize up. It's university property what she's invented, but they don't know she has. Is it theirs? Dad teaches at the same university. He teaches thinking techniques for Wealth boys. I want to take his class, but the university won't let I. He signed his contract with his retina image promising not to teach I. He taught Space instead, and Space teaches I outside of his reading group. You can't tell nobody that either."

I shake my head and cross my heart. She frowns at me, "What y'doing?"

"Crossing my heart in promise. Don't you guys do that?"

"Not so!" she replies crossly.

"So they both have jobs for life?"

"What do you mean?

"Tenure."

"Tenure?" she asks puzzled. Then her brow clears, "Tenure! The Wealth abolished tenure. To stay a professor you have to do what the university says, and the university is owned by ... by ... who is it now? Barnacle! Barnacle Wealth own City Hall too, have for as long as I remember. They're oldest, biggest in Canada. No one can beat them though Carker tries. I heard Fagin has planted enough trees and accumulated enough knowledge power to get the main east-west street where the Wealth shop. Fagin ecology may vie for university in next tree generation."

I'm frozen in shock. Hearing nothing but silence from me, she stops her carpet pulling and looks up. "What?"

"Companies own the university?"

"Companies? Don't know them. The Wealth through their ecologies own everything."

I laugh out, "Not Parliament though, right?"

"Who do you think chooses the PM?"

"Voters choose the Prime Minister, don't they? You have elections, right? We've had elections for centuries. Too many, right now," I end on a grousing note.

"We have elections. But the Wealth fund campaigns. Wealth ecologies with the largest number of new plantings are allowed to fund their candidates more. Those ecologies lease all ads, pay biggest continuous issuances to endorse them. We know who should win. Polls tell us hourly. We vote for them."

"I hate polls. Don't you vote for who you want?"

"Why? MPs do what PM tells them. Everybody knows that. Ecologies choose the PM."

"We choose the Prime Minister and MPs. They're Ministers of Parliament, not Ministers of the Prime Minister. That's why we have elections. We choose who represent us. We have our say, and after that they're supposed to run the country. I don't know about companies or ecologies or whatever they're called. I hear complaining at the office, especially from this one consultant who likes to run off at the mouth, about it not being a democracy anymore, about how the Prime Minister does everything and tells the MPs what to do, but I don't see why that should matter to me or why I should get involved? Why does he think we need to do more than go vote? We vote so they can run the country and leave us to our own lives. I don't expect them to do my work, but he and annoying people like him seem to think we should do our politicians' work. I mean, we still decide on our own who to vote for."

"Assure I? I don't believe you. In our now time's Parliament, MPs vote for the PM the same week the first cloudlight Parliament sits after the election. Ecologies tell MPs who to vote in as PM during the campaign. It's never a surprise. Did they in your time?"

"Well, no. But—"

"Ours do. Mom said in your now time, parties chose the PM. In your now time, voters had no say who was PM, electing whomever parties chose as their leaders. But ...," she shrugs. "It doesn't matter we're more democratic in law, by having our representatives vote for our PM, because MPs know who to vote for. The ecologies tell the MPs," she picks at the carpet vigorously for a few minutes before continuing: "Without the ecologies, there'd be no gardens and no economy. It's not the government that takes care of our planet, it's the ecologies. Everybody knows that."

"Why are gardens so important?"

"They represent ecologies. The more diverse a garden—more bushes and native flowers and guard raccoons—the more powerful the owning ecology, eh."

"Oh. What about other countries?"

"You mean India?"

"Sure, okay. It's not real important, but—"

"What do you mean, not important?! India is huge. They say that India is really bad on green earth and feed our greenhouse gas storms. They say they don't respond to climate change like we do and use what's left of planet oil reserves to power their vehicles. They say that's why Canada is a better country to live in. We care about green earth. We care about our planet! We make it a better place to live, not them. The stories in the continuous issuances prove what the Wealth and the PM say is true. But Dad sometimes smuggles in other issuances when he can." Hope stops speaking abruptly.

"What?"

"The stories in our continuous issuances are lies." She pauses and searches my face. I make myself look as innocent as possible. Reassured, she whispers: "They say women are equal there. Girls don't have to dress for men. And there is no Wealth or Thrall classes. They say middle class thrive there. People are free to be and say and vote the way they want. Every vote counts because ecologies don't own the economy or the government. They say they don't even have ecologies. Anyone can be what they want to be, do what they want. I hear those middle class not converting to the Wealth, wanting to be free and not oppress, are talking of moving there. Mom and Dad are. They could have tenure and be free to research and to lecture on more than what prospers the Wealth—without being censored. I'll be allowed to learn what I want. I'm not supposed to tell anyone. Don't speak of it!"

I mime zipping my mouth.

She stares daggers at me, "Not to Space."

I shake my head, "I won't. I promise."

"Everybody knows promises mean nothing. You have to swear on the Barnacle tree."

"The what?"

"The first tree the Barnacles planted to show their support for green earth two hundred years ago. It stands at City Hall. It symbolizes Canadian commitment to being green, to green earth, to living and knowing it's the most important habitat. All ecologies support green earth. But Barnacles were first."

"You revere ... trees?" I ask astonished.

Hope looks at me as if I've just said the most obvious thing in the world.

"Well, I'm not swearing on a tree. You'll have to take my word," I retort.

Hope hesitates while Atticus watches us both from his stance by the door. Hope avers, "Everybody knows a tree is trustworthy and to swear on one means you're swearing to be like it. You can't trust habitants. Habitants blighted green earth, no matter what Originals say, but I guess I have to."

"Well, thanks," I reply dryly.

Hope nods as if she's done me the biggest favour yet.

16

TEA

I'M sitting with Space and Hope at one of the tables in The Attic. Atticus is in his usual place—at Space's feet. I'm starting to wonder if he's a dog. I reach down to stroke him. His fur feels real, that mixture of softness and prickle. I fondle his ears. He cocks his head, then moves it around so I'm scratching his ears right where he wants me to do so. I remember my childhood friends' dogs doing the same thing. I stop scratching his ears. He looks up at me, raises one eyebrow, then the other, Groucho Marx style. I pat his head, bouncing it a little bit in my zeal. He's a dog. He must be. He has to be. Otherwise, what is he?

"What is Atticus?"

Space and Hope stop their murmured conversation and stare at me, Space through his inscrutable spectacles, Hope as if I've asked the stupidest question in the world. But unusually so, I won't be deterred. I must know. "Well?"

Space says, "Atticus is a dogdroid. A special dogdroid." He gestures with his head toward Hope, "Her mother created him for I, after her father asked I to teach Hope philosophy, theology, and thinking methods."

I blink at them. Dogdroid. What the heck is that? I ask it out loud.

Hope blurts, "Everybody knows what dogdroids are."

Space says quietly to Hope while facing me, "Not dumpees, Hope. That's one reason why they're left in our now time. It isn't just because of our politics, it's because our technology is so far beyond what twenty-first century habitants can imagine or have seen that after awhile they cannot handle it. That is the hope of the future boys. But you can handle it," he ends, directing the last at me.

I swallow bravely and whisper, "Sure."

"You're familiar with androids."

"No. I'm not an egghead. I don't do sci-fi and all that nerdy stuff."

"Too bad."

Suddenly I feel stupid and open my mouth to defend myself, to say that nerds and geeks and dweebs and eggheads just like to show off how smart they are, that their theories are not as important or useful as experience, real experience that people like me have. I want to say that science news is boring or irrelevant so us real people don't have to pay attention to it, unless it's the latest iPhone from Apple. Otherwise we don't need to know that stuff. But Space talks over my open mouth and says, "Knowing your own culture's science, including popular science, knowing your now time's ideas of the future would've helped you in our now time.

"An android is a human being that's artificial. A dogdroid is the same but in the shape of a dog. Human emotions and moral choices caused early Wealth trouble when they achieved a certain point in their android design. W—

"I must omit the name, it'll pollute your now time if you know it when you return. This scientist was a dog lover and created an android based on a dog, the chocolate Lab. Labradors were the most popular dog in Toronto, in your now time and in the scientist's. Labradors are loyal, loving, hard workers, energetic, playful—the qualities the Wealth were looking for, except for loving and playful. Love and friends to play with are irrelevant to the Wealth. But they couldn't design those qualities out. They switched to another dog template, but it didn't help. For their aesthetic value, golden retrievers became the popular model despite the potential for outsmarting the Wealth. Sci Wealth believed that they could keep that potential suppressed. And ... for the most part ... succeeded." He smiles a small smile.

Space continues, "Some dogdroids are ornaments, like the Afghan hound variant Wealth women take with them. The Afghan variant sticks by the side of their owner, carries purchases and rejuvenation touch-up kits, but can do nothing more. The Egyptian variant watches over Wealth men and ecology tree spaces."

I process what he's said, nod, and say: "I saw lots of golden retrievers on the streets but not golden Labs like Atticus."

Hope snipes, "Everybody can afford dogdroids. Can we discuss it?" Hope fails in changing the subject.

"All those dogdroids belong to the Thrall?" I ask. I finish, "We are discussing dogdroids anyway, Hope."

Hope says, "Not dogdroids."

At the same time, Space says, "Atticus is unique. The common-template dogdroids carry out errands Thrall do not have time to do because they work full cloudlights. Dogdroids buy Thrall food and clothing, manage money, provide safety in the home—"

Hope interrupts, "I want to discuss sending Time home. You said you wanted to Space, eh?"

Space sighs. I don't know who to look at, which conversation I should follow. Space says, "I'll get more tea." He disappears into the back. Atticus drops his head onto his paws, looks pitifully into the distance. I lean down again to stroke his head. His eyes blink; his lids droop. He snaps them open; they droop again. I keep stroking, soothing him as much as me. My eyes blur. I cannot believe he is artificial. He has the warmth, the feel, the look of a real, living dog. Yet I remember how he raises himself up, more like a human being does than a dog does, showing greater control and strength through his core. I remember how he protected us from the Wealth enforcement patrol. My stroking slows, and I blink rapidly. Atticus's face comes back into focus. He's asleep. I stop stroking and sit back up as Space carries a tray over to the table and sets it down. He pours the tea, hands around the biscuits. We sip and nibble. Hope squirms. Space finishes his cup, pours himself more tea, and says to me, "Tell I about Bikini."

"What's there to tell?"

"Tell I about what she taught you."

"It was all gibberish. I don't know. I don't know maths or physics. I'm a girl, you know."

Hope barks, "Middle class girls do math and physics." She growls under her breath, "Parsi girls do. They can't," she says drawing out the word "they" while jerking her head to the upper library, "But in your now time, girls did. Educators in your now time taught you all, boys and girls."

"I majored in English. I hated math. I only took it while I had to in high school. Me and my friends would wheedle our teacher to pass us so that we wouldn't have to learn the hard stuff we would never use anyway. If he passed us, he wouldn't have to get us again."

Hope emits a sound of disgust: "You have the chance to learn, and you throw it away? Girls in our now time don't, eh. Thrall boys have limited. Educators and the Wealth decided before they were born that they learn only what they need to clean streets, sell clothing, or power knowledge centres."

"You know science," I shoot back.

"Mom taught I. She learned from her mom, who learned from her dad, who learned from his mom. Parsi middle class school taught I. But if I'd been the Wealth or Thrall, eh ...," she shakes her head, unable to complete the thought.

Space says to me, "Recount what happened. Include all details."

I sigh, slump back in my chair, cast my mind back to that bizarre place and those bizarre people, and sigh again. I sit up and recount. The two listen without interrupting. I find their solid gazes unnerving and shift my eyes to the nearest bookcase. I finish telling the books my tale. I stop talking, and silence falls heavily. It blankets us and oppresses me.

I struggle to understand what has just happened, for I had recounted my tale in precise detail, every memory moment vividly real. I don't understand how I could relive it as if I was there again.

I'm a regular English lit graduate, I have a regular memory, yet I could see, smell, hear, remember every word she said, every equation she drew. And I hadn't realized it until I'd begun to tell it. I shiver. I clear my throat; I look down at Atticus, whose eyes are open and upon me. Does he understand? He lifts his head to look straight into my eyes, startling me. I jump, shift my chair closer to the table away from him, shift myself in my chair.

Space says, "The device she put on you sounds like the learning aid the Wealth use on their boys during first school."

"First school? Learning aid?"

"Wealth boys must learn greater knowledge than anybody else, and there's more to learn than in your now time. Learning starts at two, and adulthood starts at twenty-one in our now time, that's when the Wealth enter university. But there are still too few years to learn what they need to in order to understand green earth sustaining technologies, ecology business theory, and law before they enter university. University is for what it's always been for: plant new network connections, gain independence from fathers, and refine competitive toolboxes. They learn thinking and practical business methods to facilitate growing their ecologies.

"Learning for learning sake is considered slow and old. Educators developed a device to aid learning. It shortcuts effort and speeds up knowledge acquisition. They acquire the same amount of knowledge in less time. It is what Bikini placed on you. But it must be more advanced than ours."

"Oh."

"You remembered everything."

It's not really a question, but I nod anyway.

"D'you know what it means?" Hope asks.

I shake my head. I remembered it all, but I don't know what it means.

Space says, "Tell us the first equation she showed you."

I shake my head. I don't want to see it. I'm not a math major. I'm not a physics prof spouting stupid theories. I'm just an admin assistant. "I don't know this stuff. I just want to go home."

Hope snorts, shoves back her chair, and stomps up the stairs, smacking the library door open, slamming the library window up, and clattering down the fire escape. The clangor fades.

Space says, "Try."

"I don't want to. It's not me. I don't understand these things. It's not me."

"You want to go home?"

"Yes. But you'll get me there. You guys are smart. You have all this magic tech. Why can't you send me home?" I end on a whine.

"We don't do time travel. You have done it. You will."

"No, I won't!"

Atticus barks on my punctuation.

Shocked silence falls.

Clanging footsteps on the fire escape seep into the dead sound space my exclamation created. A heavy object lands on the library floor. Seconds later, Hope appears at the top of the stairs and takes the stairs one at a time, every footfall a decrying tome on my head.

She roars at me from the bottom step: "You want to go home? Don't look to us. Girls do that. Girls expect boys to do habitats for them. They know they can't do science, so they can't. Girls think they're dumb, so they are. They don't try, and they don't want to try. They lean on boys or middle class. Like you. And guess what? We don't want to. We don't want to and can't do time travel for you. You want to go home? You have to make it so!"

17

CONFORMITY

THE air breathes in the quiet of The Attic after Hope stomps back out. Atticus splays out on his side behind my chair, between me and the shut front door.

Space says, "Since you believe you can't go home on your own, you will have to learn to live here. You must dress like our now time girls and work as a girl. You have skills?"

"I'm an admin assistant."

"What do admin assistants do?"

"They do the administrative work to assist managers."

Space looks at me blankly. I shrug and finger the grooves in the table.

Space says, "Girls here receive shoppers into high-end stores. But you look old."

I raise my head sharply, "I do not. I look young for my age."

Space shakes his head regretfully, "You've not received the anti-aging treatments that girls receive from age twelve. They're not the proton regenerations the Wealth buy, but they are better than natural aging," Space ends, deliberately injecting insolence into his tone.

Burning blood floods my cheeks uncomfortably, "Well, I can't do anything about my skin."

"You may not wear a burka because you are not married, and they are strictly enforced."

"Enforced?"

"Burkas are encoded and tracked so that the burka company knows who has how many and may cross-reference them to marriage certificates since three marriages per Thrall in their lifetime is the norm."

"Three?"

Space raises his eyebrows. "Yes," he says mildly.

A pause in this strange conversation ensues.

I start to feel like a bug in a jar in a kindergarten class.

He says abruptly, "Stores for older Wealth women prefer girls that look old, older than anyone whose proton regenerations have failed."

"Fail?"

Space nods: "After awhile and with some practitioners, they have been known to ..."

I wait for him to finish, but his hesitation grows so long, I ask him to.

"... do strange things," he completes his sentence as if he'd never stopped. "You will have to dress normally."

My face flames in shame, and I tell the table that I can't.

"You don't want to find your way home. You don't want to wear normal clothes in order to remain here. What do you want to do? Die?"

"No!"

"Decide." On that note, Space sends his chair scooting back, Atticus leaps up suddenly, and they both disappear up the stairs. I've never seen Space so agitated. I realize my mouth is agape; I shut it with a clack of teeth. Well, I can't go back. I don't know any physics, no matter what they say about learning devices. Everyone knows math is for boys. And only eggheads know physics. I'm not an egghead. Peggy and Sue would laugh at me. I bark mirthlessly at the thought. It'll have to be a job here. I know how to work. I'm used to others who treat me like I'm a bovine mindlessly chewing its cud. How could it be any different here? I'm not old, no matter what Space says.

I square my shoulders.

I'm used to bossy bosses, and managers that look at me as if I'm gum under their shoe, and human resources who snitch on you, and division directors who make impossible demands and ream you out if you miss their deadline that they didn't tell you about until after they frittered most of it away playing Solitaire on their computer, waiting until the day before their most important project is due. During university, I worked in retail. I can do—I shake my head, I can't remember what I did. But I can be a cashier. It'll be familiar. It may be the one familiar thing about this place. I long for something familiar.

The only problem is I don't know how to pay for things, and I fear going out there and shopping alone.

Atticus bounds down the stairs with saddle bags on and skids to a stop at my feet. Are these dogdroids psychic too? Atticus thumps his tail on the wooden floor. I can't help but smile, a small smile.

He leads me to the door. I take a deep breath and open the door. We head out. We return to the same store I ran away from at a time that seems so long ago yet maybe wasn't. The same snooty man spots me and raises his eyebrows. He wends his way toward me, studies me, and says, "I see something more acceptable. But that's middle class dress. Middle class?"

I'm beginning to understand their strange way of speaking and that he's asking if I'm middle class. I don't answer and say instead, "I'd like that neutral suit." If I have to wear these shaming clothes, at least let it be the suit that doesn't invade my body and turn me into a whore or slave against my own will. Hormones are so betraying.

"I get it."

"Wait, don't I have to try it on first?"

He stops and stares at me down his nose. "Where from?" He narrows his eyes and points at my face, "Skin is not from here, not from anywhere I know." I squirm under his intense gaze. Atticus barks, and the man looks down at him. Atticus waddles up to him with short steps, almost menacing yet the waddle diminishes it. There's a message in that walk, and the man understands it even if I don't. He turns on his toe and minces away. Atticus walks backward back to me and nudges my hand.

"What?"

He nudges it again to fling it backward. I look at his satchel. He gestures his head to the saddle bag on the left. I inspect it to figure out how to open it; Atticus blows air loudly through his lips. I grapple the bag, and it flies open at my touch. I peer in and don't see anything. Atticus woofs. I reach in tentatively; feeling nothing bite back, I feel around firmly. My hand lands on a round device. I pull it out.

"Old."

I straighten abruptly, managing not to drop the device.

"Old?"

The man is back, holding folded beige fabric in one raised hand. He indicates the device with his head, "Paying with that. Not seen one since early times. Only older girls who have memories of their natural youth carry them."

"Oh."

"Get matching footwear after the purchase here."

I hand the device to him wordlessly. He takes it, presses the edges, hands it back, along with my folded new suit. I put the device back in Atticus's bag. And follow it with the suit. I take my courage in my hands and ask him where I can get a job serving the older ... I hesitate. I must remember no one is called "women" here. I force out girl Wealth.

"Marci's on Fagin. They like wrinkles and unattractive girls. It makes old Wealth feel good about themselves."

"Uh, how do I get there? I mean, how do I apply?" I ask.

He seems to have decided not to waste any more time thinking about where I'm from and accepts my questions as those from a very strange person, someone so strange it's best to get rid of her: "Like any job, go to the third. Job allocation centre. Ask for Marci's."

"Thanks."

The man's eyebrows shoot up, and I realize that was the wrong thing to say. I have his attention again. "Where from?," he demands. His suspicious face leans in toward me, and Atticus bumps into me, sending me stumbling backward and sideways and almost to the floor. Atticus appears next to me, rebalancing me, but now I'm facing away from the man. Atticus takes my hand in his mouth and pulls me out of the store, down the aisle, and to a store that sells shoes and boots. Atticus lets go, and we wander in. I stare at the unfamiliar textures of the footwear displayed on foot mannequins here and there throughout the space.

"Bought neutral suit."

I turn to see a clone of the man who'd just served me, standing with his hands clasped behind his back, a statement on his face.

He continues, "I have sandals go with that suit." He swings his arm toward a mannequin that displays a shoe with three wide, tapering lengthwise straps, the middle one attached to the sole at the toe end, the other two attached to the sole along the length of each edge. At the heel, thin, leather-like ties thread through them and round the ankle. I cock my head to perceive them better. Doesn't work. Their colour is the exact same colour of the suit. I reach out to touch it. The material is yielding yet moulded and unlike anything I've felt before. I want to get out of here. I shove down the fear. I bend my head to indicate assent.

"First time here. We shoot your feet."

"Wha—?"

Atticus bumps me hard. I shut my mouth with a click of my teeth. My fear screams in my head, and I struggle to contain it. He walks off, and Atticus pushes me to follow. I follow.

The man signals that I'm to stand before a square, heavy desk with rounded corners covered in the same material that the shoes are made of. It has a vertical ledge that prevents me from seeing its top. I stand in place, trembling, trying to control my breathing. He jabs away at the desk top, his movement visible only in his shoulders and head. He reaches toward the ledge, bending forward, and briefly disappears. He then walks around the desk to me. He hands me the pair of three-strap shoes. I take them in my hands. They're so doe-skin velvety, so comfortable in my hands. I want to stroke them. Yet they are lighter than a feather and flimsy. I wonder: how will they support my feet? My feet will ache with all the walking people do here.

"Shoes to be tried on?"

"Oh. Sorry. Yes."

He cocks his head quizzically but without the suspicions of the other man. My politeness is giving me away, and I don't know why, for isn't politeness natural in Canadians? I stop thinking and drop the shoes on the floor to distract him except they don't bang as I'd expected but land with a breath of a whisper. I step out of my pumps, and then wonder whether I'm supposed to sit on the floor to try them on.

He says dryly, "The bench helpful."

I look up and see the bench on the nearside wall. I blush, pick up my pumps and the new shoes, and tip toe over. I sit down and slide the new shoes on. I lace them up. The laces almost seem to tie themselves. I stand up and fall forward in shock. Atticus stops me. I stare at my feet. The shoes are both soft and supportive. Every millimetre of my foot is on cushiony, firm material that keeps my foot in its ideal position. Even more startling, I can barely feel the floor I'm standing on, for it's like I'm floating. I take a few tentative steps. The shoes are actually aiding me in walking. They're better than any high-tech running shoe I've worn when I go through my sporadic running jags. And like the clothes here, I can't feel them either. It's like walking barefoot, except I can't feel the hardness of the ground, and my feet don't flatten and hurt. A smile grows on my face. I love these shoes.

He says, "I like satisfied girl."

I reach in to Atticus's left saddle bag and repeat the paying procedure. I toss my pumps into the other bag. There is no way I'm taking these shoes off.

I float out the door, and Atticus trots beside me, looking amused. He leads me to the third and the job allocation centre where I join one of three lines. When I get to the head of the one I'm in, I follow the instructions I'd been given and tell the fierce woman standing at the transparent, sloped desk facing the entrance what I'm there for. She pokes and presses the transparent desk, and I school my features. I see nothing but a transparent desk, yet she is frowning and swiping. Then her brow clears. She says, "Marci's has opening; it just came open." She continues her strange interactions with the transparent desk. I'm relieved this job application thing doesn't seem to be difficult. I release my very tense muscles. I try to surreptitiously shake my aching arms.

She jabs the top middle of the desk and a beam shoots out and scans me from middle to the bottom of my feet then middle to the top of my head. At the same time, Atticus leans on my right leg and aims his nose straight upward toward my right temple. Prickles run up and down my spine; my back hairs stand on end. I strive to look innocent. The beam shuts off, she frowns at the desk, mutters incomprehensible annoyed words, jabs the top middle of the desk again. The beam shoots out again and begins at the top of my head this time. Atticus has not moved, and she doesn't seem to notice him. She's too focussed on whatever is taking place on her desk. The beam hovers around my temples. I hold my breath. Suddenly the desk sucks the beam back in. She nods to herself, presses more invisible buttons, raises her eyes to me, and says, "They ready." She frowns at me, "Wrong clothes."

"I have a new suit," I reply hurriedly. "This is all I had to wear."

She sniffs and hands me a small version of the kind of paper that Byane was carrying. It's stiff. "Hand to the mait-D at Marci's. Proper suit required. Not that one. No trouble," she ends with a glare.

I swallow and shake my head mutely. I wouldn't want to cause trouble.

18

THE JOB

IN the kitchen I ask Space how I look, and he aims his face in my direction, his hand holding his teacup suspended in mid-air, until he finally asks, "Did you look in the mirror?"

"What mirror?"

"In the bathroom."

"It only shows my face."

"The now time one."

"The what?"

Space clatters his teacup in its saucer and stands up. He unhurriedly leads me to the well-proportioned bathroom next to the bedroom he'd given me. He opens the door, and I follow him in. He closes the door and gestures toward it. Suddenly the back of the door is not wood, but mirror. I leap back and knock my left hand on the sink, luckily, not the hand holding the piece of paper the job centre had given me. "Ow," I suck my offended knuckles.

Space opens the door and leaves, closing it behind him. I gingerly take a step toward the mirror. But I'm not close enough. I chuck my head forward, not moving my body. There's something strange about this mirror, aside from it having appeared out of thin air. I move my head from side to side, keeping my eyes on my reflected self. Suddenly, I screech and rear back. No one comes to ask me what's wrong. They're used to my screeches and screams by now. I strain my head forward and squint at the mirror.

Oh. My. God.

My head did not move the way it's supposed to in mirrors. It moved the opposite way, the way others would see me move. Worse, a long line of symbols with accompanying numbers have appeared in a vertical row on the right side of the mirror. I step back and grip the sink, hard. I ignore the pain. I gather my breathing together and slow down my heart. And then carefully, slowly, I approach the mirror and see myself the way others see me. I inspect my breasts revealed under the close-fitting shirt, my bare legs, the revealing drape of my sash, my feet encased in my soft shoes, which I never want to remove. They're the only things good about this place. I grimace at myself. I try to pull the edges of the sash together over my leg, but like before the drape sways, jiggles and splays out, but it won't allow the edges to come together at all. Material with its own mind. I shiver and shut down my internal eye to my naked image. I look at the numbers. Slowly, comprehension dawns: the numbers are my heart beat—fast—and blood pressure—high—and what looks like sugar ... oh, blood glucose levels, and weight and height, and a whole bunch of vitamin and mineral levels. I don't know what those latter numbers mean. I fling open the door and hurry down to the front door.

Atticus is waiting for me.

Space walks up behind me and says, "Atticus will take you to Marci's. I'll seek a device for you to wear so that you can navigate the neutrino bridges on your own. It will take time to ... get."

"Oh."

"Keep contact with Atticus."

"Okay."

"Physical contact."

"I understand."

We stand there before the front door. Space says nothing more, and finally realizing he isn't going to, I inhale deeply, shake my arms, and wrench the door open. Atticus trots out closely on my heels and then quickly comes up beside me. He walks with his flank touching my right leg constantly, and I keep gentle hold of his ruff. Nobody bothers me. He leads me to Fagin.

When we get there, Atticus stops until I notice slight sparkles in the air. A charged curtain. An Atticus-impenetrable one, I assume. I'm lost. How do I get into the Wealth area where Marci's is? Atticus nudges my left hand, the one that is clutching the piece of paper I was given. I lift my hand to look at it, then I look at Atticus. He turns his head this way and that, raises himself up, puts his paws on my shoulders, and whispers.

If his paws hadn't been holding me firmly with his energy steadying me, my legs would've buckled, I would've fallen, then I would've run as fast as I could for as long as I could. My legs are itching to run. They're spasming. I don't hear what Atticus is saying. I don't want to hear.

He barks in my face.

I focus on his angry eyes. I quiver. He whispers, "Walk to the charged curtain, spread out the paper, hold it up, shiny side against the curtain. When you feel the curtain shimmer, walk through." He continues to stare into my eyes until I move my head up and down, up and down, up and down. He drops back to the ground, and I walk forward toward the sparkles in the air, the wall of electrons, the barrier of the future I'm living in. I do as he says. I feel the solidity of the charged curtain waver, and I step into it. And through it, Atticus right on my leg, with me.

We walk down Fagin. The buildings here are all iridescent shades of pink sand and turquoise seas and luscious ferns. The ground floor windows are reminiscent of the Bloor Street ones I know: wide and inviting, with mannequins showing off clothing, tables showing off food. But I cannot see the interiors beyond them, and I can't see through every store's seemingly transparent tall double doors, with their fat burnished mahogany handles. We stop at a clothing store. Atticus pushes me with his nose toward the door, turns around, and trots off. I watch him go. Expanding my chest, I broach the door. It shimmers out of existence. I pretend nonchalance and walk in.

Into the chest of a black-clad tall man with a haughty expression. In an ice-cold voice, he asks: "May I help you?"

I hold up my paper. He takes it, presses the top, and suddenly my replica is standing next to me and next to her, stats and information appear in a vertical row. He rotates my replica and pushes me round at the same time. When we return to facing him, he sends his eyes to my replicant then me then replicant. He inspects the numbers and information. He nods hard once. He presses the top of the paper. As he's about to slip it into his suit, a tiny chime sounds, and the double entrance doors vanish. He swivels sharply toward the entrance, plasters on a smile, and shoves me behind him, all at the same time but unnoticing of the paper drifting to the obsidian floor. All I can see is his back. As the visitor swishes by in a sea of powdery fragrance, I hunker down and pick up the paper, crumpling it into a small wad in my hand.

With the doors once again visible and closed, he turns to me, his voice all insouciance, "Marci's needs a Greeter for Wealth clients. I train Greeters. Each Wealth client has time slot: most powerful with the best husband ecologies choose; least given illusion of choosing. Only I need know the slots. Greeters treat all Wealth equally though Lower Wealth do not deserve obsequiousness. But we find Thrall girls who are Greeters cannot tell difference between better and lesser. It is good. It gives our clients illusion of power. Illusion means more spending. More we earn, better for you.

"So. Greeters treat all Wealth the same. Greeters stand by the doorway, ready to greet the Wealth whenever they enter. We have standard Thrall conditions for pay: no food and drink in the work area, no bathroom breaks, work the full shift. Greeters greet the Wealth with fresh energy, do not look at their faces, and ensure they are escorted immediately to their rooms without anyone seeing them but Greeters, I, and clothing assistants.

"Marci's is progressive—we provide Greeters with discreet, time-controlled alpha stimulators to keep our Thrall fresh. We take care of our Thrall. Most important attributes of every Greeter is to school the face and do as told. Thrall girls today educated to do that, never problems, but ...," he looks me up and down and frowns. He touches the faint lines on my face, and I force myself not to flinch. "Older Thrall preferred for their worse looks, but older Thrall not educated in good service. Which school did you go to? Job centre stats incomplete as usual."

I open my mouth and close it, trying to adjust my mind from absorbing the facts of working life in 2411 to answering his question. I'm horrible at lying. My heart races, my mind blanks, my fear surges up. It opens my mouth again, and out pops a lie: "So long ago, closed it." It could be true, I think. After all, I went to school centuries ago.

"Original small one?"

"Was." I'm learning to speak the way they do. I'm adapting. I think that's what humans are supposed to do: adapt. I'm a human. Not a dumb human, I snap silently at the boys from 3011. An adaptable one, I tell myself, trying to convince myself.

His icy voice recalls me, "Most important: schooled face. Marci's clients are never seen. Kind of Wealth who shop here not seen in public. States and Canadian Wealth coverers know not to click their likeness. Use original pre-twentieth-proton likenesses media-shopped into now time settings so no one knows. Greeters keep their mouths shut."

"Mouth shut," I repeat.

"You know results of speaking mouths?"

"I know," knowing no such thing but deciding it's probably really bad.

"First client arrives at breakfast. Marci's serves clients chef-cooked food cooked from vegetables and proteins grown in gardens north of the city. More expensive but makes Marci's the destination for better Wealth."

Vegetables are expensive? Space seems to be able to afford them. He's a good cook too, way better than me. And what's protein? Doesn't he mean meat? Why doesn't he say meat? Is that one of these things where we don't say the names of things that could offend the too rich?

I suddenly realize he's examining me and reaching out to my shoulders.

He says, "Greeters must have good posture, must ask medical care to program nanos for service work to stand with a straighter neck and shoulders back." He tuts, "But original care teams ignore posture not just wrinkles. Lax in getting girls to meet society needs."

I have no answer.

He points to a place a step behind him and near the wall. And we wait.

I think ruefully: I won't be a cashier after all. And then I wonder: what horror will come our way? The answer arrives. The doors vanish and in walks a creature that is apparently human. My jaw drops, and the man's hand discreetly and automatically reaches up to shut it. Apparently, jaw dropping is the norm.

The perfect women I saw in the garden become this? I don't hear what the man says, only his dulcet tones, but I see his hands reach out to take gently the creature's claws with their extreme ridges and exaggeratedly thick nails. I will have to do that? I want to retch. As the doors reappear, he guides her to a

Thrall who has suddenly appeared. She has a face as wrinkled as mine, which isn't much by twenty-first century standards but very much in this time. Except for the creature I just saw. The Thrall guides her from behind, down the hall, and into a door on the right.

While smiling toward the once-again disappearing entrance door, he admonishes me, "School face."

This one is worse. My jaw drops, his hand reaches out, I shrink back. Surreptitiously I straighten my sash, though it needs no straightening, anything to distract me, and feel a pocket hidden inside its upper folds. I shove the paper in it and try to mask myself.

Another Thrall guides this woman down the hall and through a door on the left; the man's face instantly turns from warm and welcoming to cold. He watches the front entrance and again adjures me to school my face. Doors vanish, the Wealth walk in one by one, doors reappear. I cannot get inured to this. I clamp my teeth together, making my jaw ache, as he reaches out to take the next one's claws in his healthy hands. Every so often, he leaves, and another like him takes his place and continues my training and Wealth client greeting until he returns.

And so it goes.

After time immeasurable, I leave. I ruminate on what I saw. Not even my hunger and thirst and exhaustion and desperate need to go to the bathroom can overcome the memory of what I saw today. The privilege and wealth that these women have imprisons them in skin that not even a rhino would love. It constrains their lives when they're perfect and makes them unfit for sight when old. I wonder how old they are and bump nose first into a charged curtain. My nose aches deeply, and I rub it vigorously to stop the tears. I want to go home. I want to be with Peggy and Sue. They would get a kick out of what I saw today. Yet it was so horrific that for once I don't want to gossip. I feel so bad for them. And for me. For in my next shift, I will have to take those rough, bumpy, cold claws in mine and pretend a warmth and caring I don't feel. That man was very good at it. He turned it on and off like a washerless faucet.

I search around in my sash until I find the hidden pocket and slip out the paper. I aim it shiny side to the curtain, and nothing happens. Oh yeah, I'm supposed to place it on the charged curtain. I push it forward until my hand meets resistance. The curtain wavers, and I walk through. On the other side, Atticus appears and grows bigger. He latches onto my right leg, and we walk home.

My next shift is the same, the man having decided that I need more schooling. I begin to find it easier, to unfocus my eyes enough so that I cannot see every proton imperfectly regenerated, every exaggerated skin cell, every mistake in colour replication. This time Atticus does not await me on the other side of the curtain, but I barely notice until someone bumps into my shoulder, hard.

I turn to shout my displeasure and see three familiar faces. My mouth freezes open. The marginally tallest one leers, "It's her. She's trying to be a good girl, but we know she isn't." He shouts and waves, "Hey, she is a non-conformist!" People stop to stare at me.

I take off.

My legs know how to run now when danger looms. They chase me. The crowd does not part; instead legs stick out suddenly here and there to trip me up. Spittle flies at me. I develop feats of leaping and weaving I had no idea I had. I zip toward the gardens, and my shoes give me unexpected speed. Suddenly, I'm approaching an intersection. Think, think, I tell myself. I hadn't put the paper back in my pocket but had absent-mindedly held onto it. I wonder. As I run, I flip the paper back and forth to find its shiny side. I reach the neutrino bridge. I hit it with the paper. I'm through it, but now unlike the crowds, I'm with the cars. The cars don't know what to do. Chaos invades their ordered progression as I dash between them to the other side of the street. I repeat my action with the paper when I reach the charged curtain separating people from cars, but only when I'm through do I see the boys waiting there, on the other side, for me.

The neutrino bridge is faster.

Obviously.

"Hey, alien," they yell as they launch themselves at me. I dodge under their arms. I vault sideways around a stuck-out arm and catapult myself into the garden near me. I race to the next intersection. And this time when I enter the Wealth lanes, I run along the length of the street instead of crossing it.

There are no crowds to slow me down.

Horrified, the Wealth stare at me through their windows, as the cars stall or speed up to keep equidistant from me and the cars around them. At the next intersection, I dash across the street. This must be old Bay Street, but it's nothing like what I remember.

The boys aren't here.

Still, I don't ease off my race.

I hear a far-off shout, but I'm too far away. And they can't catch me. At Wellington, the old buildings with their alleys and ancient backways let me search for Space's place from their hidden sides. I see Byane disappearing up a fire escape and run toward it. So intent am I on keeping track of where the fire escape is that I stumble over a fat, furry form. A snarl hits my ears as I feel air swipe across my calves. Another raccoon! I regain my footing quickly and leap forward, feeling but not seeing the raccoon speed up to catch me. I can see in my mind's eye the way those striped beasts scurry along the back lanes in my neighbourhood after a tiny dog they hate, the way they knock over garbage bins and strew bones down the walkways, the way they scream and shriek at each other in the trees until one falls down to his death. Why hasn't this advanced Toronto gotten rid of these nasty creatures? I shudder at the memory of cleaning up raccoon body parts off my backyard table one sultry summer morning. I feel hot breath on the back of my ankles, and I lurch forward to grab at the fire escape. I scramble up the metal steps and fling myself through the open window, landing chest first on the floor.

I skid to a stop.

I pause as I mentally check myself over. I feel bruised but okay. I push myself up to a standing position and brush myself down. I straighten and see: Space half-standing up out of his chair, Byane and his group twisted around from their seated positions, staring at me, Atticus wagging his tail where he stands next to the door. Only Hope has more interest in her book than in me.

"Hi," I wave feebly at them and then fall back to the floor, starving.

19

REALITY

SATIATED from what Space has fed me—I was so hungry, I barely noticed what he'd placed before me and have no memory of it except that it was food—I'm sitting in the chair I've come to know as mine. Hope and Space are in their chairs, and I'm not sure where Atticus is except he isn't here. Byane, Brittayne, Michael, and Marie had disappeared but are now streaming back into the room through the window. Byane and Michael leap over the back of the couch and land squarely on the seat. Brittayne and Marie go around the arms of the couch and take their places sedately. That's when I notice Brittayne is carrying a bag that's like a bole from a tree with a handle, except the sides move and the small opening widens as she raises it to Byane who takes it. He reaches in and pulls out packages wrapped in wax paper and hands one to Michael, one to Brittayne, one to Marie. They unwrap the wax paper, but the paper makes no crinkly sounds and is as rippleless as plastic when opened up. I lean forward to take a look. "What is that?" I ask.

"Food," Byane replies.

I frown. Each has something different. Marie raises a flat, wide milky-looking chocolate bar and nibbles it delicately. Michael bites off half of a portobello mushroom covered in waxy cheese. Byane and Brittayne have the same thing: slices of toasted baguette loaded with chopped tomatoes. But a funny thing: all have clean hands. No cheese stains skin with fat; no tomatoes drip oil onto chins and clothes.

I say, "It looks like real food … but it … it doesn't act like it."

"It's not," Hope sneers.

"What do you mean?"

"Here," Byane throws me a bruschetta. I catch it awkwardly in both hands, against my chest, yelling, "Hey!"

I look down to wipe at the oil stain, except there is none. I scan my shirt and my sash and see not a drop. And then I realize my hands are telling me this is not food. I cannot feel the smooth slide of oil or the heaviness of tomato bits. The bread has the feel of rough crust, but it's not quite right. I take a tentative bite. The crust crunches, the tomatoes drip. Yet when I reach up to wipe my chin, it's as clean as it was before. I chew. It's spongy.

And then the monochromatic flavour hits.

I can't help it—fake food spews out of my mouth.

We all look at it on the floor.

I needlessly wipe my face with the back of one hand as I turn my mouth down, stick my offended tongue out, revolted at what's left in my other hand. Byane looks at me with disdain. Brittayne and Marie giggle. Michael swallows his other half of his pseudo-portobello, while Hope twitches the corner of her mouth up. The girls and Byane finish their snacks. They all fold up the wrapping and put it in the bole-bag Byane holds out. I toss my food back to him. He catches it easily but glares at me before dropping it in the bole.

I say to Space, "I'm sorry. I didn't expect it to taste like pasty-California-tomato-burnt-oil-bland-bread mushed together. What is it anyway?"

"What we eat," Byane retorts as he hands the bole back to Brittayne. "Better than twenty-first."

The bole shrinks closed.

"No way," I retort back. "Not even greasy diners serve food this bad. What is it?"

"It's ordinary food," Space replies.

I don't get it, and Space finally registers my confusion.

"Food is programmed."

I wrinkle my brow. I envision a vending machine with stale white-bread sandwiches and say so.

They wrinkle their brows and query: "A vending machine?"

"You know, that thing at work you put loonies into, press the button of what you want from what's displayed, and it gives you a sandwich, except only after you kick it."

Hope guffaws and turns it into a cough.

Space says, "As you now know Time, we don't eat at work. Food is dispensed in the home by nutrition printers."

"Huh?"

He sucks in a deep breath and explains: "Food comes from nutrition printers. You fill a printer with the basic building blocks of all food: protein, carbohydrates, fats. You program in what you want, including vitamins and minerals prescribed by your personal habitant base. It prints your meal out in ten minutes to look traditional without the mess of traditional food. Any leftovers must be disposed of in the home. The law requires every habitant to dispose of their own waste through recyclers and power generators."

My mind reels at the latter, so I focus on the food itself. I ask, "Is that what you've been feeding me? Because it didn't taste as bad as this."

"I prefer traditional food. I cook. The Wealth have special chefs to cook for them and own multi-hectare food farms—mine is modest and on my roof—but Wealth kids prefer to slum it when out and about," he nods toward Byane.

Byane shrugs and grins.

"Space has prosperity to eat and compost grown food," Hope adds softly but not so softly that I can't hear her.

Michael swallows and says, "Space gave traditional bread once. Hard to chew, made tongue explode. Like real food."

"Too much flavour for you, eh, Michael?" Hope asks rhetorically.

He sticks his tongue out at her. She rolls her eyes. I look down at the mess on the floor and wonder how to clean it up. Space reads my mind and heaves himself out of his chair. He walks over to the door. I twist around to see what he's doing. He taps the wall next to the door and a display pops into view. He presses a broom graphic, and I hear a hum start in the direction of the window. I whip around to look. A flat stone disk hovers into view. It rotates, its edge going from matte to shiny, and halts when the shiny part is aimed toward the mess. It accelerates forward and stops over the mess. For brief seconds a muffled sucking drowns the hum. It ceases. The disk spins back and accelerates past the couch. The hum stops abruptly. I stare at the clean floor.

Silence descends; no one wants to break it.

Space, back in his chair, shifts to face me, "It is time for you to adapt since you don't want to go home."

At first I'm confused. Weren't we talking about food? And then I click in. I don't want to talk about it. I say so.

"We must."

"Fine. Of course I want to go home."

He says, "Going home means you have to do it yourself. You don't believe you can. Your alternative is to stay in our now time and live like we do. But it is dangerous. Atticus is mine. He cannot be with you all the time. You cannot live in my space, in The Attic forever. We live a long time in 2411. You are still a young adult—"

I choke—and turn it into a cough. Young? Me? Hadn't he said earlier I looked old? And anyway, I'm about to turn forty. No, I have turned forty. Somewhere in the ticking time after I found refuge in The Attic, I must've turned forty because time moves in 2411 as it does in 2011, and time ages humans. But when?

"You see, you cannot stay focussed, like a young pup who needs constant reproving to pay attention."

I straighten in my chair, dismiss my forty obsession from my mind, and refocus on Space. "What?"

He shrugs his shoulders and raises his palms to the ceiling.

Byane says, "Girls do what told."

"What?"

Hope says, "She's not Thrall."

Byane says, "Not middle class. Men only tolerate middle class girls not obeying." He rakes Hope up and down with his eyes. She glares at him. They bore their eyes into each other. They stare. And stare. And stare. It's hypnotizing, and I find myself not blinking in concert with their battle. Neither will give in. And then Brittayne jostles Byane's arm, and he blinks.

He snaps at Brittayne, "Know place."

She replies unaffectedly to the bookcase behind Space, "Do."

He eyes her suspiciously, and she drops her head to inspect her sash's pleats. Hope snuggles into her wing chair contentedly.

Space says, "Byane is right. She is not middle class, and as such must live like a Thrall girl." He turns to me and says, "Time, you must live on your own. People don't share dwellings in our now time. Middle class have leeway in what is tolerated. Up to this moment in time, my dumpees have been left undiscovered since most die soon after arrival. But you have achieved more: more time and a job."

I mutter, "It's awful. They won't let me eat or drink or even go pee during my shift. I must not move from my post ever. Don't they have unions here?"

I receive blank stares in reply. Byane slaps his thigh, "Unions! I know unions. Business class teaches them as example of when capitalism hampered and good sense gave way to sentimentality. Twenty-first have unions?"

"Yes. They protect us."

"You're in a union?" Hope asks.

"Uh, no."

"Why not?" Hope asks.

"Well, we don't need them."

Brittayne says, "But ..."

Byane slaps her, "Hush."

She hushes. I frown. She resumes pleating.

Hope admonishes Byane, and he glares at her again. They are about to recommence their staring match when Space barks, "Stop." He turns to me, "There are no unions here. The Wealth don't want them, and the Thrall don't know about them. The middle class keep their privileges of education and independence by not agitating for them. It's win-win. You have a job, and now you must find a place."

I open my mouth and close it. I open it again, and again I close it. I start to feel like a fish stuck in foaming water at the beach, and I finally force my vocal cords to work: "There must be a better job."

They all say in chorus: "Isn't." Space continues: "Working for old Wealth women on Fagin is the best for a Thrall."

Byane says, "More than dumpee good for."

Hope scorns, "You maintained you can't get yourself home. You're not good enough, you said. Ergo, you acquired job you're qualified for."

"I—," I stop speaking. And slowly close my mouth and slump into my seat. I stretch out my legs and pigeon my toes. She's right. I reflect on my sash and see my long bare legs. I play with the pleats. My sash falls to the inside of my left leg, and I don't adjust it. It's amazing how quickly I've become used to this suit. I no longer feel naked; it almost feels normal to be so exposed. I try to speak, clear my throat, and whisper, "How do I find a place?"

No answer. I look up to find Byane staring at my fully exposed leg and Brittayne covertly despairing. A gleam appears in his eye, and he grabs Brittayne's thigh near her hip. Space barks, "Byane. You know the rules in my place."

"She—"

Space points at the window, "Out."

Byane obeys the command and forces Brittayne up with him by shoving his hand underneath her sash and standing up at the same time. Space stands up abruptly. Hope becomes engrossed in a book fast, while Michael eyeballs Marie, and she awaits his lead. I blink at this bizarre tableau. My brain refuses to comprehend what my eyes are seeing. Space takes a step toward Byane and grinds out, "Your father will receive an anonymous—"

Byane removes his hand like it was scorched and holds it up in a pacifying gesture, "Old attitude, Space. She's Thrall. She's girl. She's for I while I want her. But for Space, I do I business in private." He goes on, but his words become a buzz in my rejecting ears.

From behind her book, Hope throws lightening bolts at Byane while Marie watches Michael like a dog waiting for a command from its owner.

Space's menacing blank spectacles and aggressive stance are his reply to Byane's long speech. Atticus wanders in to stand beside Space and to watch Byane.

Byane grabs Brittayne's hand, and she follows him out the window. We don't hear any clanking on the fire escape, and

Atticus barks once. Feet clamber down the escape, faster and faster. One set sure, the other stumbling. Space strides over to shut the window. Michael clears his throat. Space opens it, and those two clear out as well.

Space returns to his seat, and Atticus wanders toward the window.

"Uh ...," I have no words. What did I witness? What is going on? Are girls ... my mind refuses to take in what it has perceived. A niggling thought enters it, and I voice it.

"They are not sex slaves," Hope affirms. "They are Thrall girls."

I look at her puzzled. She breathes out heavily, "You haven't learnt?"

Space reproves her, "She's a dumpee."

Hope declamates, "Even so. In our land, everybody is a habitant. But multiculturalism taught us that we must tolerate differences. Sci Wealth taught us certain divisions are natural because most societies had them. Patriarchy is natural, eh. Matriarchal societies disappeared. They weren't natural. Green earth did not design girls to understand certain concepts. Green earth made girls weaker. Green earth gave boys logical brains suited to ecology and science thinking, the two most important habitats of life. Only they lead to prosperity for green earth. Green earth evolution proves boys and men are made to lead. That's what they say, eh," she draws out the word "say" and rolls her eyes disgustedly. "Sci Wealth also say boys can incorporate more knowledge. Boys need to learn more knowledge in our now time than in yours. For centuries, educators segregated boys and girls in school. Boys needed attention when girls got too powerful. Segregation proves boys excel faster and learn more in less time than girls. To help girls, educators constrained curriculum to what girls learn naturally: languages and service. Girls know how to please and how to communicate, eh. Ecologies need those skills to benefit men to prosper ecologies and innovate. Girls can't invent. Everybody knows that, eh." Do I detect a note of sarcasm? "Other cultures came to Canada who also have girls do what they do best: keep men happy. Proves green earth evolution.

"Productive men care better for green earth. Happy men are productive men, eh. Girls make men happy through service. Wealth girls serve men with words after marriage. But Thrall girls are no use to their husbands in that way. Thrall girls must breed workers to care for our city and to provide mental energies, eh. No one immigrates to Canada anymore, and we can't power our ecologies and thought technologies without habitants.

"Thrall girls serve ecologies by producing children. Marriage is not necessary, eh. But it's hard for single Thrall girls to raise children. We are an independent country. The Wealth expect everybody, girls and men, to look after themselves and not expect others to do their work for them. Independence breeds strength. Single Thrall girls with children cannot work. Doctors program Thrall girls' nanos to keep them sterile until they're married, and Thrall men have to remain married as long as they have children under twenty-one. Wealth men acquire several wives to give them an edge. More wives, more rivals can be spied on. More prosperous, more wives. Also having more wives keeps smarter wives in line. Wives competing for a man's attention are less likely to stir up trouble."

Yup, definitely sarcasm.

"Thrall girls look for good Thrall boys with the best jobs. They cannot work at marriage start because they're popping out babies. The Wealth require four per Thrall girl to balance population and not deprive ecologies of workers. Wealth girls do not get pregnant. They don't like mess, and it would deprive husbands of their service, eh. Chosen married Thrall give two of their own to the Wealth and work as nannies.

"A few now times ago, more boys were being born than girls. But the Wealth noticed it was bad for ecologies and Wealth safety. My parents' generation was the last that was unbalanced.

With mine, we're back to old, eh: forty-eight percent female, fifty-two male." I open my mouth to object then think why bother. "Brittayne is trying to get into the Wealth by pursuing Byane. It works," Hope shrugs, "sometimes. But she's not being hundred percent good. Boys are so thick. They don't notice little rebellions. But Byane starting to pick up on hers."

"What rebellions?" I ask.

She looks at me like I'm the stupidest person in the world. "You didn't notice?"

I shake my head, puzzled.

"Marie doesn't either. Thrall girls, eh? History books state it was same in your now time."

"What? What do you mean?"

Hope jerks her head to the window.

I exclaim, "Are you kidding me. Girls don't—don't service men."

Her eyebrows rise in disbelief.

"Not like that. They don't dress like—like—," I gesture to my sash.

"I saw photos of Catholic school girls in Byane's history picture book. And I saw women in black burkas."

I'm speechless. I don't know what to reply. Words tumble through my mind as to how it's different. Girls have rights. Women are called women. Rich don't have special enclaves. And then an errant thought pops up: no, they have gated communities. I brush it aside. It's not the same as commandeering Bloor Street for their exclusive use. Anyway, in my now time, I can be anyone I want to be. I don't have to be some slave who isn't allowed to eat or drink or pee because some ugly hag will get upset if I do.

I scowl at myself. "Hag." Where'd that word come from?

I blush as a thought reproves me: "hag" is a word as deriding of women as this society is. And then I wonder: can I really be anyone I want to be? Is that what I did for myself? I shake that thought away. Of course I did. Father just had unrealistic expectations. Just like these two do now. I'm no mathematician. I'm bad at math and physics. How can I build a time machine alone? I studied English lit, not science, not computers. I make a face and recall one newbie who showed up last year at work who was definitely a computer techie. Peggy and Sue and I used to poke fun at her every day and her loser Blackberry. We had iPhones, the cool smart phone. She wasn't even up with the latest *American Idol* judge escapade. She used to say she didn't watch TV as if that was a good thing. Peggy and Sue and I didn't believe her. Everyone watches TV. She was just trying to be superior.

Suddenly, I feel stupid. And trite. And trivial. That smart girl had left the company after six months; then the day before my kidnapping, I'd learned she'd gone to work for Blackberry but not as an admin assistant. She was in product development. I blurt out, "Do you guys have Blackberries?"

Hope replies with a blank stare. Space says, "Fruit?"

I sigh. No Apple. No Blackberry. It's like the gadgets we all covet never even existed. I feel ephemeral, transient, like my life is a whisper of shattering atoms in the stars.

20

AD MAN

GHOST light permeates the air under the iron-grey sky. Hope and I walk along quiet sidewalks, their surfaces scarred with the final imprints of drying autumn leaves. The houses we pass are familiar to me; they're the houses of old Toronto neighbourhoods. They look like nineteenth- and twentieth-century homes, yet they hide technological advancements the iPad generation would covet. But I don't. I want to go home where the tech is familiar and either cool or out of touch.

When Hope had asked me to have dinner at her parents' house and to wear the clothes she'd given me, I was relieved to get away from The Attic and Marci's, the only two places I ever seemed to be in, and to put on something different. The neutral suit never needed cleaning, but I was tired, oh so tired, of wearing it.

Hope leads me to her front door, and we enter.

A sing-song female voice calls out, "Andia, is that you?"

"I brought Time," Hope replies. I look a question at her, and she whispers out of the side of her mouth, "Parsi name." She makes a face. "Means Hope."

I have no time to reply, for a woman comes into the hallway, wiping her hands on a dish towel, a broad smile wreathing her face and her black, thick hair, although pulled back in a pony tail, waving and sticking out all over. A man follows on her heels, trying to get by her. And when he does, he smothers Hope in a hug that embarrasses her. She struggles; he grins and lets go.

"So, this is Time?" he says, turning to me and taking my hand in a vigorous two-handed shake.

Hope rolls her eyes. I'm so startled I don't shake his hand back. He pauses, clasps my hand harder, and says, "Welcome. Welcome. I'm Andia's father, Rustum. And—"

The woman pushes him away, taking my hand away from him, covering it with both of hers, saying, "I'm Asha, Andia's mother. Welcome, Time." She lets go of my hand and sweeps her arm to the rear. "Come, come into the kitchen. I'm almost done cooking."

"You're cooking?" Hope asks with disbelief.

"Of course. What is wrong with your mother cooking. Tell I that?"

"Nothing, nothing," Hope mutters.

Asha bustles back down the hall, and the fragrant smells emanating from that direction entice us to follow her. The kitchen is large and chaotic with an island in the middle and three counter tops and cabinets surrounding it. Pans litter the granite counters. Granite is popular in every time, I smile to myself. Sue would love the heather purple of this granite. I look around. All I see are smooth, uninterrupted counters.

There is no stove.

As I approach the island, I see that one saucepan has stew bubbling gently in it, the thick sauce a saffron-yellow. I step back startled. I try not to inspect the counter underneath the saucepan too obviously as Hope chats animatedly with her parents. How is this stew cooking?

Hope says, "At least she didn't scream."

I jump. The others laugh but good-naturedly. I smile tentatively. I point at the pot. "How is it cooking?"

Asha looks into the pot, "Ah. It is done. It is perfectly cooked."

"That's not what she means, Mom. In her now time, they had special equipment in fixed locations."

"I know what a stove is, Andia. Who do you think gave Space his? I was only joshing her," she smiles.

I say brightly, "I hear you're going to India."

The kitchen hushes, and I suddenly remember I was to tell no one what Hope had told me. But surely it's okay to say so to her parents?

Asha frowns at Hope and queries, "Andia?"

Hope looks at the floor and rubs it intently with her toe.

Rustum adds his voice, "Andia?"

Hope defends herself: "I must tell someone. Time will not be here long. Who will she tell, eh? She doesn't know anybody or anything. I can't wait to move. I will study in public. I won't hide. Habitants won't stare at I's dress or care what group I belong to. No man will tell I how to dress or where to work or how to live. I's vote will count. No Wealth will decide I's government. The Wealth won't track I or tell I what to do. I can be who I want to be. Government prospers habitants to create and invent for green earth's benefit even when doesn't prosper Wealth. Did you see that story Zenobia smuggled in through her vine about invention to eradicate GMOs permanently? That's genetically modified organisms, Time," she says the last in an aside and continues before I can respond, "And that small article about Indian scientists cracking walnut of how to rid green earth of xenoestrogens. India knows GMOs and xenoestrogens make habitants sick. They don't think it's right Thrall and middle class must buy special nanos from the Wealth to mitigate effects. No Wealth. No enslavement to GMOs. Their scientists can invent what they want. Why do you have to invent things only the Wealth want? Best, we won't live under clouds and greenhouse gas storms for the Wealth to hog sun. We should go, go now, and tell everybody."

Asha says, "You know it's dangerous, Andia. We told you to keep that private."

"What's private? Only old think privacy exists. It's not like it's a crime to move."

Silence.

Silence stretches.

It stretches until it feels like cat gut screeching.

I must say something: "I haven't told anyone. I only said it here because you already know because, well, you're the ones going." I smile with my mouth, begging forgiveness with my eyes.

Rustum says, "Very well. All is forgiven. We will forget about it now."

"Why are you going to India?" I can't help myself, the question slips out, and I slap my hand over my mouth.

Rustum says, "It is okay to ask. We cannot be fully thinking beings if we are not willing to ask. Asking is good, I tell my students all the time. But do they listen? No. But you, you are listening, I see. And you wanted to know why. Why? Why are we going? We are going because I want Andia to blossom her true potential, and it is impossible for Asha to be the engineer she is. She is a woman. They tolerate her because she's middle class, and we Parsis know how to buck the system and make it work for us. But she is treading into Wealth areas, areas of ecologies and money. I tell her to be careful. Does she listen? Not so. Still, she is sharing it with others. She is talking and working with habitants in other countries. The Wealth like this not at all. They are wanting, always wanting total control. And they are not happy. When they are not happy, the government is not happy. As you know, we have some privacy, but—"

I interrupt, "What do you mean some? Aren't there privacy laws? It's not like we need them though; they're such a pain with all their rules, all the forms we have to sign. I don't see why privacy is important if you have nothing to hide. Only criminals need privacy."

All three look at me pityingly. Hope says, "Thrall have no privacy. The Wealth like it that way. If Thrall consider rebelling or using goods in non-Wealth ways, the Wealth will discover and can squash it. The Wealth like privacy for selves but believe Thrall and—"

I flash to that Facebook guy's photos being splashed all over the TV, how Facebook's founder's own privacy was violated and how upset he was about it, though he'd been busy revealing everyone else's stuff. We had all laughed about it at work.

"— middle class—"

I blink back to the present. I say, "I'm sorry, I didn't catch that."

Hope sighs exaggeratedly, "The Wealth have wealth enforcement patrol to retain privacy and live apart. They don't like middle class having privacy, but we know how to switch our birth chips to privacy mode. The Wealth have programmers who try to reveal what we hide, but they're no match for us," Hope finishes smugly.

Asha says sternly, "That's enough, Andia."

"It's true," she replies sulkily.

Rustum says, "Now, now, let us not fight. We have a guest here."

They all look at me and smile. Asha says brightly, "Come, let us eat. All is ready." In no time, serving dishes are filled with sauces and rice and yogurt mixtures and condiments, and we're being swept into the dining room that opens into the living room, through whose front window I can see the darkening day.

Yet the street outside isn't pockmarked with artificial light; instead light fills the air at pedestrian level, above which darkness reigns. I'm about to go investigate when Hope's parents call to me to sit, sit. I sit.

Andia's mother points out the dishes to me. Hope scoops massive portions of all the dishes onto her plate with mutterings about having to eat the nutrition-printed glop they serve at university. Happy slurpings replace talking. Since I began this time trip, I have eaten many more home-cooked meals than I ever had had at home. I long for home, but I will miss this goodness. I dig into vegetable pilau, basmati rice, tofu tandoori, raita, mango chutney ... they must be vegetarians, as I've seen no meat dishes. I ask.

They look at each other nonplussed. Rustum suddenly says, "Ah. Of course, your diet was quite different to ours. You were eating meat. We are seeing it as not good for our green earth. Only the Wealth eat meat, and only on Feasts like the Holidays and Bunny Day. And they have quite the suffering for it." They all laugh.

"No one eats meat?" I ask, appalled at the thought.

"Not so," Hope replies. "It's bad for green earth. Don't you know that?"

Asha says, "Don't be insolent to our guest, Andia."

Hope slumps and forks up a giant load of rice.

"It's okay," I reply.

Asha says, "It's not 'okay'—is that how you say it? We want our guests to be welcome. It is not your fault you come from a barbaric time when habitants didn't understand how important green earth is to our survival and how bad you were being to it."

I choke on my tofu. Hope giggles and says under her breath, "Now who's being unwelcoming?"

I say, "I don't think eating meat is going to kill the, the planet."

Rustum clears his throat. Hope mutters "oh-oh, you've raised the lecture." And Asha says, "Not now, Rustum. Be mindful of our guest." Rustum nods and contents himself with: "Eating meat per se will not kill the planet, you are right. But it is how you are treating the cows and the pigs and how much you are eating that will and, as is common knowledge, almost did. Now, as our forefathers discovered, it was not food culture and aqua culture alone that caused—"

Asha warns, "Rustum."

Rustum says contritely, "Oh, of course. Sorry, m'dear, I forgot that we're going to try to get her home, and she mustn't know these things."

"Thank you."

I lean forward and say, "Did you say—Are you—Are you going to try to get me home? Really?"

"Didn't Andia tell you? As soon as she told us about you, of course we knew we would help. Isn't that right, Rustum?"

"Of course. It goes without saying, m'dear. You are not belonging here. It isn't your fault you ended up in our time. We will do all we can to help," he smiles upon me. "Well, perhaps not we, more like Asha and Andia will. They're the science brains in this home. I am merely a humble thinker."

"Oh."

Asha says business-like, "But first we must make sure you are not suspected as an alien. It is all very well for you to wear middle class outfits when you're with Andia. But not when you're alone or on the job. Your speech is ... well, I know it is difficult to change. We can't do anything about the nanos— it is too dangerous."

Hope bleats, "But Mom—"

"We will talk later about that, Andia. But we can and will ensure you see what we see. It is too dangerous for you not to use the neutrino bridges or be oblivious to what is around you any longer."

"Oh."

"Eat up."

I eat. The huge meal is followed by desserts of all kinds. I haven't seen anything sweet like this in ages. Chocolate cupcakes, and small squares of intense nutty sweetness, and fruit pies. I've hit heaven. I stuff myself and waddle away from the table on a sugar high. We have our coffee in the living room; they talk, and I listen. As the light outside fades, the lights inside glow on. Their luminescence reminds me of fireflies at camp.

I grow warm and safe.

"Right, Asha, shall we outfit our guest?"

That snaps me awake. Outfit? My sense of warmth and safety vanishes.

Asha stands up and gestures to me, "Come. Andia, stay and talk with your father." Hope sits back down, and I follow Asha to the basement.

The basement door looks like any other, but Asha uses a complicated sequence of staring into the door, planting her hand on the middle surface, and then punching a code into a hidden box—I assume it's a box, for I cannot see it—next to the door. It swings open, and we descend into a brightly lit cavernous space filled with gleaming shelves and instruments. Of torture, a voice in my head adds. I push the thought away.

Asha leads me to the end of this space through another similarly locked door that had looked initially like it was part of the wall and to the table that sits in the middle of that room. On it sit tiny objects. But she ignores those, picks up the finest tweezers I've seen, reaches for a tiny rectangular glass plate, and slips the bottom tweeze of the tweezers underneath a sliver of a computer chip. As she raises it against the light, I see through it; only the computer chip-style design is opaque. It is gold. She says, "This is ready. When I first heard of you from Andia and Space, I immediately created this tattoo for you. I knew you could not survive in our now time without a birth chip. We cannot give one to you, but this old-time tattoo will do. Since no one will suspect any one here doesn't have a birth chip and the tattoo will mimic it, you won't be caught easily." She aims the tweezers at my right temple, and I flinch.

She says, "It won't hurt," and reaches again for my temple. This time I quiver but don't move. She pushes back my hair. I feel the cold of the tweezers on my skin, feel a soft whisper sliding down as the tweezer warms and then leaves my skin. A slight pressure, a "there," and it's done. I raise my hand to touch it, but Asha grabs and holds it. "A moment," she instructs. The whisper sinks into my skin. I feel bile rise and gulp. "Is it? ... is it?" I cannot articulate the question: is it part of me?

"It is on your skin but cannot be seen. I've programmed it with camouflage. You must keep your hair over it, for Wealth enforcement patrol will see it clearly with their visors if your hair is not over it. Thrall and the Wealth will not. It's old tech, but old tech is more invisible than new."

"Oh."

She pulls me to a wall. A mirror appears, a realistic mirror like the one at Space's. I lean forward, pull my hair away from my temple, move my head this way and that. I cannot see it, I cannot see how it makes me one of them, but I know it's there, repulsively part of my skin.

"You'll get used to it. And now you'll be safe. Andia will guide you; you will see."

"Okay."

She smiles and puts her hand on my shoulder, "We will get you home. You will need to lead us, but we will help."

I nod. Lead? How can I lead? But I say nothing, feeling my heart tighten, feeling more and more like I'm becoming an inextricable part of this world, feeling overwhelmingly that home is receding away like a lost shore.

We return to the other two, and Hope and I say goodbye. We walk through the quiet neighbourhood in the artificial sun.

"Where are the lights?" I ask.

"Lights? Oh, the light beamed from space. They use neutrino bridge technology to send light from satellites down to streets. The satellites gather sunlight, and they use your kind of GPS technology to pinpoint locations to turn on light. They change. On Feasts, our neighbourhoods, the middle class ones, regain their darkness to allow us to see stars and celebrate outside."

"Neutrino bridge?"

Hope sighs exaggeratedly. Really, I'm so glad I don't have a teenager. They seem as irritating in this time as in my time. And then I remember Hope is not a teen; well not in my time. She is a teen here. Maybe age isn't a function of physical years but mental ones. I ask her again.

"Wasn't it in your now time they discovered neutrinos move faster than light?" she queries.

I shrug. Why would I know about some physics thing? I say so.

"Because physics habitats are important. They're not hard," she replies, saying the last word heavily. She continues: "Neutrinos move through matter. Neutrinos move in and out of other dimensions without affecting those dimensions or ours. To move a habitant or object from one side of the street to the other without being hit by Wealth cars, you connect to neutrinos, and they take you to the other side. Same with light. Novatastic, eh?"

"Uh, sure. How do you do that?"

Hope shrugs, "Post-grad work. I'll be lucky if university Wealth let I into that," she ends morosely.

I reflect for a bit as we cross a street normally. And that's when it hits me: I've not seen any cars in our walk through her neighbourhood, either when we came or now. "Where are the cars?"

"Cars? Here?" Hope laughs and laughs.

"Okay, okay. I get it. Only the Wealth have cars."

"Even so!"

"So why don't you use traffic lights, you know, the normal way, to get people to cross streets? Generally, people don't get hit at those kinds of intersections."

Hope looks around and lowers her voice, "The real reason for neutrino bridges is so they can barricade the roads with charged curtains and force Thrall and middle class to cross in specific locations. Neutrino bridges and charged curtains allow cars to drive non-stop, unimpeded by habitants, bicycles, or streetcars. Wealth cars self-drive, keep equidistant from cars in front and behind, and negotiate with other cars for when crossing intersections. Wealth cars weave in between each other. Ingenious, eh? They sense habitants and moving objects and avoid them, but the Wealth don't like anyone to slow them down, least of all Thrall." Hope pauses. "I heard this crazy story at university. Some Thrall breached the charged curtain and ran down the street, beside the cars. Nova'd the Wealth out."

"Nova'd?"

"Even so. Scared, like how a Nova would scare you if it exploded right in front of your eyes."

"Oh."

"Wealth enforcement are hunting for the Thrall who did it and are trying to figure out how they did it. But there's no birth chip trace. Weird, eh?"

"Weird. So where're we going," I ask studiously looking frontward.

Hope isn't to be distracted. She chuckles quietly then says, "Round this corner, we rejoin public city. Brace yourself," and her chuckle changes its tone to nasty.

I look at her perplexed, her face easily visible in the artificial sunlight. Yet for all their advanced ways, the neutrino-bridged sunlight still casts those creepy night shadows that our primitive artificial lights do. She says we're here, and I turn my head forward.

And raise my arms in horror to block out the cacophony.

Ahead are the same streets and same buildings that I'm used to seeing in this now time, but everywhere there are ads: blinking ads, musical ads, building-height ads. And there are signs: street signs that hover and move to stay in your vision, that have multimedia presentations about the name on the signs; warning signs to stay on the Thrall walks; shopping hour signs; "enter here" signs. And there's an ad that looks human, talks human, looks solidly male, and is walking right toward me telling me about the latest sale at the sewing store for those who like to make their own suits and to enter here—he waves his arm to the side—for a chance to win the latest machine just by playing with my five fave friends, telling me he's happy to set up the connections to bring them in, all I have to do is tell him who they are. And here he cocks his head and asks why I don't have my five fave set up already, but not to worry, he can remedy that, he has access to habitant base of all the middle class in Toronto, although if I want, he can also access the habitant bases in other Canadian cities and ten major States ones, all included in the one low price. If one of my five are outside of those cities, it'd be an extra low-low hundred dollars per city-search to find their birth chip code and bring them into my five fave. He is willing to serve me immediately, and here he stretches out his hand toward me.

Suddenly he's right in front of me, his hand almost touching my chest; he rotates it into a fist bump. All I have to do is bump his ready fist, and the payment is made, my five fave are set up, and I can play the sewing game, and here he sweeps his hand toward the side again, and I glimpse a room full of laughing, chatting girls, holding materials of shimmering hues, machines humming around them, music thumping in time to the beat of the needles thrumming up and down, up and down, up and down. I love sewing, but I haven't done it in ages. I want to see, and I take a step toward the room. The man encourages me to try a sample embroidery game. I can enter the room free with no obligation to try a sample. It's easy. I step through the opening into the room, and the room encloses me. The girls nearest me turn their heads and invite me in. They gesture with their hands excitedly to ask me who has the best square of quiltwork. One holds up a gleaming gold square to her chin, the fabric falling to her knees. It sways gently in an unfelt breeze, its embroidery of waves and peeking sunlight entrancing me, pulling my hand close to feel it. It feels like a gentle wave foaming over my fingers. The girl on my other side turns me toward her so that I can see her square of forest green with enticing tree shadows and glimpses of deer, their ears swivelling to hear my voice. I get lost in her embroidery. Their cries of "pick one, pick one" crescendo in my ears. The Ad Man whispers from behind me, his breath hot and erotic on my neck, that all I have to do to be part of the game, to win the newest machine that's not even in the Carker Centre stores yet, is to pick the best embroidery. The debit will be taken from my account. I won't even have to do a habitat. All I have to do is fist bump, and I can continue to play with the girls and the fabrics and the new machines for as long as I want, but to really benefit, all I have to do is have him set up my fave five—

A hand grabs my shoulder hard. I stumble backward and land against Hope.

The room is gone; the Ad Man is gone; the cacophony around me remains.

Hope grips my upper arm and drags me back around the corner. We're in the quiet of her neighbourhood again. She grimaces, "I thought I'd lost you. What you see?"

My heart begins to race; my breathing becomes frantic.

She thrusts a threatening finger in front of my face: "Don't. Scream."

I shake my head no, and she lowers her hand. Suddenly, I'm aware of how tired my eyes are, how angry my brain is from the bombardment and from being pulled out of that room. Hope reaches under her hair and does that dit-dit-dit thing with her fingers on her temple. She grabs my hand and moves my fingers in a similar pattern on her palm. She gestures to me to repeat it. And I do. She mimes for me to tap it on the tattoo her mother had stuck to my temple. I place my suddenly-very-fat fingers where I think the tiny rectangle is, and she adjusts them. After a few tries, I succeed.

Hope says, "We can talk. I turned off the tracking. Memorize the temple pattern so you can turn it off when you need to. But do it only when emergency. You'll need it to walk to your job and back and to cross the neutrino bridges. Do not use your job card. What you see?"

I swing my head back and forth, my body shaking so hard I cannot think.

She grabs my head with both hands, narrows her eyes, and looks right into mine, "What game did he offer you?"

"Game?"

She releases my head, crosses her arms, and simply looks at me. I blurt it out. She says nothing, and we stand together in the quiet of this street with its old houses—centuries old, not decades as in my now time—and older trees, the bridged sunlight lighting up her hair and reflecting off her eyes, making them deeper, darker. I sigh long. This peaceful middle class street is a balm. My body releases its angry tension. My heart slows down. My breathing returns to normal.

"What happened?" I ask.

"Our now time happened," she replies.

"I don't understand," I respond.

"Simple. This is how we live. You get used to it," she shrugs.

"But where did it all come from? What was he?"

She stares at me before rolling her eyes, "You are dumb." She taps my right temple, and I reach up to feel it. "The tattoo," I say doubtfully.

"The tattoo," she counters. "I have a birth chip, eh. All habitants get one embedded after the umbilical cord is snipped.

Your tattoo is like our birth chip; it lets you participate, like
Mom said."

"Participate?"

She sighs exaggeratedly, "How do you think the Wealth keep
Thrall obedient? They don't need police or alcohol or drugs;
they have games for shopping. You go shopping and play a
game. Or you go reality contesting and win small habitats for a
chance to buy bigger habitats. It's fun. It's addictive."

"But ... but when we went shopping at Carker Centre, there
were no games."

"Carker Centre is traditional. You buy like in old, eh.
Nostalgia and merchandise make you feel good. Remember?"

My body remembers, and I blush.

Hope rolls her eyes, "You're old."

"This is not my time," I remind her.

"In I now time," she says, emphasizing I, "the time you're in
now, the merchandise keeps you happy, in whatever way makes
you happy. Carker Centre starts the happiness through
nostalgia, and their suits keep you happy every cloudlight you
wear them. Some habitants have five."

"What do you mean? You only have five suits?"

"That's much."

"That's stinky."

"Stinky?" she laughs, "our clothes self-clean. I forget your
clothes are primitive."

I process this. Something she said earlier pops into my mind,
and I ask, "What did you mean you don't need police? Don't you
have crime? And what were those patrols if not police?"

"I told you shopping and contesting addict Thrall. They
occupy Thrall when not working. They keep them spending so
they can't stop working their long cloudlight shifts. You
attended a game. Did you want to leave, eh?"

I shake my head no, shamefully and a little fearfully. I had
been so easily sucked in, had so wanted to be part of that group,

to have my opinion mean something, to change people's lives. Only now do I realize my opinion was for something meaningless and transient. It seemed so important in that moment, so trivial in this now moment. I say, "Is that what they're doing when they stare into space, at Space's place, playing games or, or ... what did you call it? Contesting?"

Hope nods, "When Michael isn't working, he's reality playing and spending all his work money on the games."

"But why don't they move when playing the games? Did I move? I must've moved."

Hope shakes her head slowly, "Not so. The game sends a signal to immobilize the player. Rare habitants are immune and walk."

"Like sleep walking."

Hope's silence is her reply.

"Do they play games all the time?" I ask.

"Since Michael hooked up with Byane, he spends less time in game rooms, but he's not dangerous to the Wealth because he's following Byane around, doing what Byane says. And the Wealth, they always have their own interests in mind. What they do is not criminal."

I squint at her to detect a sign of sarcasm. I see none, yet ...

She continues, "Marie and Brittayne are on each other's fave five. Thrall girls have special codes built into their birth chips so when their men want them, their game rooms disappear, and they can't re-enter until their men aren't near them anymore." She frowns in thought, "Though I think Brittayne has discovered how to circumvent that so Byane doesn't notice."

"Oh."

"Marie plays for shift lengths. She travels from one reality contesting to another, racking up sale points so she can go shopping and play games. Sometimes she'll shop right through her host ad—"

"Host ad?"

"The man you saw, he's your host. He customizes games and reality for you and guides you through them and shopping. He brings you what you like and learns from your choices. Wasn't he going to set up your fave five?"

"How did you know?"

"You don't have one," she snorts.

"Oh."

"Marie likes Carker Centre too and visits with other girls at shift ends."

I stand there pondering. "So." I ponder some more. "So, basically you're saying, there are no police because the Thrall are too, uh, enthralled with shopping and playing with their friends to think about it. But what are the patrols for?"

"Wealth enforcement patrols. They keep the Wealth safe."

"That makes no sense."

"We went close to Wealth neighbourhood. Remember, eh? Thrall immune to game immobilization sometimes end up near Wealth borders. Wealth enforcement shoos them away."

"It seemed more serious than that."

She looks at me sideways. She says, "Wealth enforcement keep middle class in line. They know we know how to think. They censor continuous issuances to prevent us learning how non-Wealth dominated countries work. They monitor birth chips for failure. About two percent of the population can't be addicted, and Wealth enforcement watches them because they're the ones who can lead. But many don't realize they can't be sucked in, and they like being like their friends."

"Why don't you?"

"Boring."

I think she's nuts. Shopping is not boring, and then I think of that room and how much it affected me. I shiver. As long as people are happy, why would they rebel? But what about money? I ask her.

"The Wealth discovered how to pay Thrall little but spend lots."

"The debt must be crushing."

"They spend lots because Wealth enforcement set up algorithms for Thrall to win enough reality contesting to keep them shopping and playing games. No Thrall can earn enough to pay for all their shopping. The Wealth contribute to a pot they call 'Safety Central' to fund the algorithms. Safety Central pays off Thrall debt without them knowing about it. No one has debt. The food they eat is cheap. Machines make all our clothes. Thrall work in service or knowledge centres, and there's nothing else for Thrall to do after work. Educators and parents taught Thrall to think education is boring and learning is the worst. So they're happy."

I nod slowly, "When do you get the chip?"

She huffs at my inattention, "When you're born, remember? The doctor injects babies with nanos and implants the birth chip. It sends out tendrils to monitor your whole brain and records your aging, your health, where you live, whether you skip Thrall school—no Thrall has skipped school in decades since they included that program and started implanting everybody with birth chips."

"But—"

She silences me with her hand and very seriously shakes her head. She continues, "It records what you say and to whom you say it." I mouth a silent "oh" and am slightly freaked out. "It records where you go and when, your job, and most of all your consuming habits. At first your habits will be your parents', eh?"

"What do you mean? Babies don't shop."

"Sure they do!" She sees my look of disbelief. "Babies develop their own taste preferences. Their birth chips are hooked into their parents' chips until they reach adulthood, twenty-one. Babies' birth chips program the babies' preferred ads into their parents' chips. That way when parents think they're going to get their kid mushy peas, and the kid really wants prunes, a host ad will pop up and correct them."

I shiver.

She shrugs, "You get used to it."

"I wouldn't." I have to move but am afraid to move from this safe spot. I cast around for a reason to delay. I suddenly remember how she'd called herself "Parsi," a word I'd never heard before. I ask.

Hope huffs, "You sure don't know a lot. We were around in your now time, millennia before. You heard about Persians?"

"Yeah, they're from Iran. Muslim."

"No! Parsi!"

"Oh."

"Muslims stole our land, but we Parsis are ones who made it. The originals, the real Persians. Zarathustra was our prophet. He meditated years. Received illuminations. When he came out of his cave, he showed people how to be good. He said we have free will. We decide to be in truth or in lie. He taught ritual and words are not enough, you must start in your thoughts. Then come out good words and deeds. He wrote millions of verses guiding us, teaching us how to turn toward good thoughts and away from bad thoughts, telling us about what was and what to come. He made men and girls equal in marriage, even in battle. You heard of Cyrus the Great?"

I nod.

"He created first human rights code. Was a good thought. We were thinkers, intellectuals Dad said we were called. We help people too. It's what we're supposed to do."

"That's why your mom is helping me?"

Hope doesn't respond. My head hurts, all this thinking, all this learning new, all this discerning and deciding. I'm not used to it. I feel unaccustomed curiosity but weary beyond measure to ask more.

I shuffle my feet in a side-to-side rhythm I cannot hear as my arms sway limply in sync.

Hope waits.

My thoughts track back to what lies ahead, and I ask the ground, in spite of myself, "If these things track everything, and if only you and a select few know how to turn them off, how come no one knows about Space's classes?"

"Space established a shield around his store, eh. It's a dampening field. Nothing gets out or is let in that Space doesn't want. It lets others play their games, while feeding false scenarios to the birth chip about where they are. Mom worked on programming with him. But its biggest safety is in Wealth attitudes. The Wealth believe their habitant walls are foolproof against reprogramming. We keep a low profile. Space vets his chosen students and warns them not to reveal through behaviour that they're learning in his group. They don't know about the habitant wall—except I," she says with conceit. "I'll never tell."

"You just did. Anyway, I don't get it. What's the point?"

"Point?"

"Of all this effort, of going to Space's, listening to bad history and boring books being read out loud when it's so dangerous?"

"Knowledge."

21

I WANT TO GO HOME

I want to go home. I want to go home. I want to go home. The words repeat in my head, repeat and repeat, all the way through the Ad Man calling me incessantly to rejoin the embroidery room, past multimedia street signs singing the virtues of their new Wealth sponsor—Pecksniff is now Payne Street—under demonstration banners for new regeneration techniques, all the way from Hope's neighbourhood to Space's place. I'm thankful the tattoo can't read thoughts. I'd suddenly had that fear just before Hope had turned her chip and my tattoo back on. She'd replied that when they'd enabled that ability in birth chips, the influx of thoughts had overwhelmed the information analysis centre. It had shut down. And suddenly the Wealth didn't know what Thrall were doing. They decided it was better to know what Thrall were doing than try to know what they were thinking too. They shut down the thought-reading ability.

They hadn't needed it anyway to keep society controlled for two generations.

I want to go home. I want to go home. I want to go home. Like a metronome, the thought repeats itself until I open the door to Space's library and blurt it out.

Space glances up from his book. He places his forefinger between the pages he's reading, and half-closes the book. He gazes at me through his blank spectacles, and I repeat my desire, strongly, firmly, determinedly.

Space says, "You will need to retrieve those equations."

The thought wails in my head, I can't! But I say, "Okay."

Space says, "You're not a mathematician or a physicist."

"Bikini thought I could do it. Hope's mom said she'd help me."

Space says, "The journey is yours alone."

"In the final phase, but who says I have to do everything else by myself?"

Hope says, "She saw our now time."

"Asha's device worked?" Space queries.

"It worked. I instructed her to go through neutrino bridges by herself to test. It worked."

"We'll begin."

I don't ask him how he will, but I know he's helping me now because I believe it. And because I want to work with people not have them do all the work. Needing people is not depending on people, I finally understand.

Space searches down the side of his chair and fishes out a rumpled bookmark. He replaces his finger with it and puts his book on the precariously growing pile on his side table, stands up, whistles, and strides out the library door, along the hall, and down to the store floor. Atticus bounds out from the back of the store and joins us as we sit at the table furthest from the store window. It's gloomy back here. The light reflects off of Space's spectacles in half moons. Hope recedes into the dark. I blink, trying to adjust my eyes.

"In this darkness, you will focus on what you have learnt," Space instructs as he reaches into his shirt pocket and extracts a piece of paper that looks similar to Byane's: folded, wrinkled, translucent white. He unfolds it and slides it over. I eyeball it. What am I supposed to do with it?

I say, "I need real paper and pencil."

"That will do," Space replies.

I look at it, look at him. Hope snatches it with a huff. She presses the top left corner, and it pops up into a notepad with little squares top to bottom, side to side, like I remember those pimply boys in high school geometry had. It made good doodling paper for me. She reaches into her kilt pocket and pulls out a stylus and tosses both toward me. The stylus lands, bounces, and rolls. I snatch at it, and it rolls right past my darting hand and off the table and into Atticus's mouth. He arches his neck up, and I take the stylus from him. I surreptitiously wipe it on my skirt. Atticus looks disgusted and sits down next to me. Somehow his head is above the table, high enough to see the pad that shines so brightly in this dim store and my hand hovering over it with the stylus. The texture of the pad distracts me. It feels like it's repulsing my hand ever so slightly. I miss the comfortable roughness of paper, the way its warmth tells me this is real, the paper is real, what I'm about to write is real.

I can't focus.

I begin to panic.

The harder I try to ignore this electronic pad that doesn't look electronic, that doesn't have the smooth glass feeling of a computer screen, the kind of electronic I know, the more my thoughts scatter into the air.

Space says, "Close your eyes. Return to that room. See Bikini. Do you see her?"

I start, "What?"

"Close your eyes," he repeats gently. "See Bikini. Do you see her?"

I close my eyes. I see her. I say, "Yes."

"See her at the board. Do you see her?"

"Yes."

"See her begin teaching you. What is the first thing she writes on the board?"

I open my eyes to answer, and Space points at the non-real notepad while saying, "Write it down." I draw the first sketch Bikini had drawn. I don't remember what it was about, but I remember the sketch and swiftly reproduce it. I stop. There had been no familiar scratch of pencil on paper, no slight indentations appearing as I drew. I lift my stylus. I shudder. I can't remember what comes next.

Space says, "Close your eyes. The technology is irrelevant. All you see is that board. All you see is yourself drawing what was on that board. When you cannot remember any more, close your eyes, and go backward into that now time. Return to that future room, see Bikini?"

I close my eyes and say, "Yes."

"See that board?"

"Yes."

"See her standing in front of it; watch as she writes the equations."

I drop my head and return to that room, to Bikini beginning to write her equations. I keep the memory going, and when I can see the next sketch of dots and the energy source she spoke about, I open my eyes and sketch that swiftly on the notepad. It looks exactly as I remember in my head. I close my eyes again and see more. And each time I close my eyes, I recall greater snatches of sketches, then whole equations and names of things I need. My hand moves unceasingly across and down the pad. I fill the first page. I flip it, no longer thinking that this is not a real notepad, that it isn't supposed to have pages, because I'm so immersed in that 3011 lab with Bikini and caught up in copying what she'd taught me.

My hand begins to cramp; I shake it and carry on. I flip another filled page and another one.

With a sigh, I throw down the stylus and sit back. I massage my aching right hand. Space reaches over for the notepad and slides it toward himself. Suddenly I can't see it. He makes a flipping motion and bends forward as if perusing my drawings and equations. Clearly he can see it, yet I cannot. I blurt out my puzzlement.

Hope mutters, "Space's dampening field shortens length light can travel, eh," as she scoots her chair over to Space and rests her chin on his shoulder to read along with him. I don't move, but I stretch across the table, crossing my arms to support my aching head. The notepad becomes visible to me again. Atticus remains with me. And a hush descends. Not even the flipping of the pages emits a sound.

I can't stand it as I watch them read so intensely: "You understand all that?"

"Physics is advanced, but Mom will understand," Hope replies without looking up.

"Human beings are capable of comprehending what they want to when given the knowledge," Space replies without stopping his reading. He flips another page. I try not to shift on the chair or shuffle my feet. Atticus lays his heavy head on my lap, and I sit up slightly as my hand automatically reaches down to stroke him. It calms me.

Space straightens as he slips his hand underneath the first page and flips the lot back onto the notepad. Unlike real paper, none of these pages have curled with the indentations of my writing or from having being flipped. They lie perfectly flat on the pad as if they have never been written on. I could wish for such well-behaved paper at home.

Home.

My heart suddenly sings at the thought, that maybe, really, truly, I can leave this nasty time and go home. Home to my crabby boss and gossipy Peggy and Sue.

I knit my brows.

Space interrupts my reverie, his voice suddenly loud, "Your mom?" he asks Hope.

"She told Time she'd help. She can supply energy source. It's hush, but I overheard her telling Dad she's discovered how to create energy out of quantum particles without an energy supply. That'll do, eh?"

"What about ceramonanocarbon tubes?"

"She has zetta of those," Hope replies flippantly. I wonder. But I resolutely push my doubts away. I won't indulge them.

"We can architect the ship. You have a good hand at drawing," he says to Hope, who squirms, "and I can supply most of the materials you need." Space adds, "My antegenerations have been storing habitats in the basement and not removing old ones as they bring in new ones. I can make space down there to build the ship where no one can see."

"You have enough space? And, uh, where's the basement," I ask, looking around at the bookcases.

"Space expands to what you need," he replies. "The basement door is over there; it's the lower half of the bookcase to the far left."

I look over and see way back in the caliginous corner underneath the stairs a narrow bookcase at the end of the row of regular-sized bookcases.

Okay then.

"Time will lead. These are your equations, Time, you're the one who learnt them directly. We will rely on you to guide us in what to do and in which order."

Terror snatches my breath. Can I really do this?

Space continues, "We won't tell the others. It is safer for you, Time, that only three of us know. You must be quiet on this. We are used to not talking, but you come from a gossipy time." The reflections on his spectacles grow to full roundness as he leans toward me. I rear back, the bars of the chair back pressing into my back, as I face the fact that I've never kept a secret in my life and gossiping is my favourite sport.

Maybe I can't do this. Maybe I have to stay here.

But I don't have anyone to tell this to, I recall with relief. So I won't have to control my mouth.

But they still want me to lead. How can they want me to lead them? They're so much more advanced than I am. How can I guide humans who are centuries beyond me in technology that's centuries beyond them. They seem so confident in themselves and in me, but even as I saw the equations, even as I copied them and felt confident I had not left one dot out, I didn't understand what I was scribbling.

No, I can't do this.

No, I have to do this.

I'm not going to doubt. I'm not going to doubt. I am going home. I am going home. I am going home. I keep repeating my mantra resolutely, trying not to let the first flush of my determination dissipate.

22

CHASES SHARPEN
THE MIND

SPACE says as I walk through the library door, "Hope is waiting for you in the basement."

I'm tired, cranky, hungry, very hungry, thirsty, and Toronto still has no public bathrooms. I open my mouth to complain that she can wait a bit longer when Space shuts it with the words: "She has a sandwich for you."

I race down the stairs to the store, jog around the tables to the back of it, find the hidden door-bookcase, open it and shut it behind me, and scramble down the stairs in search of that sandwich. Hope hands it to me without a word. I gulp it in two bites. She hands me a glass of milk. I swallow it in one long stream of gulps. I'm not satiated.

Hope says, "Space will bring down more food when you've had time to digest. You'll sicken yourself if you eat too much at once after a shift. We all know." She makes a face at an unpleasant memory.

"Here. I've drawn some sketches," Hope waves her hand over the scarred refectory table she's standing at the end of. The table dominates the plain area, and it springs into light. An architectural drawing of a strange ship appears on the table's top, an incomprehensible egg-shaped bunch of lines and arrows and tiny, perfect printing.

"What do you think, eh?"

"Uh, it looks fine," I answer, stretching my cheeks with my hands, wondering when Space will bring down more food.

She blows her hair up in exasperation, "You gave us equations."

"Yeah, but it doesn't mean I understand them."

"Time to learn. Time." She chuckles at her use of my name.

"Ha, ha," I respond. I then sigh and rotate the skin around my temples, "I'm too tired for this."

"You'll never not be tired. You can't quit your job. Drawings aren't hard, eh. Now look at them!"

"You sound like Bikini," I grumble. "Memorize," I mimic sarcastically. "Memorize!"

"I'm asking you to look not memorize! CEO, who's adult here?"

"Fine." I bend my head down toward the drawings, trying to ignore my rumbling stomach, my cotton-wool eyes. But my mind wanders where my hunger leads, and I dream of a large waffle with a perfect sphere of vanilla ice cream on top, lusciously drowned in chocolate sauce, and buried in a bevy of strawberries. No, better. A heaping fluffy mound of mashed potatoes, topped with shreds of old white cheddar, hunkered next to two slabs of steaks, blood oozing out the edges, pepper littering the top, and a giant Yorkshire pudding nestled up to their sides, gravy spilling over its cup. I lick my lips.

Hope shouts in my ear, literally, "Are you listening? I've architected, and you can't even look! Can't even listen!"

I jump and yell, "Don't shout in my ear!"

"Listen! Important! Don't you want to go home? Don't you want to direct your own life? If you won't help you, why should I?"

"I don't know. Why should you?"

She shouts back, "Because I care. I want to help. Nobody helps nobody here. Only parents help; only middle class help others. But I don't exist in middle class now I'm at school. I'm between Thrall and the Wealth. I'm nowhere. Haven't you noticed?" She sweeps her arms out into the empty space of the basement. "Zetta habitants live in Toronto, in Canada, on this supernova land mass, but none of us know each other or want to know each other. We fear future—and present—if we did. We fear obligated to help. We fear thinking about somebody other than I. We don't know how to care after generations of not caring. I want to know how. I hate now time existence. I hate being a girl. I want better life. Bikini is right: you can help our now times. You must!"

"No, I don't! And I can't anyway."

"Why you here? To say I can't? What's end game of your existence?"

"I don't know! I don't know why I'm here! What does it matter why, anyway? Maybe I'd be—"

"Don't say it!" she screams, fear filling her emittance. "Don't say it," she commands. "Other dumpees did. You can't!" Tears squeeze from her eyes.

"I can if I want to! I'm just one person! I'm only one person, only a stupid admin assistant. I know how to type memos and manage my boss's schedule, nothing else," I yell back.

"One habitant can change life!"

"Oh yeah? Like who?" I demand, knowing the answer but not wanting to admit one person can change the world.

"Steve Jobs."

That stops me. I thought she was going to say Ghandi. But Jobs? Some rich guy who made cool gadgets but didn't change society or bring down dictatorships or bring peace at Christmas or show us a better way to be? Jobs? Well, I'm not Jobs. I'm not a computer engineer. I never will be a math whiz; if it kills me, I won't be one!

I say, "Jobs didn't change the world. He just created Apple."

"Apple? What's with you and fruit? Dumb! Jobs created iPods, precursors to our birth chips. His inventions—"

I tune her out. Figures someone like him created this hellish tattoo or chip. I can't let go of what she said. Well, okay, maybe Jobs changed the world, but he was consumed with tech. I'm not him. And I'm not Ghandi either. I'm not trying to liberate a country. I don't have his smarts or his courage. I just want to go home.

"What you want? Home or stay in our now time?" Hope's voice interrupts and echoes my thoughts.

"Yeah, I do want to go home!" I turn away from her on my final word and run up the stairs to the store floor. Atticus is standing at the top.

I command him, "Let's go for a walk, Atticus."

Atticus wags his tail and follows me to the front door. I yank it open and slam it closed once he's out. I walk south, away from the legions of people and toward buildings from my time. I can see the edge of the old post office across the street from where I am. I try to cram my hands in my pockets, but this suit has no pockets. Only this stupid sash that leaves my legs exposed. A wind blows up and ruffles its pleats, puffing the top part of the sash away from my chest. Goose bumps rise along my arms and legs. I shiver and cross my arms. I increase my pace. Atticus easily keeps up with me. The sash flattens against my chest, and wherever cloth, shirt or sash, touches skin, I feel a warmth flow from it into my skin and thence into my core. I put my head down and hurry along, trying to ignore the strange dichotomy of warmth and shivering limbs, the cacophony of advertising playing music and movies all around me, my Ad Man walking up to me, chirpily selling me on the wonders of buying more suits to complement my neutral one. I can even create my own designs in their brand-new room featuring their updated suit sewing machine. I only have to help five habitants choose the material for their custom-made suits. I race walk away from him, my thoughts, and my unhappy stomach.

We reach the next main intersection. I raise my head. And I see the street signs: Pawkins and Napoleon. Huh? Wasn't Yonge something else? I wrack my brain but cannot remember. Something Dickensian. It doesn't come, and I shake my head. It doesn't matter. This is Yonge and Wellington. I know Yonge Street. I know Wellington and Front and King and Bay and Queen. No, Wellington is behind me. This is Front. Front! Front! Front! These new, changing names are stupid; they're confusing me. I want to shake my fist at those signs, the signs that don't exist except in my head, in everyone's heads. They're not real. This place is not real. I swing to the right and see:

The Hockey Hall of Fame.

The same sculpture stands outside it as in my time: a line of laughing, screaming hockey players garbed in helmets and hockey jerseys, leaning over the wall of the players' bench, one with his leg thrown over. I can see the hockey rink, hear the crowds cheering, the players heckling, the banging on the boards. I walk up to it and reach out to touch the bronze. Its coldness reassures me. This is real. This is, no, was my home.

I hear players calling me to join them; I turn around unsure. A road hockey game is in progress behind me. All girls. One runs out of the scrimmaging at the goal net toward me. She wants me to join them. She waves her stick at me, raises it two-handed above her head, declares it the best, the fraggiest stick ever. If I buy it, I can join. I'll be as good as them. I can be part of their team, their group, their play. She beckons me to join them in a test scrimmage, to see how novatastic it is. I take a step toward her, wanting to play, not to think, thinking I don't need to test the stick out, I want it now, then wondering how I can buy the stick and play hockey all day. I always was useless at the game, even floor hockey, and the others would boo me off the floor. But here I can be a part of a team that wants me, but how do I pay for it? Suddenly, the Ad Man is in front of me, saying all I have to do is fist bump him.

Atticus bumps into me.

I stagger, and the team is gone. It's just an empty road with the odd Wealth car passing by. I start as I realize I'd confused the virtual world with the real one. I wrench my gaze from the road back to the bronze players. I focus harder on the sculpture. As long as I stand close to it and look only at it, touch it and interact with it, I can't see the lie that I can be part of a team. I feel a tap on my shoulder. I ignore it. It's not real. The Ad Man whispers in my ear that there's a sale on for a pair of shoes that will give a pleasing contrast to my suit, but it's only on for a limited time so I must hurry. I shrug off the pseudo hand. It clamps itself to my shoulder, trying to pull me around to look at it, its associated voice telling me my friends will be novatastic in their new shoes while I won't. They'll laugh at me if I don't keep up. I won't be part of the crowd. The hand is so compelling. My heart beats harder. How can something so artificial have such a physical presence?

This world frightens me.

Atticus leans against my leg, and suddenly the hand vanishes. I say to Atticus, "Thanks." I smile down at him, and his mouth opens, his lips stretch into a grin, his tongue hangs out, panting. He woofs gently. And I uncross my arms to reach out and pat his head. The motion soothes me. I notice the sidewalk here is like the old concrete ones I'm used to. It's grey and mottled with discarded ageless gum. "C'mon," I say to Atticus. "Let's go back."

A voice rings out, "Where d'you think you're going?"

I raise my head sharply and see them. The three boys from the future. They're wearing mufti. Oh God, I breathe out silently. "Atticus," I whisper. He's suddenly between me and them. A growl emits from his throat.

Guy says derisively, "You can't think we're afraid of him, a primitive dogdroid!"

"You should be," I answer with more bravado than I feel. I take a careful step backward.

He snarls, "We told you what would happen dumb human if you disobeyed us." They stride forward in tandem. Atticus leaps at them. They startle back, and I take off, back up Yonge Street. Dodging the Ad Man, dodging the few human beings who're walking on this part of Yonge. I see the red frontage of The Attic growing closer as I flee the boys.

"Dumb human, we'll catch you! You can't run faster than we can. You can't escape us." Guy's voice is near, and I lean forward into the wind, lengthening my strides and putting more weight into the take off. My shoes respond and spring me forward. I run faster. Atticus is suddenly right on my heels yet not tripping me. He's a solid presence that Guy and his boys will have to get through to get to me. I skid and swivel as I reach The Attic's front door. I yank it open, and Atticus and I rocket through. I slam it shut, almost catching Guy's hand. He tries to open it but cannot. The knob won't respond to him. He bangs and kicks at the door, swearing. At least I think he's swearing. I don't understand the words, but I understand his anger.

"Dumb human, we're letting you go this time. But I warn you: try to get home again, keep defying us, and we'll be back." I hear them trudge off, and I sag against the nearest table, putting my hand to my chest to calm my heart. Atticus remains standing, watching the door vigilantly.

Space says behind me, "What are you going to do?"

I have no energy to jump. "Eat and then go look at Hope's drawings," I reply. "But we need more help, Space. We can't build that thing alone. I don't know what I was looking at, but I do know it's complicated and needs people to build, more than two people, especially when one of the two is me."

"It's not safe."

"They know anyway," I reply, gesturing with a flailing hand to the disappearing boys outside. "So what does it matter?"

"It's not safe for I and Hope."

I shake my head, "Your group is not safe either, Space. Yet you hold it. They can help me, us."

I can feel Space thinking. At last, he says, "I'll ask the boys."

"The group is more than boys."

He says matter of factly, "Girls can't help. And of the boys, only Byane will be useful. But boys understand these things innately unlike girls."

"I'm a girl," I reply, using their language, yet not feeling like a girl but a weary old woman who wants to sit in her comfortable rocking chair in front of a fire in her well-worn home of bricks and wood.

"You have no choice. This is your journey," Space replies. "Hope is middle class; she's bred to be like boys. The girls won't help. They can't. We're not asking them. And they won't expect it or want it."

I shrug. I'm too tired to argue. Two more is better than just me and Hope.

23

THE EGG

THE wind rattles The Attic's front window and slams into the front door. It howls down the street. If anything, it's stronger than when it blew me in after my shift at Marci's, my bare skin blasted frozen, the covered part of me warm as toast. These clothes are ... interesting. When I arrived home, no, not home, The Attic, Space's place, Space's not mine, Hope was not yet here after classes; neither was Byane. And so I'd been able to eat a decent meal, slowly, enjoyably after my shift.

The front door swings open and smacks into the bookcases then slams violently. Space and I look at each other while Atticus continues to snore under the kitchen table. I tiptoe over to the stairs and peek over the banisters but see no one. I go down, one careful step at a time, and still see no sign of life. And I can't hear anything over the wind banging imprecations against the battened down windows and fastened door. Perhaps whoever came in is in the basement. Space has said his store is safe; Hope corroborated. Atticus isn't perturbed, so ...

I tiptoe to the basement door and open it quietly. I hear a drumming overhead, and I peer around the staircase to check that the front window and door are still intact. They are but now I see streams of snow flying horizontally by the window, whisking people south down the street whether they are facing north or south.

Space says to me over the banister, "This greenhouse gas storm has been brewing for some time."

"I'm glad I got in when I did in one piece," I reply. "Why are they like that? I don't think I've seen totally horizontal snow before."

He shrugs, "It's common."

I flash back to what Hope had said about storms and nod. Another reason to go home. These kinds of storms are beginning to happen in my time but can't be called common. Yet. I turn to go down the stairs, Space on my heels. Atticus is still snoozing, I surmise. Space closes the basement door behind him, and the quiet is profound.

Until Hope yells, "Where is I protractor?"

Space slips past me, hunches down next to the table, picks up the protractor, and hands it to her. She says nothing but merely takes it and continues with her drawing. The basement door opens, letting in the thundering sounds and ionic smells of the storm. Byane jogs down the stairs and shakes off shoulders of snow onto the basement floor. He's not wearing a coat.

"Aren't you cold?" I ask.

He looks at me with contempt.

"Wipe that expression off. Down here I'm the boss. You look up to me." I'm surprised to hear those words leaving my mouth. It makes me feel good, empowered.

"Suit warm."

"You still have bare skin."

"Suit on to full-body coverage," he answers then sighs at my questioning look. Hope intervenes and informs me that suits contain a portable charged curtain that can be powered on to keep the cold out. Girls' suits have those too. And she ends with an impatient can we get on with it.

"Oh," I reply, feeling deflated. No one had told me. I could've been warm all over. I sigh deeply then shrug it off. I must focus.

We all gather around Hope's drawings of *The Egg* that'll take me home. That's what we've decided to call my time ship: *The Egg*. Hope points to the skeleton and structural elements that will be made of the ceramonanocarbon tubes; she outlines with her finger the neutrino field; she indicates the location of the energy source. I can finally discern which is the front and which is the back of *The Egg*. Hope says, "Mom has energy source. She has a prototype that will work for Time. Byane," she admonishes, "you can't tell anyone!"

He sneers at her, "Girl, don't tell I."

"Don't call her girl like she's an object," I tell him off, channelling my fearsome grade one teacher. "She's the one who took my equations and created this drawing out of them. You've done nothing worthwhile yet."

"Equations are future's," he drawls at me.

"They're not yours either, and they came out of my head," I snap back. He doesn't back down; the sneer doesn't leave his face. Standing nose to nose, I feel a resolve rising in me not to back down either. I cannot remember the last time I stood up for myself. Try never, I think, as I continue to stare into his contemptuous eyes. I see the contempt change into puzzlement then frustration then fury then dawning respect. My eyes are itching from dryness. But I won't concede to his superiority. I won't, I decide, because he isn't. He's human like me. Seeing that, making that decision feels good. Again, I feel power surge through my arteries and nerves. I straighten my spine, lengthen my neck, intensify my focus. Byane blinks. He looks away. I smile to myself while he mutters to Hope, "I won't tell. I want growth."

The standoff resolved, we resume our planning, and I say, "We need to figure out all the materials that are necessary and divide up who will acquire what. I'm not from here, but I can co-ordinate our acquisitions."

Hope huffs, "As I said, Mom will give us her prototype. She'll make it work first."

Byane says, "I get the ceramonanotubes—"

Hope interrupts, "I can acquire those. Mom has—"

Byane interrupts back, "Dad's company has a subsidiary in the nebula program that owns the manufacturing rights to the tubes and has a part stake in the company that makes the ceramo particles and another part stake in the company that matures the required nanos. My Dad's youngest brother runs the monitoring section of the subsidiary and can plant the books. He does it all the time." He suddenly realizes he's spoken in complete sentences like middle class. He continues, "How think Dad grow ecologies to grab Carker Street?"

I blink in confusion. "Wait. Don't you mean Carker Cen—"

Byane cuts me off, "Keep up. Dad's ecologies soared on earth exchange. He was awarded Pawkins. Longest in world. Symbol of Carker ecologies' tree strength. Will be mine; make it flower," he smirks.

"So why are you here?"

"Ecologies aren't everything," he grumbles.

"That's sacrilege, what you say," I counter.

He looks at me, wariness in his eyes.

I soften my voice and ask him what Hope asked me: "Why are you here?"

He looks off into the distance, slides his eyes at me, and they change. His entire body relaxes into the relief of a decision: "Ecologies are boring. The way we are is boring. I feel dead. The only time I was alive was when my Aunt dragged I to India to live there during the monsoon season. We holed up in apartments, communities of families. We played board games, talked about everything from politics to education to philosophy to best green earth practices. They have different cultivation methods. Then we'd venture into the rain—I hadn't been poured on before and it excited I—and rescue habitants. I learned to speak like middle class. It was so strange, so enervating. But when I returned, Dad was furious I spoke like middle class. He thought my ideas worse. He said the Wealth were greater, didn't need to waste hot air on many words and dangerous ideas," he peters off as he returns in time to that memory. He shrugs his shoulders and says, "I get tubes."

I frown, caught on a word he'd used. I say, "Don't you mean 'invigorating' not 'enervating'?"

He frowns. "No. I mean more vigor not less."

I blink perplexedly then remember an old linguistics prof talking about how words change their meaning to the opposite over centuries. "Oh. Right." I reset my mind and ask: "Where do we get the neutrinos?"

Space says, "I have a source."

We all accept that, and I ask, "What's the interior made of?"

"Carbon fibre," Hope replies.

"Old," Byane scoffs.

"Cheap," she retorts.

"I get anything."

"Perky."

I snap, "Enough." Taking a steadying breath, I say, "What is the best material for the job, not the cheapest or the hardest to get but will provide a safe interior?"

Hope says, "Carbon fibre will—"

Space says, "Carbontubes proliferate more."

Byane says, "Algae extrusion gives best malleability and strength."

"That sounds gross," I reply.

Hope and Byane roll their eyes at me.

"Glad to see we're in agreement," I mutter. We pause in thought, "What are the most important attributes for *The Egg*'s interior?"

"Strength," Hope answers.

"Smoothness," Space replies.

"Malleability and strength," Byane asserts.

I think about it and ask, "What's the cheapest?"

"Carbon fibre," they reply in unison.

"Carbon fibre it is," I assert, not wanting to strain my host's resources any more than I have to. Byane looks disappointed. And I look at the drawing again and point to the inlaid furniture: "What are these made from?"

Hope shrugs.

I suggest, "We could use the algae extrusion for those?"

Byane perks up. Hope leans forward to study the console and chair intently, "Barnacle idea. We need malleable strength for appendages. But they should be tied into walls of equal malleability and strength—"

Byane murmurs, "I get algae extrusion for whole *Egg*."

"—so it'll support your mass—" she looks up critically at me then back down to the drawing, "—times the gravity forces. I'm unsure we can protect you from those."

Space says, "I have the antigravity suit from *The Mars Explorer*."

"Oohh," Hope says, "Third one?"

Byane looks upon Space with envy.

I scan their faces and decide to feel honoured.

I disrupt the Space reverence by saying, "So the first order of business is to quantify and procure these materials. Hope, how much do we need?"

"Paper?" Hope asks, reaching her hand out. Byane pulls out a pink piece of folded paper. Hope takes it and spurts, "Pink?"

"Latest," Byane replies self-satisfiedly. "Here," he reaches over to fold it up into thirds, and suddenly it's a small notebook with an attached pencil.

Hope's eyes widen. She flips open the cover and scribbles on the first page.

"You already know the numbers?" I ask incredulously.

"Even so," she replies proudly. "No number escapes my head," she says as she taps her head, "I'd already calculated quantities."

"Oh."

She hands back the notepad to Byane. Space fishes in first one pocket then another then his shirt pocket before finding a crumpled piece of paper and a stub of a pencil. I smile. Hope takes the pencil, examines both ends, decides which end will write, and scribbles on the paper. She hands them both back to him.

"Right," I slap my thighs. "We're in business. I'm going to have my *Egg*!"

24

THEM AGAIN

FLAT clouds loom overhead and the air has a fuzzy look to it as I walk home from work, weary, hungry, and very thirsty. I've become used to the crowds, people shoulder to shoulder, voices fading in and out as groups pass me by. Hope had cut my hair in the acceptable style. Hope and her mother weren't too happy with the colour and were concerned about my skin colour too, but I didn't want to be entirely subsumed into this culture. I don't want to become them. I flash to a news story that wouldn't leave the front pages of every newspaper in its box that I passed every morning on the way to work, the story about an honour murder of three girls and a woman in the Kingston Locks by the parents and brother of the girls because somehow the girls and woman had dishonoured the family by their dress or normal behaviour or something. Everyone in the office had talked about it each morning during the trial, even Peggy and Sue. I hadn't believed it was true. It had been just another domestic violence case, if that. Shame burns my heart and slows my feet as I gaze at the shadow-darkened pink granite. I hid my sight from the truth then, and now ... I don't want to accept this now time as the truth, for if I did, I would be saying, if to no one else but me, it's okay.

I turn these thoughts over in my mind, about who I am, about who I am becoming, how I'm being influenced by this time, by this way of being, into seeing my time clearer, thoughts I'm not used to having or pursuing in depth, not since ... not since university and over-the-table dinner conversations my father insisted on having. At the time I hated them; in this time, I miss them. I sigh. I lift my head, try to swing my arms, lengthen my strides, move away from contemplating my life and toward Space's cooking, but my muscles refuse to move faster. I settle back into my thoughts, and to my surprise, I'm relieved. I'm liking this thinking; it's connecting me to my school days when I had felt so alert and popping with energy, ready to bounce into the future. And that reminds me: I'm supposed to be thinking over Hope's question.

I sag at the enormity of it.

They had found most of the materials, and they are stacked in a separate storage room in Space's basement. Hope wants me to decide what to tackle first: the exoskeleton, the engine, or the energy source? It seems like such a simple question, but cloudlight shift after cloudlight shift has sapped me, and my mind refuses to focus, refuses to make a decision. My head hangs down, my eyes taking in but not registering the path I'm on as my feet automatically take me back to Space's. I try again to consider Hope's question. But my thoughts prefer wandering into images of roast beef, mashed potatoes, pizza, a Dagwood sandwich, a root beer float, a vanilla cupcake with a swirling mountain of chocolate icing—

My stomach growls. It's being doing that most of the time since I began working. I'm perpetually hungry, and I down glasses and glasses of water whenever I'm not at the job. And after I eat and drink, all I want to do is sleep. Yet I must work on *The Egg.*

Egg.

I wish I had the energy of an egg.

But I don't.

How can I do this when Marci's drains me, when walking along this ad-laden street with ads approaching me as I pass by every store—and there's no city block that is not one store after another—when Ad Man is my yapping companion, when keeping up with this weird culture requires me to be constantly vigilant? I cannot do this. I cannot supervise making *The Egg.*

"There she is."

I cannot even fathom doing anything to aid our *Egg* building except to sit and watch.

"Get her."

But they don't want me to do that.

"There are too many."

"The crowds in this nasty time won't care."

I have to find the energy somehow.

"Get her."

Can't be done, I'll have to tell them. Maybe during my first cloudlight shift off I can work on *The Egg.* We can build it in spurts. I perk up, then wonder: when will my next cloudlight shift—? Days! The word is "days"! I don't want to adopt their language, yet it's creeping even into my thoughts, and I hadn't noticed. I exhale loudly. I haven't had any time off, and I'm thinking more and more like them. Shift on, shift off, is the rhythm here. Are they all like this? Does everyone work like this? I blow out a mournful stream of air as I see time unfolding before me in unending shifts.

I smell garlic sauteéing. I raise my head and sniff appreciatively into the wind that's blowing the blurry air around. Pasta. I close my eyes to smell the enticing aroma more fully.

Hands grab me.

I struggle, but I have no strength. It's the boys. They've got me with no Atticus around to protect me. I had heard their voices, I suddenly realize. But I hadn't paid any attention. Just like last time. Anger at myself blows out as quickly as it had flared. I half-heartedly open my mouth to scream out help. But what's the use: the crowds are murmuring at the extra jostling but are carrying on with only a backward frown, annoyed at the inconvenience of being deviated from their paths not at a girl being manhandled.

A hand wraps around my neck over my Adam's apple, and my voice won't work. A stiff tiny square of something irritates my skin, and the hand is removed. I gulp in air. The square of something on my neck presses in. I drop my chin, bulge my neck, but nothing I do will dislodge it. I cannot make a sound. The three hold my arms tight behind my back as they hustle me off Yonge, no it's now Payne Street, no Carker, onto Fagin. I frown. I thought Bloor was Fagin, but now Dundas is?

I have no time for distractions, no time to quit, I admonish myself.

Struggle!

I wiggle my shoulders, drag my feet. But the boys have me firmly, and firmly they move me forward. There are no graffiti-lined alleyways between the buildings here; only quiet treed spaces filled with strolling people and the burka-draped gardeners. We'd stick out if they took me down one of those, and so they hustle me along. The fight goes out of me again. Where is my adrenaline? Isn't that supposed to kick in, no matter how drained one is? Mine is gone apparently. Might as well go with it. I let go of all my muscles, and I become a dead weight. The three swear and have to stop. It's a good time to get free. But I'm a dead weight because I'm literally a dead weight. I make an attempt, but my muscles are too feeble against their fresh energy levels. I let go more; I envision myself as an iron ball; I make myself so heavy that they must gasp and struggle to hold me up and to pull me along through the uncaring crowds.

I lose track of space and time.

We're in that place where I started, where empty grey buildings look down upon cracked sidewalks and old road, where no people walk or hang out. They let go of me and surround me.

One of the boys raises my head by my hair.

Guy sibilates, "I said to you to stay here, in this nasty time, the time for you. I said not to try to get home. No girl disobeys me." He slams his closed right fist into the corner of my left jaw. Consciousness swims, and I fall back against the boys.

Guy puts his face into mine so closely I cannot bring it into focus. He hisses, "You will not get home. I won't let you."

They commence beating me up. My arms rise instinctively but futilely to protect my head.

Mercifully, the second blow, one to the angle of my right jaw, obliterates consciousness.

I wake up to the sight of a white ceiling. It's glowing and moving toward my feet quickly. I blink several times. Pain appears and punches me in my face, my shoulders, my arms, my chest, my legs. I close my eyes and try to disappear into unconsciousness again.

A voice behind my head says, "She's awake."

I open my eyes to see a face looking upside down at me.

We whisk under a lintel and a lower ceiling glows down upon me. I close my eyes. I feel hands expertly examining me from my feet up. When the hands reach my face, light glows redly through my lids. The hands push my hair back.

A male voice says, "Bring the magnifier here, I feel something."

Warm breath tickles my temple.

"What is this?"

I feel a body press against my left side. A female voice says, "It's one of the old tattoos. My grandmother has one."

"Remover," he commands. The pressure on my left side eases then returns as an arm reaches over, brushing my lower ribs, setting up lances of pain. The doctor quickly pokes my temple with an instrument. Ripping pain shoots along my skin, shocking open my eyes.

He hands the instrument back to the nurse and says, "Analyze that. Bring me the nano programmer."

I don't like the look of the doctor, and I close my eyelids quickly. I hear shoes squeaking away, clinks, shoes squeaking back, and the small smack of something being placed in a hand. The light remains on my face, but now I feel a prickling sensation on the top of my head. The prickles move down.

"What is this? Who is she? She has no nanos, and I detect an abnormality in her molecular density."

"I haven't seen that."

He replies automatically, his thoughts focused on this conundrum, "I've seen it once before. He died."

My heart contracts, and I flash back to what the boys had said about transportation and time travel, how their nanos would repair their particle density but nothing would repair me. Terror engulfs me. I struggle against opening my eyes, against saying anything. I gulp and realize that the small square of something is not on my neck anymore. The boys must've removed it. 3011 tech can't be seen in 2411. Hysteria threatens to burble out.

The male voice, the doctor I surmise, says, "Put her in isolation."

We're moving again. And although I'm lying down on a soft, supportive bed, the slight jerk as they accelerate it shoots the dull aches into overdrive, shocking me into screaming out. It is a bit late for my voice to work.

"Be quiet."

I moan through clenched teeth, "Pain. Pain relief."

"Thrall don't make demands."

"I'm not Thrall."

"Who are you?"

I don't answer. The ceiling goes by faster, and it's making me dizzy. I squeeze my eyes. But that hurts. I watch the ceiling again. We zip through another doorway into a glass-enclosed space, through a sliding glass door, into another glass-enclosed space, through another sliding door, which seals with a hush. They swivel my bed around, pull me backward, and then stop the bed. An orderly appears from behind my head, walks past me, his white suit with pleats so short they end just below his waist, and toward the glass door, which is flush with the wall. It disappears sideways into the wall as he approaches; it reappears to slide closed behind him. A female nurse and a male doctor walk into my view and look down upon me, one on either side of me. The nurse's sash and short shirt are all white with a single blue stripe along the outside edge of the sash. The sash ends ... I look away, embarrassed. I tell myself it's because it's so white that it hurts my eyes. The doctor is in a male suit, also white, but creamy white with a very long skirt to his tunic and sharp pleats. The medical sign adorns each side of his v-neck. He wears no hat, but his locks are tied back. I look up into their faces. Their eyes looking down at me are suspicious.

The doctor says, "We need to inspect her skin properly. I'm wondering what colour it is. Let's deal with her injuries so we can see her better."

"How?" the nurse asks.

"We'll use EEG stimulation to flood her body with endorphins while I prep emergency nanos for injection. They'll restore her molecular density while repairing her injuries."

"How?"

"After that last one died, I reviewed my notes and saw where I went wrong. It'll work this time."

"Nanos in short supply. CEO Barnacle required after he tore left shoulder in tennis match. He ordered five minutes healing time. Had an ecology meeting. Needed extra nanos to make it."

The doctor swears and strides through the obedient door, commanding over his shoulder: "Seal the room and start the endorphins. I'm going to prove my theory right. I'm getting those nanos."

The nurse follows the doctor to the door and places her palm on the wall on the right side of the door while leaning in to the wall. She speaks, "Isolation five."

The wall repeats, "Isolation five, activated. Who access?"

"Nurse Oliver, Doctor Smallweed, orderlies."

The wall confirms, "Doctor Smallweed, Nurse Oliver, orderlies access. Isolation Five."

The closed door hisses and becomes a clear part of the wall. The nurse walks out of my view, and after a little while I feel her place a lacy cap on my head. Cold gel seeps out of it and covers my head. The gel warms up, and I no longer feel it. My pain starts to fade, and I feel good. Warmth floods my body right down to my cold toes; she removes the lacy cap. I reach up tentatively to feel my hair. My arm is stiff yet doesn't ache or burn. My hair is in clumps and feels rough and dirty. I let my arm drop, and I fall asleep. Somewhere in my dreams, I feel a prick and then tumble down into black water.

When I awaken, I'm alone in the room. I scan my body with my mind. I feel ... normal. For the first time since my time here, I feel normal. The tiny tickles of pain that had become background noise in my consciousness are gone. I feel light, free. I grin. I want to shout. But then I doubt: is it real? Maybe I'm dreaming.

I raise myself on my elbows and look down. I'm covered in a sheet made of the same material as my suit except it's white, glaringly white. It doesn't shift as I move, yet doesn't pull on me either. It keeps me covered and warm. I sit up fully and push it down to inspect myself. My naked self. I burn in embarrassment. But I soon forget that as I look at my white skin.

I have no bruises.

I pat my chest.

It doesn't hurt.

I slide my right hand along my left arm's smooth, unblemished skin.

It doesn't ache or burn or hurt.

I pat my punched jaw on both sides. It's not tender. It's strong and sharp on the corners.

I probe my right temple with my fingers and find the tattoo gone. Then I remember the pain of the tattoo being ripped off. I remember their questions and suspicions. Fear leaps into my breast, and I carefully pull the sheet back up and lie back down. I contemplate the ceiling and wonder what will happen to me.

I'm hungry.

Yet for once, I'm not thirsty.

I wonder what emergency nanos are. I remember the doctor had said something about an injection, and revulsion fills my mouth with bile at the thought of smart foreign objects wiggling through my bloodstream, pushing their way into my cells, manipulating my functions. I can feel them crawling on my skin, and I start flailing, trying to shake them off.

Stop it! I command myself. It's all in your imagination, I adjure myself. I will myself to calm down and decide: if I ever get out, I'm going home!

Energy flows through me, snapping my mental processes, fuelling my body. Life energizes me in a way I haven't felt since childhood. I sweep the sheet around me and in one fluid motion sit up and swing my legs over the side of the bed. Clutching the two edges of the sheet together near my neck, I duckwalk up to the clear part of the wall and smack into it because the door won't open. Duh, I mock myself. I inspect the wall to the right of the door, trying to see where she'd put her palm. I was sure I had seen a rectangular input device there. But I see nothing now. I touch my temple. Of course, with the chip gone, I cannot see the virtual part of their world.

Virtual.

I think about that word and how it means something so different here than back home. Here, virtual interacts with humans physically. Back home, it's all eyes and ears, but nothing physical like solid print books or solid buildings or solid signage. Or solid touchpads, I add sourly.

I wander around the room, my eyes scanning every detail, my ears alert to any whisper of sound. The room is white. Sunny snow white. The only furniture in it is the bed they brought me in on. I look down upon my feet. They're bare, yet they're not cold. This floor is warm and smooth and glacial ice white with not a seam or textural gleam in it. I climb back into bed, rearrange the sheet to cover me up to my chin, and ponder the ceiling that lights up the room and throws no shadows.

I'm hungry.

I have no idea what to do.

I hear the door swish open. I raise my head to look.

It's Space in a white orderly suit.

With Atticus right behind him, carrying white saddle bags with red crosses on them. I sit up quickly.

Space raises a placating hand, "Lie back down." He tosses me a suit, "Put this on."

I wiggle into a neutral suit under the sheet. It's not easy, and I'm afraid of ripping it, though that doesn't slow me down. But this cloth doesn't rip. It pulls and shifts and retreats into place as I hustle on the shirt and then the sash. With a sigh, I flop back and then go to get up.

Space says, "Lie down. Pull the sheet up to your chin. Close your eyes. Not like that, relaxed. That's it."

I feel the bed jerk; I hear Atticus's paws click before us. The doors swish open and zip closed behind us. The bed turns, moves forward, turns, moves forward. I lose my sense of direction. I'm disoriented.

Space whispers in my ear as we're moving in a forward direction, "Get up as soon as I touch your head. Don't look around, don't hesitate, follow Atticus."

He continues to push the bed forward. All of a sudden, I feel his hand on my head. I leap out from under the sheets, spot Atticus trotting away, and run to catch up. When I do, I match his trotting pace. Space is on my heels. We speed up. We fly through an outside door and join the crowds on University.

I steam south, outpacing Space, causing Atticus to jog to keep up with me as his saddle bags morph from white with red crosses to regular shopping ones. I cannot wait to return to Space's basement to make that *Egg*.

25

WHO AND WHAT

I storm down to the basement where Hope and Byane are leaning over the architectural drawings of *The Egg*. They stand up, and a smile wreathes Hope's face. She tries to be nonchalant, but after a brief hesitation, she launches herself at me and strangles me with her arms, her head digging into my neck.

I stagger back and reach my arms around her tentatively. Dampness washes my neck. She lets go and roughly wipes her eyes. She returns to her place, mumbling "glad you're home."

Byane blurts out, "Novatastic."

I take it he's happy to see me too. Atticus thunders down the basement stairs behind Space's light feet. Seeing them, I start to wonder how they found me. I ask.

Space says, "Atticus found you."

"How?" I ask, puzzled.

"Don't dogs have sensitive noses in your now time?"

"Well, yes ..."

"Dogdroids are based on dogs. They do too."

Hope says, "You're not telling the truth."

Space clears his voice, glances at Hope, then back at me: "Asha didn't want Hope to disappear, like some middle class girls did in the now time she was born in. They disappeared those girls to keep them from polluting Thrall and Wealth girls, but they abandoned it after a decade. It made middle class militant, more like to share ideas. Better to keep them complacent. But Asha worried. She refined her dogdroid noses to search for one molecule of scent in one hundred square kilometres and follow it. Atticus has that nose. We had your molecules."

I draw out an "I see." I absorb this information for one more second, then return my attention to why I came down here so urgently.

I say, "Hope, you asked me what's next."

"I said—"

I hold up my hand, "I know, I know. I'm paraphrasing. Being beaten up in this godforsaken place, being ignored by the crowds except for how we inconvenienced them, being held prisoner, has made me mad. I'm mad. I'm steaming mad. I'm—?"

"We get point," Hope interrupts, rolling her eyes. "You're mad." She pauses and squints at me, "You're not crazifying, are you?"

"What? No! I'm mad, as in angry, enraged, frustrated, furious. Mad. Angry mad, not crazy mad. What does mad mean, anyway?" I ask in a quieter voice.

Hope shifts her feet, Space says nothing. Byane finally says bluntly, "A terrorist. Don't have them in our now time. The Wealth rid green earth of them." He stops speaking, and I decide I don't want to know how.

I clear my throat and begin again, "I'm finally angry, angry enough that it doesn't matter if I'm not a physics major or whether I'll turn into a geek. That doctor was frightening, but he healed all my time and physical injuries. I've never felt better, and he and the beating up opened my eyes. The only thing that matters is to get home and to get out of this nasty time. I'm raring to go."

"Nasty time?" Hope ejaculates.

"That's what the boys call it. I'd say their time is nasty too. Everyone is nasty—except you guys. I want to go back to my familiar home, where real things are real, where people care, where dogs don't talk, where men and women don't understand each other but like each other, and girls don't need to be sex objects or have to hide themselves—"

"But—," Hope raises her hand.

"—because they think that's what men want. I want to go back to when food was real and workers got to pee—"

"But—"

"—and health care was screwed up but not a jail. I want to go home, and I want to go home now. So, Hope, you asked me what we should do first. I say we begin on all of them first."

"But what you said isn't—," she stops and looks at my determined face. She decides to drop her objections, whatever they were, to what I'd said and changes course. "We can't do," she informs me.

Byane says, "Impossible."

Space says nothing.

"It is possible if we get more help," I counter.

Space says, "We can't afford the risk."

"We ask the rest of the group."

Byane blows a raspberry.

Hope rolls her eyes.

Space flashes his blank-eyed spectacles at me.

Atticus creeps backward away from me.

"They won't talk. And they can help," I maintain stubbornly.

Byane scoffs, "How? Girls no use here. Michael hasn't shown."

"Michael is a Thrall, and his job keeps him away. Does he work for your Dad's company?"

"How matter?"

"Because if he does, you could second him."

"What?"

"You know, say you need him for your work. Be mysterious. Be hush-hush. Make it sound big and important but that you need a slave to do the dirty work. Isn't that what the Wealth do? Treat employees, I mean Thralls, as slaves? Get some powerless person to do the dirty work and take the fall?"

Byane gazes at me. I return his look coolly. He nods slowly, "I can do that."

"Good. He'll join us but under my conditions," I reply, emphasizing "my." I continue: "I'm not going to have anyone go hungry or thirsty or needing to pee because of the work they're doing for me. We treat every human being here the same: with respect and great expectations." As I'm talking, I'm thinking: where is this coming from? Where am I getting this tone of authority, this sense of I'm in control? It's so foreign. And fun.

"But one more is not enough. We need the other two too." I refrain from using the word "girls." I'm so sick of it, sick of objectifying and diminishing one-half of the population with the simple use of a word that has connotations of child-like, property, and uselessness to it, when what it should really mean is a female child. I resolve then and there that if—no, I admonish myself— when I get home I will never use the word "girl" unless I'm also using the word "boy" in a playful, community way or because I'm referring to a female child under the age of eighteen. I sigh. It'll be good to get back to an era when adulthood begins at eighteen not some random older age. I shake myself out of my reverie and land in the middle of Byane's counterattack:

"... girls can't help!" he ends triumphantly.

"That's it? That's the sum of what you have? Pathetic. That's a facile argument and you know it." I can tell from Byane's face and Space's small smile that Byane doesn't understand my vocabulary. Good. Power to me. I motor on: "We need Brittayne and Marie because we need the extra hands. Maybe they're not math whizzes, but neither am I—"

"But—"

I hold up my hand to Byane's face: "We need them. They can help you and Hope. One each. Marie will be your helper, and Brittayne Hope's."

Byane snarls, "Brittayne is mine. She'll work for I—if I allow her."

"Brittayne is not yours. She's a human being, not a widget. She will work with us. Hear. My. Emphasis." I stop and bore into his eyes before continuing, "With us—because we need her. And she won't work with you because you'll waste time having her meet your needs not having her work to get *The Egg* operational and me out of here."

Hope stifles a laugh, and Space's smile widens to visible length. Byane glares. "Girl—"

"Stop right there. I'm a woman. I'm older than you. I'm more experienced in matters of life than you are. I know more than you because I know how humans are supposed to be and what they're capable of. Space and Hope's parents know more than me because they're older, and they have lived in a time that blares the dichotomy, but you don't. So don't think you can dictate to me or get away with your rationalizations." Byane's eyes disappear into pinpoints. I glare back and continue: "We need them. They are human beings with all the abilities of human beings to learn and adapt. They're going to help."

Hope says, "I don't want to agree with him. I like how you treat him like Thrall. But I hate girls. Girls are dumb."

"You're a girl," I remind her.

"Middle class!"

"You're female. They're your sisters. You were a girl till you reached adulthood ...," I pause and wonder: "Are any of you adults? Officially?"

Space says, "Officially adulthood begins at twenty-one. Unofficially, it's forty for men. Never for girls. Girls cannot help with this kind of project. Hope can because she's middle class and has been educated all her life; her parents expected her to learn. But Thrall girls are trained to meet men's needs not to learn for themselves. Doing this," he encompasses the entire room with a sweeping gesture, "is beyond them. We cannot ask it of them. And they'll get in our way."

I can't tell if he's being argumentative or believing what he's saying. I counter, "Anyone can learn if you give them a chance."

Space's blank face hides his thoughts. Byane and Hope's reflect the strength of their beliefs. None of us give way. We all stare at each other. And stare some more. I finally close the argument: "We're going to ask them—I am going to ask them because I want to go home now! And I can't get home if we build first *The Egg's* exoskeleton then the engine then the energy source then ... it will take three times longer than if we do them all at once. I can't keep safe from those boys and from this society, especially now that they know I exist. They removed my tattoo. Won't they discover who gave it to me? And what will happen when I don't show up at Marci's? I dare not go out again. The boys will get me, and your ... your Wealth enforcement patrol is probably looking for me too."

Suddenly the three of them stand up straight. Fear enters their eyes, and they look at each other. I press home my point, "If they find out who gave me the tattoo, won't it just be a matter of time before they backtrack and find out you were here, Byane?"

Byane opens his mouth, looks anxiously at Space, and asks, "How good is The Attic safety?"

"Barnacle. But it's been compromised by her sojourn in the hospital. They know what she looks like. Wealth enforcement patrol will begin to track her tattoo and will find Asha. They will also view the CCTV footage."

Byane appears astonished. He blurts, "But ... but Dad elevated I in charge of holding celebrations when CCTVs declared dodo. He took down the last one in the goodbye-to-the-past event."

"It was show. They rely on birth chips to track Thrall, but they replaced the visible CCTVs with nano ones as a back up," Space answers, gazing upon Byane sadly.

Byane shakes his head, but Space doesn't waver. Byane finally believes him, and disillusionment droops his features. Space looks away; Hope looks down at her drawings. But I keep watch upon him and see: anger at the cynicism of the Wealth, at his father's betrayal; then bitterness that he was treated the same as Thrall; and lastly red-hot revenge rage at being kept in ignorance by his own father, though he is a Wealth and is his inheritor. Crimson floods his cheeks; sparks brighten his eyes; revenge puts a rod in his back. He snaps, "Get the girls."

Space and Hope jerk their heads up at him, look at each other in bewilderment, and Hope says, "I don't know ..."

His voice rough, Byane says, "I don't either. But he treated I like Thrall so I'll treat Thrall like the Wealth."

Space aims his spectacles at me, and they drop ever so slightly. I see respect and pride in the top slits of his icy eyes. I smile back, rather pleased with myself.

26

GETTING ON

I'M sitting down low in my Barcelona chair in Space's library, Space is in his chair, and Hope is hugging her knees in her chair, her chin on top of them, eyes on the floor. Byane is resolutely staring into space; he's playing a game, probably something to do with acquisitions and mergers. It's like those McDonald's movie tie-ins. See the movie, buy a burger, get the toy.

Michael is following Byane's lead while the two ... I will not call them girls. I won't. But as I watch them, I think how girlish they are as they wave some sort of small, straight pink wand over their nails to try out various colours and patterns. Brittayne is inspecting her choice of pink stars on midnight blue background. From her face, I gather she doesn't like it.

They're waiting for me. I'd hoped Space would speak to them, but he'd been short and terse in his reply: it's your *Egg*, you ask. But what do I say? How do I ask? I realize as I hunker in my white weathered chair, formulating and discarding words in my head, that I'd never asked anyone to help me, ever, for anything vital to me. Sure, it's expected to ask for participants in group projects at work, but group projects are meaningless to me personally. And to life. Peggy and Sue are like that too. My boss has no problem asking me for help with buying his wife birthday presents or setting up holidays for him and his family, but then that's my job: to do his work and his bidding.

My parents used to ask me for help because it was expected that a child aids a parent. In any case, as my mother used to josh over and over, I took so long sparking into life and then being born, I owed her. But when she'd call for help, she always used to begin with an apology, "I'm so sorry, dear." It echoes in my memory, although I can barely remember the things she used to ask me help for—usually silly things that eventually I understood were more about being able to see me. She was starving for companionship. That hadn't dawned on me for so long, being tied up with busywork, surrounded by people all day, gossiping. I grimace at the memory of the wild conversations people's relationships at work used to engender. Amy in marketing was always a source of good gossip, flitting from director to manager every month or so. No one gossips here—people being thoroughly engrossed in their own selves—that I find myself sickened by all the horrid things I used to say about Amy, the foibles Peggy, Sue, and I used to laugh maliciously over.

Malicious: that is the word.

That's when it hits me: I'm afraid to ask these three for help because if they fail, if they show themselves to be who Space, Byane, and Hope say they are, then I will be the butt of gossip, of finger-pointing by the two who think my idea is bad. I shift uneasily in my chair.

Then I remind myself: I won't be the source of gossip because people here don't gossip. They simply put you down and return to their games.

I don't want to be put down either.

Atticus's slow-moving paws click in the quiet space as he pushes open the door and comes to sit next to me. He raises his snout to my face and leans his head against the chair arm. His eyes liquefy with pleading and reassurance. I smile at him. He waggles first one eyebrow then the other. He shifts closer. I continue to smile but do nothing else. He raises his back haunches, lifts his right paw, lazily extends it forward and places it back on the floor to get his nose around the chair arm, and flips my hand up with his snout onto the back of his head. I stroke it, front to back, front to back, front to back. He sits back down and snuffles. He drops his eyelids and stretches his neck forward, his head seeming to rest on air. I stroke from the front of his head to the back of it, down his neck to his shoulders. And repeat. After awhile, he settles down on the floor, leaving my hand hanging. He looks up at me and crooks his eyebrows. I laugh.

And speak.

I say: "Brittayne, Michael, Marie, I've been talking to the other three about a project we're working on and saying we need more help. I want your help."

Michael continues to stare into space; Marie nudges him with her leg. He frowns down at her nastily, and she jerks her head in my direction. He touches his temple and looks toward me. I repeat myself.

Michael says, "You mean I."

"No, I mean all three of you."

Brittayne and Marie look at each other then at me, confusion written all over their faces. They point mutely at themselves.

"Yes," I reply, "all three of you."

"Girls no help," Michael scoffs. "Unless do something for a man. That's what trained for." He narrows his eyes, "I assist men all cloudlight long, Wealth men. I don't do for girls."

I suppress a sigh, "No, it's not for men, for Wealth men, although the way we'll do it is for you to be seconded to Byane."

"What?"

"Seconded, I mean, he'll tell your boss he needs you to assist him full time so that you can help me."

"Why'd I want to do that?"

Why does anyone want to help anyone? I shrug my shoulders, and a movement takes my eyes away from Michael. Byane has crossed his arms and is gloating. Annoyance flares up in me, and I think: I have to answer Michael's question in a way that would appeal to him. Help for him is working. And work for a Thrall is non-stop from beginning of shift to end, with no break. I turn down my mouth at the unpleasantness of working life here. A memory of Mother thanking me with a smile so kind and grateful it lit up her eyes, all because I'd cleaned up her garden after the neighbour's dog had gotten into it for the umpteenth day in a row and had stayed in it until his owner had gotten home from work. The dog had been a prodigious pooper. I was annoyed, tired, dirty the summer afternoon Mother had called me. My only thought was a shower and, if I was lucky, catching the end of *Survivor*. Helping my mother had cost me watching the penultimate episode. But her smile had vaporized my irritation in spite of me wanting to stay in a bad mood, in spite of me seeing it as a chore, in spite of me seeing her as a burden.

I smile.

I smile right into Michael's eyes and put every ounce of gratitude I can muster into my own windows of the soul.

He startles. He swallows. He looks away. I turn my smile wattage up and compel him with thought alone to look back at me. He does and blinks.

I say, "Please?"

His eyes widen in incomprehension.

Space says, "It's an old vocab habitants used to use when asking favours."

Michael croaks, "Favour?"

"Favour is an action done for no gain," Space defines.

They all stare at him except Hope. She hangs onto her knees grimly.

I speak up, keeping my smile firmly planted on my face, keeping that feeling of gratitude going so that my eyes don't lose their smile either: "In the twenty-first century, people—habitants—did favours for each other all the time. It's what friends do for each other, but the best was when strangers did favours for you. Even small favours can insert a happy moment into a hard time, like when a tall, strong woman grabbed my overstuffed suitcase to race it up to the top of the stairs at the train station. She waited until I'd caught up, handed it back to me, and walked off so quickly that I had no time to thank her."

"Thank?" Michael asks.

Space says, "It's what the recipient of a favour says to a habitant who's done them the favour. It's a way to show gratitude."

Byane makes a noise, "Gratitude!"

Hope barks and we all jump, "It makes green earth worth living in. But you wouldn't know that. The Wealth expect habitants to slave for them."

"So middle class."

Hope lifts her head and glares at him, "So? Better than the Wealth."

"What's thanking like?" Michael asks.

"For losers," Byane asserts.

"For strong habitants, habitants so strong they don't need to compel others to work or help them," Hope retorts. "For winners."

"Well," I reply, ignoring the sparring two, "It's like this. I ask you if you would please help me build something. I really need your help. Without your help, I probably won't be able to complete it before I'm caught by your Wealth enforcement patrol. Please, please, please," I beg.

Michael shifts uncomfortably. He turns his head away from me, he sneaks a glance back at me. I smile, "Please?" He jerks his eyes away, but they slide back. I smile wider, and I say, "I will be very grateful if you say yes. I won't be able to thank you enough." His face flushes, and his lips stretch then shrink back then widen into an upward curve, and his eyes drop shyly.

"That's so awesome. Thank you, Michael. Thank you so much!" I pour it on. And then I continue, "Brittayne and Marie, will you help me too? I really need all the help I can get, and I know you can do it."

Michael jerks his head up: "You're lumping I with girls?" He looks over to Byane, "The Wealth accept?"

Byane shrugs and says, "Time thinks they can help." His features darken, "Dad will see what it's like to be betrayed though Time will fail."

Michael glares at me, "I don't work with girls."

Brittayne pipes up, "I do what Byane tells I."

I say, "We've agreed that you'll help Hope."

"Hope?! Don't work for girls."

"I'm not a girl. I'm a woman," Hope retorts.

Marie whispers, "What can I do?"

My impatience rears up, but I shove it back down. I cannot get angry at these people. I need their help. Anger and exasperation are a waste of breath. I inhale deeply. I exhale till my stomach is hollow. I speak calmly: "Okay, people. We need as many hands as we can get. I, Time," I say, laying the emphasis on my personal pronoun, "the dumpee from the past, I need your help to get home. I'll be stuck here forever if I can't get home, and if I stay here much longer, they'll find me, and if they find me, they'll find you." Michael, Brittayne, and Marie sit up in alarm. "The only way for them not to find me is if I'm not here."

Michael grumbles, "Use them."

Brittayne and Marie look worried and scared but nod. Byane rolls his eyes. Hope glares at me. Space watches Michael.

I follow Space's gaze and say, "I need your help too, Michael."

Atticus heaves himself up snorting and scrabbling his toenails for maximum noise on the floor. He has our attention. He points himself at Michael, his tail sticking straight back while his head and eyes bore into Michael's eyes. Michael cannot look away. He compresses his lips. Atticus doesn't move. Michael compresses his lips harder, anger flares up in his eyes, anger that hides fear. Atticus stretches his neck to its fullest extension, never removing his eyes from Michael's.

Michael's lips part, he exhales, "Even so."

I flop back in my chair, relief sighing out of me. Atticus turns and departs. Hope, Michael, Marie, Byane, and Brittayne huddle into themselves. But Space quivers with eagerness at this unexpected future.

27

IN THE BASEMENT

THIS is it. We're all together: Thrall, the Wealth, and me. Oh, and middle class Hope. All here to build my *Egg*. I feel portentous. Space leads us past the drawing table to stand in front of the wall. I should know what's going to happen next, but I'm thinking maybe he's there to talk about the droopy skin-coloured garment with arms and legs hanging on the wall, the one that appeared since I was last down here. A helmet hangs over it. Space ignores it. Instead, he raises his hand to the wall, a pad appears out of the wall, scans his body from hair to feet. He tells it to open, and a door emerges and slides open. We walk through the door.

I exclaim, as I halt, causing the others behind me to bump into my back, "How big is your basement?"

He turns to smile enigmatically at me before guiding us through a cavernous room with grey walls and a ramp to nowhere. A table with three large metal canisters on it and a box with a semi-transparent container encasing it stands next to the ramp. There are no windows.

Space says, "We will build *The Egg* here."

"Where does the ramp go?" I ask.

"Outside."

I peer at the wall; I walk closer. It's still just a wall. I turn back and say, "I don't see any doors."

"They will be there when we need them," Space replies and then walks through the wall opposite to the door we came through. I screech, a small screech.

Hope scoffs, "Optical illusion. You have those in your time, eh?"

"Um, yeah." The others follow Space: Byane with energy, Michael on his heels, Hope not wanting to be left behind, Brittayne and Marie hanging back, walking as slowly as they can. When they're all gone. I inspect the wall, first with my eyes and then with my hands. My eyes are deceived; my hands are not.

I walk through as Space is saying, his voice echoing in the vaulted space, "... engine."

"Why not build the engine in the same room as *The Egg*?" I ask. "It's not that large."

"We need to test it."

"Oh. Right."

Brittayne tentatively raises her hand.

Michael berates, "Not class. Girls don't ask questions."

Brittayne's hand falls.

"What's your question, Brittayne?" I ask her with an annoyed glance at Michael.

"Girls not speak," he orders.

Byane berates Michael, "Brittayne belongs to I."

Michael chastened, mumbles, "I saving Byane from saying what Thrall know."

"Brittayne knows she has to ask permission."

I tell them off: "No one has to ask anyone's permission to ask a question."

Byane asserts, "Brittayne and Marie do. They're I and Michael's."

"God! What about your declaration to treat Thrall like the Wealth?" I ejaculate.

"She girl."

Byane's vacillating rationalizations and language are beginning to spin my brain like a washing machine at the end of its cycle. Doesn't he know who he is? I half-close my hands and drum my knuckles on my cheekbones. My head cleared, I say, "Brittayne, ask your question."

Brittayne looks over at Byane, who shakes his head. I grind my teeth. This is worse than an obedient child who always looks to controlling mama. I glare at them both. But then I see mutiny stir in her eyes, and I pounce: "Brittayne, no question is dumb. Ask it."

Brittayne parts her lips to speak, but Michael leaps in and mocks, "I ask question, teacher?"

Byane laughs and mocks, "All questions are welcome, Thrall."

Michael laughs with his mouth but not his eyes. Brittayne tries to speak over them, but Michael drowns her out: "What is an egg?" he asks in a falsetto and mimics Brittayne raising her hand. Byane laughs and shimmies his shoulders. Brittayne tries again. I strain to hear her but cannot. Hope storms out, back to where we came from, the brittle laughter of the boys ringing after her and in all our ears, like out-of-tune bells. Brittayne takes in a lungful of air and tries to ask louder. But a lifetime of breathy speaking and keeping her voice low prevent her from shouting, which is the only way she could be heard. I have no such problem.

"Shut up!" I bellow. My bellow echoes around the room, slamming off the ceiling onto the walls, off the walls and into the boys' ears. They stop talking abruptly. I demand: "How old are you? Two? Don't answer! I want to hear Brittayne's question!"

Michael opens his mouth, and I bellow again, "Shut up!" I glare at the two of them until I'm satisfied they won't speak. I nod at Brittayne. But she's cowed. I say, "What's your question, Brittayne."

She puckers her delicate eyebrows, confused.

"I mean, just say or ask what you want to ask."

"Who build engine? And ... what *Egg*?"

"Oh, right. *The Egg* is ...," I begin. I relate the story of how I was taken, how Bikini showed me how to build a time ship, how I want to go home, how Hope's parents offered to help, how Space has given me space, how Hope has the knowledge, how Byane has the connections, how we've acquired the materials needed, and how we're calling the ship "*The Egg*." She looks as confused at the end as she had at the beginning.

She says, "Don't build engines."

"That's okay," I answer. "I don't either. That's why we're going to work together, all of us," I sweep my hand out to indicate everyone. I don't see Hope. And then I remember that she'd left. I say, "Let's go back to the drawing room." I lead them back through the wall, through *The Egg* room, and into the room where the drawing table awaits us. Hope is leaning over it with a ruler and pencil, vigorously ignoring us. I clear my throat. She straightens up and looks at me with a "What?" expression. I pretend I don't see it and ask, "What would you be better at: making an engine or making *The Egg*?"

"Engine," she replies and resumes refining the drawing.

"Okay. Then Byane will build *The Egg* with the help of ...," I was going to say Marie, but I'm thinking maybe I should mix it up. Make them all as lost as me. It's mean, I know. But I'm not in a kind mood, and I'm fed up with them and with myself. Maybe myself the most for not paying attention back home and again here, letting the boys take me twice, for wasting so much time doubting myself, for the trivial person that I was content to be, for settling for mediocrity and the superficial acceptance of those around me. "Tcha," I blurt. Rumination time is over. I continue: "No, Space will build *The Egg* with the help of Marie. Hope will build the engine with the help of Brittayne. Byane will make the neutrino wall and set up the energy source to communicate with *The Egg*. And Michael will work with me coordinating everything."

They burst out with objections. They cannot believe my assignments. I'm stupid, foolish. Girls can't do anything.

I don't care.

My aloofness finally gets through to them. Their voices die down.

Space says, "Interesting assignments. Are you building a society or a ship?"

"Both," I mock tersely.

"I think you are," he answers back.

I blink at him. I'd been facetious in my answer. But I look around at the mutinous and scared faces and wonder. A surge of power at what I've decided upon sharpens my eyeballs and mind's eye; it makes me feel wicked, wickedly arrogant like the Wealth. Doubt worms up. Perhaps I should pair them up as we'd talked about originally. But I so want to make Byane work, to make him feel like a Thrall, and he'll never feel that if he has someone to command as he always does. I want Michael to learn some humility and to realize working for a "girl" won't emasculate him. I want Hope to respect her own kind, and Brittayne seems to be getting some spunk to challenge her into doing that. And Space is the only one kind enough to be with Marie. No. These pairings are good.

I clap my hands loudly. They jump. I smirk at me startling them for once and say, "Let's get going."

28

BUILDING TIME

"WASTE I time building engine. Use magneto elevator!"

Michael commands me.

I grit my teeth, pretending to know what he's talking about. "What. Is. A. Magneto. Elevator?"

"Public engine. Reach exagame points, visit moon in ship off magneto elevator."

I call upon my patience and explain, "We can't use a public facility. What am I going to say, oh excuse me, I need to lift my time ship to space? Great way to keep it secret."

"Byane, make it happen."

"Byane's not God."

"CEO, Byane's the Wealth."

"He's not a CEO."

He rolls his eyes, "CEO, she stupid."

The penny drops. He used "CEO" like we use "God"; he wasn't saying Byane was a CEO. I can't stand it. Emphasizing "not," I say, "We are not using an elevator. You're supposed to help me coordinate, not waste my time with useless ideas."

"I don't waste time. Girls waste. Men like I know best."

"I listen to you, we blow my secret and tell the whole world I'm here—and you too."

That shuts him up. I pass my hand wearily over my damp forehead. I turn to Hope and see that they're all watching us like crowds at the Coliseum. I gather I'm the gladiator. This time I won. I sigh and ask, "Hope, what kind of engine are you building?"

"You don't need to know."

"I do."

"You're twenty-first century, you won't understand."

"Then make me."

"Pbbfflliitt!" Hope splutters. I wait. Finally, she instructs: "*The Egg* has to get off the planet, and physics behaves the same way in our now time as your now time. Gravity fights us. We fight back with force. We need power for force. Magneto elevator works best, but it's public. Even if Byane booked launch with you substituting for him, there's safety zone, and you needing to look like a boy." She rakes me up and down critically, "You can't pass for boy. Everybody knows Byane. I don't know how he hides getting here," she frowns at him.

"Continue," I chivvy her along.

"I'll architect rocket engine."

"You mean, you and Brittayne," I correct wearily. And then I wonder: where will she get the rocket fuel? I ask.

"Tsk. We don't use fuel like in your now time. It's anti-green earth."

Oh, silly me. Bad us. I don't say it out loud but simply stare at her wide-eyed until she sighs heavily and says, "We can't use solar since we must hide *Egg* until ready." She sighs heavily again in answer to my now-puzzled look. She explains: "The engine needs time to charge when using solar power. So I was thinking ..."

Byane snorts, "Girl thinks?"

"Oh, shut up, Byane," I yell.

Hope has kept on talking, "... bend space—"

"What? Bend space?"

"Bending space will take you from planet surface close enough to sun to use neutrino source."

Maybe I shouldn't have asked, but her look of superiority and Brittayne looking as lost as me goads me on. "Explain."

"We create a heavy point, like gravity, that bends space around us. What looks far away to twentieth century like you will be a few kilometres away in our moment time. Then we blast engine to propel you through space before heavy point disappears. Mom's engine. One problem. Mom has only achieved her invention to stay stable for ten seconds."

This sounds like a Hollywood movie, where the hero has some impossibly short time to do something that realistically would take hours. My disbelief shows. Hope spittles laughter. Byane laughs with her, but his laughter is forced, and I feel better knowing he's as lost as me.

Hope points at me and sputters out, "You bought it." She gasps, "I watched your TV, eh. Space worked one of his old devices to show I during one of your cloudlight shifts. They," she snorts, "they make up these impossible time habitats. I," she grabs the edge of the table to hold herself up, "I made one up for you. Ten seconds, I made it up," She leans on the table, like a fish out of water, gasping for breath. I feel stupid but school my face to look like I hadn't been fooled and am not bothered. We both know she's not fooled by my insouciance. She pulls herself back up. She clears her throat. "Works. Mom's engine stable but didn't inform university Wealth yet. She worries they'll abuse power." She breathes a final chuckle and says seriously, "It stays stable for many moments time, enough to thrust you to your space destination and forward in time."

"You mean, time travelling in to the future?"

"Don't be dumb, eh. We're all going forward in time."

"Oh." I absorb what she's said and ask the obvious: "What power source do you use?"

"Strong force. Also to create neutrino source."

I have no idea what she's talking about but ask, "You have it?"

She shifts her feet and hems and haws.

"I gather not," I say drolly.

Hope mutters, "Entanglement."

Byane says sarcastically, "Easy."

"You got a better idea, eh?"

"How're you going to acquire entangled particles?"

"Brittayne will."

Brittayne squeaks, "What?"

Byane scoffs, "Girls can't deceive. It takes a real Wealth man."

All us females snicker. Byane and Michael look at each other uncertainly.

I say to Byane, "I thought you were going to show your Dad Thrall are as good as the Wealth." I ignore his muttered, "Thrall not girls," as I ask Hope, "What do you need Brittayne to do?"

"Girls serve sci Wealth when they're building a new power source 'cause business Wealth won't let them leave until they're done. They're starting on one today," Hope replies.

Byane frowns, "That's Wealth-only info."

"Middle class know everything," Hope says with conceit. "Brittayne goes in, pretends to service, knocks out sci Wealth multiplying anti-neutrons and anti-protons, gets particles."

Byane asserts, "She won't. I won't take her."

"She doesn't need you."

Brittayne's head has been swivelling from Byane to Hope to Byane to Hope during their exchange but stops at Hope, horrified.

"Where is it?" I ask, thinking it's at one of Ontario's nuclear power plants, hoping it's the closer one at Pickering.

Hope says, "Gride Station."

Byane says simultaneously, "Transition Road."

Brittayne says simultaneously, "Far!"

I say, "Huh?"

Hope says, "Gride Station is furthest station on Fagin-Nickleby line." I sort through my memory and decide that must be the Bloor-Danforth line. "Transition Road is at Scarborough edge," she finishes.

That would be a bad trip in my time but maybe not now: "Gride Station is near Transition Road?"

"No," Brittayne wails. "Take I all cloudlight."

"There's no Gride Station in my time. Where is it?"

Space says, "It's at the old Scarborough border with Toronto."

"But, but ... that's Kennedy," I gasp. And then I remember the subway line-ups, "That'll take her eons. Why doesn't she drive there? Oh yeah, only the Wealth drive. Well, Byane will have to drive her." And then it hits me, "Wait a minute, they make bombs in Scarborough?"

"Bombs?" Hope asks, then the penny drops. "Not so! They make particles to create energy. No bombs. We're not primitive like twenty-first century!"

"I won't drive her," Byane interrupts petulantly. "This twenty-first century idea is stupid, stupider than Thrall. It won't work."

I interrupt him, "The subway will take too long. I saw those crowds. It'll take her way too long to walk there too."

Brittayne gestures away the subway problem, "Only stupid Thrall wait subway train. I don't. Drive I, Byane."

Byane's jaw drops at her gall. She suddenly realizes what she's said and steps forward, hand outstretched, to placate him when I jump in: "There used to be buses in Scarborough."

Hope considers, "She could take Nickleby extension bus. But she'd still have to walk. Only the Wealth have business on Transition Road and only Thrall girls go there when they go. They won't provide buses for Thrall girls."

"Well, a bus partway is better than nothing. And I bet Brittayne, you don't wait for buses either?"

She shrugs, "Of course not."

Byane angrily bursts out: "Where's she going to hide the particles?"

"I hear the sci Wealth in charge likes, um, aids. She'll have a bag," Hope replies.

Byane grinds out, "No girl of I ..."

Brittayne says simultaneously, "I don't do aids."

Hope and Byane ignore Brittayne, so intent are they on bickering. I think about what these aids are. "Ohhh," I suddenly realize as I remember that day Byane took out Brittayne and how angry Space was with Byane and how aids must be related to that, uh, activity. I say to her, "You're smart. I bet you could mimic using aids without really using them so he passes out with anticipation before you have to do anything, um, icky."

Brittayne nods solemnly. I suddenly have this idea she does that with Byane. I manage not to laugh out loud. I raise my voice over the bickering ones: "We have a plan for the engine. I'm not sure what it is. But I know Brittayne and Hope will get it done. Do you have any questions, Michael?"

Michael shakes his head sullenly. I silently send a prayer up of thanks.

"What about *The Egg*?" I interrupt Byane.

Byane stops mid-word and looks at me as if I'm a cockroach that has suddenly crawled up onto his shoe. He deigns to reply, "Hope will input exoskeleton design into my birth chip. I'll program ceramonanotubes to work together, and they'll form into *The Egg*." He shrugs like it's no big deal. I refrain from saying "oh" and nod knowingly instead. He adds, "Brittayne not getting particles."

"She is."

Fury puffs out his face, bulges his eyes in their sockets. I want to ignore him but speak rapidly to him instead: "I want to go home. You want me to go home so your Dad won't find out you're studying with Space. The fastest way is for everyone to help me. No one can get those particles but Brittayne. And you said after what your Dad did that you'd treat Thrall like the Wealth. So do it. Do what you say because it's in your interest too for Brittayne to get the particles." The fury drains from Byane's face. I briefly feel bad for reminding him of his Dad's betrayal and am about to add that she's smart enough to handle some man but clamp my mouth shut on that. "Smart" and "Brittayne" in the same sentence would probably infuriate him all over again. Instead, I turn to Space and ask, "What about the neutrino source?"

"Asha has sent it over. It will go into a compartment that is bolted on the outside of *The Egg*. I have a compartment in my storage. We will program the exact time and space in which the source will activate and your now time to which it will destinate *The Egg*."

"Is that, uh, hard?"

Space replies with no answer.

"How will Marie help?"

"She will follow I."

Marie looks relieved.

I'm weary but I muster up enough energy to stare into his stubborn spectacles. Space has the grace to look away. He thinks about it and says, "She can buy explosive bolts. I don't have those. It would be difficult for a Thrall to buy those, but she can say they're for her man's special needs. No one questions that. There are other things she will need to buy." He pauses. "We will have to space out her purchases to avoid suspicion."

"Program her birth chip to show her as other habitants. I do that when I get bored," Hope offers.

Space nods slowly, "That will speed things up."

I say, "Great." I force energetic enthusiasm into my voice and say, "This is a really good start everyone." I look over at Michael and ask him if I've forgotten anything. He squares his shoulders like a peacock about to dominate the garden, meaning me, with his gaudy display, but one glance into my fed-up eyes, and he decides to be prudent, "What about food?"

Laughter bursts out of me, and I nod. "Good question. Space can't cook because he'll be building; I don't know how; and half of us don't like printed food."

Marie offers tentatively, "I c ... I cook ... after ... after purchasing."

The boys' stomachs rumble on cue, and a hint of respect creeps into their eyes. Byane says, "Go cook."

"No," I counter, feeling that a bit of hunger will be good motivation to speed them along. I say to Marie: "Get Hope to reprogram your chip and purchase what Space needs first. Then we can eat."

Byane says, "I eat when I want to."

"Good for you."

Marie looks from me to Byane and back to me. She looks over to Michael, who looks at Byane and then at me. He knits his brows and considers me. Something shifts in her, and she says to Hope, "Program chip."

29

FLIGHT

"I acquired permission," Byane says as he walks into the basement pulling on the handle of a round ball that is hovering above the ground. Atticus follows him in, crosses the room, and disappears through the other door. I look up from the drawing table where Hope and Space are marking off the last two completed items. Brittayne, Marie, and Michael are in the room with the ramp, checking the connections between *The Egg* and its engines, scanning for leaks in the exoskeleton, confirming the neutrino source is ready.

"You have the truck?" I ask.

"We don't call it truck," Byane replies impatiently but without malice. Building *The Egg* together, learning to work on his own, seeing the girls accomplish their tasks, has engendered grudging respect in Byane. He talks to me as a Wealth and almost the same way to Michael, if not yet to Brittayne and Marie. I smile to myself and think he'll get there now, whether he wants to or not. I feel potent seeing what I've set in motion;

satisfied too. I stand up and ask him again how we're moving *The Egg.*

He gestures to the hovering ball, "It's not large-item mover. Before you say again, no not boat either. We use tug to pull *The Egg* forward. *The Egg* is not heavy, except for the energy and neutrino sources. They're small—"

"But dense. I remember. That's why they're heavier. But wouldn't a truck be better?" I refuse to use twenty-fifth century wordy words for truck. "It'll hide *The Egg.*"

Byane shakes his head, "Large-item movers don't work during cloudlight."

"Not even with special permission?"

"Not so," he replies shortly.

I'd thought that was what he was getting permission for. I guess his influence as the son of big Wealth goes only so far. I prudently keep my mouth shut.

"Tug is superior." He adds, "I said I'm pulling a new boat design. I said I was architecting one in private for Canada Day Wealth races."

"They bought it?"

"Everybody architects new boats in private. The Wealth have places everywhere in Toronto to architect them hidden. Everybody wants to architect fastest one. It's common," he shrugs.

"Will I be able pull it?"

"Thrall always walk it. But it'll move as fast as you can run. I got permission for Wealth assistants to take it on the Wealth roadway down to our private slip. I gave Hope key."

"Key? Will we have time to unlock gates and open them?"

"In her birth chip, key is in her birth chip," he says with great exasperation.

Oh yeah. They don't have regular keys. How stupid to forget. I shrug off my negative thoughts because another thought hits me: "How will we avoid showing Wealth enforcement or the boys The Attic?"

Space drolls, "Neutrino door."

I examine his face and suddenly I understand: "That ramp goes to one end of a neutrino bridge! Oh, like a door to a neutrino bridge. No, a door that works like a neutrino bridge."

Space smiles.

"But ... but it looks like a wall."

"The wall looks like a wall until I power on the neutrino door. I built it from scratch, using old tech, in case of an emergency. It isn't our now time's standard. But it's charged and ready for you."

"Thank you."

Brittayne flies though the ship room door, Marie and Michael on her heels. They're red from excitement and exertion. Brittayne announces that they're all done. Michael says he triple-checked the connections. Marie breathes that there are no leaks, that it's safe. I'm not sure about that, but my stomach hollows and my chest tightens as I suddenly realize: it's time. We stand around the table, looking at each other. It's that awkward moment between a job done and the pending fear and excitement of an unknown journey about to begin.

Byane breaks the silence, "Greenhouse gas storm is blowing in public Toronto."

"What do you mean?"

Space sighs, "The Wealth Weather Creator has kept Wealth neighbourhoods sunny longer than normal to accommodate the extended Feast in honour of Barnacle winning a point in his favour in Supreme Court. It will be appealed to Ecology Court, but until then, they celebrate. The clouds have ballooned over our area, and the magnetic poles are moving faster, generating greater cloud cover. The clouds are unleashing rain."

"And wind," Byane adds. "Can girls handle it?" He looks to me and Hope.

I counter, "Can boys handle it? And the 3011 boys too?"

"Petal of flower," he snorts.

"If you think that, I'm doomed."

Michael pipes up, "We have plan. We know what Bikini looks like. We distract boys. Show Time." Brittayne and Marie disappear back into *The Egg* room. We wait and suddenly twins of Bikini come barging back in. I suck in a breath. Only after intense scrutiny do I see they're not her.

"Wow," I breathe out. "You look just like her."

Michael says, "They stop tug, girls stop boys."

I nod slowly, "Maybe not for long, but long enough."

Byane says, "I and Michael run interference because I win foot races—Michael has to keep up with I—and I know our now time better than they. We won't allow them close."

Space says, "Atticus will be between you and the boys the entire way to Byane's jetty. They won't get past him."

"I haven't seen any weapons, but ..."

"He's a dogdroid," Space says as if that is answer enough. I wonder if Atticus is made of Kevlar.

Space steps toward me and takes my arm. He pushes up my cardigan sleeve and places a small disk on my skin. I feel a tiny pinprick then a cold rush. I shiver. Byane had found a supply of emergency nanos his father had secreted in his office. Space had retrieved one of the short-lived emergency nanos that the doctor had injected into me before it had biodegraded. He'd analyzed its programming and replicated it in these emergency nanos. They will last long enough to repair my molecular density once I get to the other side, but I cannot have blood tests for a week at least, not like I see my doctor for anything other than an annual anyway. He reminds me to put on the anti-gravity-cum-protection suit as soon as I enter *The Egg*.

"I guess, I guess I'm ready. We're ready." Tears flood my eyes, and my throat closes. I walk around the table to Brittayne and

Marie. I reach over to encompass them both with my arms. They rear back and look at each other then me questioningly.

"Hug?" Marie asks.

"Children parents hug. Not adults," Brittayne says.

"In my now time," I inform them, my arms still out, inviting them to hug back, "adults hug goodbye." They hesitantly reach their arms around me, and as I tighten my hold, they hug me properly. Suddenly, they're crying, little uncertain sobs as if the emotion is foreign. I join in. When their sobs diminish, I let go and wipe my eyes. They watch me and copy my motions. We smile at each other. "Thank you," I say.

Byane says, "Whatever that was, not doing it."

"It's called hugging. Don't the Wealth do it?"

"Only middle class married and parents with children."

Strange world, I refrain from saying. Michael suddenly shoves himself away from the table and around Byane and throws his arms around me. I stagger back. "Thank you," he says into my ear, lets go, and returns to his spot. I look after him with my mouth hanging open. A hand pats me on my shoulder, and I turn to see Byane standing next to me. I grin wolfishly and fling my arms around his waist, catching my hands in his thick ringlets of hair. I give him the biggest bear hug I can and am satisfied to hear all the air in his lungs push out. I let go and stand back. He blushes as red as a boiled beet.

"I'm ready," I tell Space.

Space takes the tug and leads us to *The Egg*. He positions the tug in front of *The Egg*, presses the top of the ball, and *The Egg* slowly rises a little and then stops. Space instructs, "It needs a centimetre clearance. But if the tug has to go higher over the ground, it will raise *The Egg* the same amount." I have to be content with that. He shows me how to pull it, and they have me practice. *The Egg* is my arm length taller than me, is as wide as my two arms outstretched, and is as long as three lengths of my body. It easily moves around the room; I feel no resistance as I pull the tug and thus *The Egg*. Satisfied with my performance, Space walks back into the other room and soon a hum fills the cavernous room, bounces off the walls, its echoes interfering with each other like wavelets in a pond. The wall at the top of the ramp shimmers, and that's when I see where Atticus had got to. He's sitting at the top of the ramp, waiting for us. Space returns and takes the tug from me, and we troop up the ramp after him. Space holds up his hand, and we stop. Brittayne and Marie walk up to stand beside him. Byane and Michael move to stand behind them. Atticus pads over to me, stands up, and puts his paws on my shoulders. He looks right into my eyes, and mine begin to swim. I don't want to say good-bye to this friend. He licks my face from chin to forehead, a big sloppy dog-like kiss. I laugh out loud; he woof-laughs in reply. He drops down to his four paws and returns to his place. Space clears his throat quietly. I wipe my face and turn toward him. He releases the tug handle into my hand, and while they all take a few steps forward, I stay put. Hope comes to stand beside me. We look at each other and then at the others. Space removes his spectacles. His icy eyes are large and penetrating. He says, "Welcome home, Time. I'm glad you didn't die."

I smile at him. "Me too, Space. Me too. Thank you."

Space nods, replaces his spectacles on his nose, turns, and walks through the wall. And the words "He was a truly perfect noble knight" slip in. Chaucer's words fit Space. The others follow Space through the wall. I take hold of Hope's hand with my free one, suck in a lungful of air, and on the exhalation start running—right into the wall.

We pop out on University Avenue, under a deluge of rain. I blink and spit out water as the wind blows it into my face then rotates round to blow it into my side. We run and splash south down the right side of the road, the others right in front of us, Byane, Michael, and Space hiding Brittayne and Marie from our view. Cars decelerate and veer all around us. The centre line of trees and fountains peter out on our left, and we cross King. Somehow the tug keeps *The Egg* firmly behind us despite the wind blasting its force against it and us. Hope calls out over the howl, "Brass. Why did Space put us so far away? Barnacle and Brass! We have to run all the way to Pawkins and Dodger! I'm soaking!"

"Since when do you care about walking? You walk all over Toronto. Even in the rain!" I yell over the gale.

"Only because I must."

"Well, you must now too," I scream, the wind hurling my words into the driving rain.

I see Front ahead. Front is filled with smooth-running cars and no traffic lights. Although the crowds fill the sidewalk space between the charged curtain and the gardens, the road is clear and easy to run on. I'd changed into my twenty-first century clothes but am wearing my twenty-fifth century shoes. The rain is whipping my wet skirt and washing the dirt off the fabric. It makes it hard to run, but at least I don't have to contend with those cheap pumps. I'd bought them unthinkingly, shoes like everyone else's. But after the bliss of wearing these twenty-fifth century ones, I'd rather walk barefoot back home than wear my pumps again. I'd left them behind, a souvenir for Space.

The road curves eastward toward Front, and suddenly I see Guy standing legs wide apart with his two boys on either side, cars deviating around them like water round a rock, while the rain and wind don't seem to touch them. They're wearing personal charged curtains.

"There he is," I yell. Guy has eyes only for me and doesn't notice the others angling off to the right, dodging behind a car, and weaving toward him so that they can surprise him from behind while Atticus puts himself firmly in front of me. Hope and I slow down to a trot. Guy looks contemptuously at me and shouts, "You can't get around me. We will catch you. You're not going home."

I keep trotting toward him, cudgelling my brain to figure out some way around him and hoping Atticus will show me. Marie pops up behind the boy on Guy's left and strokes his head.

Somehow her Bikini-style hair remains untouched by the rain and doesn't move in the wind. He startles, uncrossing his arms. She pulls his head toward herself as she walks away from Guy, and the boy uncomprehendingly follows.

"Hey!" Guy turns to his first boy and meets Brittayne's subservient gaze. Her hair too is perfect, as is her body. The other boy swivels his head then his body to watch in envy. They're all distracted enough for Atticus to weave to their right, my left, into the oncoming traffic, with me and Hope following close on his tail. *The Egg* floats past their turned backs. I'm so thankful these cars have no horns, only affrighted passengers who say nothing, they're so shocked. We veer on to Front, soaked and buffetted.

Hope grumbles loudly, "We're only at Dodger."

"Run," I retort. She lets go of my hand, darts in front of me and onto my other side, and grabs the tug handle. We race down the curving street, water splashing up to our knees, water tattooing on our heads, while Atticus slows down to get himself behind *The Egg*, between us and the boys.

"Get her!" I hear Guy's faraway voice blown toward me by the wind. I didn't see what happened after we'd passed, but Byane and Michael must've gotten in their way too for them to be so far behind.

"Faster," I pant. We increase speed and fly toward Yonge, our heads down against the wind, my skirt plastered to my legs, my cardigan clinging to my chest and arms. I wrestle my skirt with my free hand to hike it up above my knees so I can run freer. The wind gusts up underneath it and folds it up against my thighs. I struggle to release it from between my thighs. I succeed at last, and I lengthen my steps. Hope keeps up. We skid round the corner and suddenly the wind is buffetting us south. I hear thudding steps behind us and then a yelp and a crash.

Hope yells "Don't look" as I'm about to turn to see what had happened. I obey. I hear swearing, growling, and another crash over the howling wind and drumming rain. My heart is racing faster than my feet. Is Atticus down or the boys? In a sudden lull in the gale, I hear steps darting and dodging on the watery street.

Hope bellows, "Can't you run faster?"

"No," I gasp out.

"We should've made you run every day. You're slow."

I have no breath to retort. I barely notice that there's no highway overhead and that overstuffed gardens of leaning birches, rhododendrons, and roses bisect Lake Shore as we stream past them and across the wide boulevard. A wet leaf smacks into my cheek. I leave it there, pumping all my energy into my legs and lungs. I register in the deep recesses of my mind that *The Egg* isn't whipping out of control but remaining behind the tug obediently, the tug undeterred by rushing air or plunging water. The footsteps are gaining. We hit Queen's Quay, and I almost stop, for it's not like the street I remember.

"Don't stop!" Hope shouts, "We have to cross Payne first!"

I put my last ounce of energy into my feet, and my shoes spring me forward, cutting through a sudden cold gust and rain that's like tiny drills flinging themselves horizontally. We cross Payne and sprint through the charged curtain guarding Byane's place and smack right into a silent forest under dappled sunlight.

I stumble in the sudden change from storm to sun. I look back at *The Egg* as I regain my footing, praying it'll fit in between the trees. It does barely; branches hit and fling off it, shattering their leaves to the ground, spraying the earth with droplets off the tug and *The Egg*. Behind *The Egg*, Guy is heaving on the other side of the charged curtain, his angry eyes pinning me. I falter to a standstill. I feel like a frozen mouse. But, my inner voice asserts, I'm not a mouse. I'm a woman. My resolve reasserts itself. I reach up and peel the wet leaf off my cheek. I fling it to the ground. He lowers his eyelids down slowly, and Atticus skids in the puddle behind him, spraying his back and grabbing him by the ankle. Guy's lids shoot open, and he screeches with pain and frustration. I'm relieved Guy couldn't use his thought power to get through the charged curtain.

Hope lurches me onward. The trees soon hide the view of him and Atticus fighting, and we slow down to guide *The Egg* carefully through the thickening forest. Suddenly we're out of the trees and on the edge of a gleaming boardwalk. We step on to it. The boards beneath our feet are made of a shock-absorbing material the colour of freshly stained white cedar. The Toronto Islands stand green and gold across from us. The water sparkles, and white dots bounce and fly over the waves.

Hope breathes out, "I've never gotten this close before."

"It's beautiful," I gasp out.

She nods then her face turns business like. She says, "We must send you home."

"But how? They can see us," I pant.

"Not so. Wealth jetties have charged curtains that obscure Wealth owners from view. The Wealth like to see but not be seen."

I swallow hard to slow down my breathing. "Are you sure?"

Her look admonishes me. She says, "Hurry up, eh. Atticus may fail to keep Guy away. He could arrive any minute."

I shake off the beauty of this place while Hope touches her temple. She follows the instructions only she can see, and I assist. We pull *The Egg* into position. It's supposed to point straight to the sun. She commands me to "Get in!" She releases the tug, and *The Egg* floats gently to the ground. It doesn't even thud when it makes contact.

I nod and head for the back side of *The Egg*. I stop and look at her. She doesn't move. I walk back, determined not to cry again. I fail. I sniffle as her visage wavers in my sight. We hug. I wipe my eyes with my cardigan sleeve and walk back to *The Egg*. As I'm about to enter, she calls out: "Wait."

I turn, hoping for ... hoping for something.

"Shoes," she says pointing to my feet.

Oh. I consider my feet. I don't want to give up my shoes. Suddenly I hear crashing through the trees. I rip off the shoes, leap into *The Egg*, take the two steps to the console, hit the button I was told to hit, the one that would activate *The Egg*'s programming. Air hisses out, and I can feel a seal closing me in. I grab the skin-coloured suit off the seat and push my legs and arms into it against the rising air pressure. I pull the edges of the front opening toward each other. I shake my appendages inside the suit to try and make it comfortable as it seals itself closed. A layer of air fills up between me and the suit, and then I feel prickles as electrons and protons fill the space. The original helmet was more protection than I needed and unwieldy too; instead Space had crafted head gear similar in material to the suit, and I slip it on. It seals itself to the suit, and immediately the breathable air generator wheezes on. I sit down, and a charged curtain surrounds me making me one with the chair.

I wonder if I can move. I wonder if we're moving.

I lean forward slightly and am relieved I can move. I extend my right arm to touch the smooth white console. A Lake Ontario-grey square appears with symbols representing time and space; soon after the coordinate numbers appear in the colour of orange-clay. When they turn green, that means I'm home, Space had explained.

A bang reverberates the side of *The Egg*. I freeze. *The Egg* lurches to the side, and the charged curtain keeps me firmly in the chair. Suddenly many voices permeate *The Egg*'s skin, all yelling and swearing. A chorus of barks overrides them all.

Silence.

Someone rights *The Egg*.

The charged curtain eases.

I shift in my seat.

I wait.

The departure time is programmed in; I cannot change it, for it must be precise in time and space to the sun's orbit and the earth's moving magnetic poles. We timed our race here to take into account any delays the boys would create but that would still get me here before departure time, in time to be sealed up in *The Egg*, so that when the engine came on and it folded space, I would be in *The Egg*. We arrived before guesstimate time.

The wait is nerve-wracking.

I feel a small jerk.

I feel great gravity in the form of the charged curtain becoming stronger, pushing me firmly into the chair moulded for my frame, not allowing me to move.

I feel hot.

I wonder if I'll become one with the sun, if I'll return to 2411 or some other future, if I'll truly, finally get home.

I wonder where I'll end up

I feel particles of me disappear and reappear and am relieved.

30

THE FUTURE BEGINS

DECELERATION begins. My molecules coalesce. Little feet prickle my cells. I check the display, and to my relief, it shows the coordinates in green. I'm home. The charged curtain around me shimmers blue then disappears. I hesitate to move. But nothing happens. I don't float or vanish. Relief floods me.

Ignoring the busy multitude of prickles in my cells, I leap out of my chair and head to where the door is. Hope's advice arrests my hand: "Remember to look out before you open the door." I press *The Egg's* wall next to the door, and a human-size display of the outside pops onto the door surface. It's like I'm standing outside. I scan the area.

It's the same alley!

At the end of the alley, the occasional person hurries by. I focus on that part of the display, and Queen Street zooms in closer. A couple saunter past. They're wearing twenty-first century clothes! I'm so ecstatic I jump up and down, clapping and yelling and turning round and round.

"Yay!" I scream, thrusting my right hand to the ceiling.

I settle down and inspect Queen Street again, just to be sure. Sunlight lights up the sidewalk and glints off of glasses—glasses!—and purse buckles—purses! Everyone is carrying a paper coffee cup encircled in cardboard. My smile stretches wide until my cheeks hurt. I inspect the rest of the alley, and the display responds by focussing on what I'm aiming my eyes at. The same graffiti, the same littered ground. I leap into the air and thrust both hands up. "Woot!" I yell out.

I dance again. I can dance in here because no one can see me. My heart sings; my lungs burst with happiness at breathing the old, familiar polluted air. Well, not yet, but soon. My muscles are tensing in anticipation of running down the alley and all the way home.

Hope's voice interrupts me. Literally: "Remember to self-destruct."

Even so. I smile at the old-future term for yes. Yes, I must remember to self-destruct, not me, *The Egg*. I giggle. Hopefully with its destruction, those 2411 terms will fade into memory but not the experiences and the people.

I return to the console and press my full palm down while looking at the surface to the left of my hand. Hope's voice says, "Self-destruct on." I lift my hand up and look around one last time at the future. When *The Egg* senses that I have gone through the door and there is no life inside, it will annihilate the interior particles and anti-particles, the neutrino shield will hold until all the particles are gone, and then the force binding the neutrino shield will also disappear, and poof, all the neutrinos will be gone. Or something like that.

I spin slowly, taking in this symbol of a future time. Times, plural, actually. Two now times. I hadn't thought I would feel it, but nostalgia pangs me. I miss Hope and Space and the others already. I miss the ease of so many things of that time. I miss my springy, soft shoes. But I don't miss the gender wars.

I walk purposefully to the door and through it. I don't look back. I won't look back. Oh all right, I can't help it, I have to look back.

I twist my head to look over my shoulder.

I see nothing but the alley.

I knew I would see nothing. Still, it's a shock that suddenly there is nothing to remind myself of my journey, not even my clothing in a way, which in my future-stained eyes looks antique.

I turn my head forward, straighten my shoulders, and take a big step forward. And feel a small, thin fragile bump under my toes. I retreat my foot and look down. My iPod touch! I'd forgotten all about it. I pick it up, press the Home button, and after a heart-stopping delay, the lock screen flashes on. Smiling, I stuff it into my pocket and walk forward, uncaring of the rough concrete, the litter under my bare feet. When I reach the end of the alley, I turn left instead of right.

I'm going home.

As I walk, I drink in Queen Street in the early morning. The slant of the sunlight. Sunlight! The way the men and women are dressed like men and women. Oh, except for that one veiled in black from head to toe. I shiver in memory. What is her life that she feels her very being must be hidden? And behind the isolated woman, what is that girl's life—for surely she is a girl, a real girl, not a woman being treated like a child and kept down like a child—to want to cover her outward essence in ink and metal pierced into flesh and deadening black leather? And what is that woman's life like, the one across the street, that she agrees and unthinkingly wears boring suits ill-fitting for a woman because some human resource office decided that they were appropriate for work? I had been that woman. My skirt today, my own today time, my today in her now time, with its splashy roses and flashy white background was a rebellion when I'd put it on this morning or last year or whenever that time slice was. But normally I too conformed.

My feet follow the familiar path home as I ponder what I see newly.

I trot up my front steps and espy the morning paper. I remember suddenly that I had not had the paper with me when I'd gone to work. It had been late arriving. I stare at the rolled-up newsprint, remembering that morning so long ago, when my impending fortieth birthday was my biggest worry and wonder: which paper is it? I bend down, pick up the paper, straighten up, hesitate, strip off the elastic band, and unfurl it. I look for the date.

I blink and put my face closer to the page, widening my eyes.

It is today's date.

The date I left for work.

I slowly turn and walk down my front steps, one by one, staring at the date on the paper in my hand. I stroll down the narrow path between the houses until I get to my back yard. I stumble into my weathered Muskoka chair, scattered with fall leaves, uncaring that they will stick to my white skirt. I am sick of white.

Tomorrow is my fortieth birthday.

Yet have I not reached and aged past forty already?

How old am I? Am I the age that I was in this time before I was snatched, or am I as old as the time I have experienced?

I feel older.

Yet those nanos inside me re-densifying me are already settling down and that feeling of strength and vitality that filled me after the hospital episode is returning.

I feel younger.

I feel like I'm that university student again with a future that excites me. Yet terrifies me. But this future I will thinkingly choose.

I will have my lunch with Peggy and Sue. And then I will quit my job. I have better things to do, purposeful soul-filling things I can do, I have come to realize, simply because I am human—not a *dumb* human—but a human being like all the people I have met, from those ignorant twenty-fifth century boys who chased me to the complex Hope to the enigmatic Space and especially to the desperately brave Bikini. I don't know what I will do after I quit my job, other than feeling liberated from prison. But I will know it when I see it. The first present I will give myself are Continuing Studies programs from every university and college in Toronto that I can take. The second will be to find volunteer opportunities, something to do with girls. Real girls. Non-adults. And something to do with boys. Girls and boys cannot see each other as individuals, instead of as opposing genders, unless both learn to see the other as human beings like themselves, like I'd taught those Thrall and that stubborn male Wealth to see. I smile, and happiness stuffs itself into every fibre of my being.

I finger the edges of the paper, feel its sharpness.

"Ouch," I suck my offended finger and grin around it.

With a slurpy pop, I release my finger from my mouth and put my entire palm on the surface of the paper. I caress it. I feel its roughness; I even imagine I can feel the bump of each letter, the shape of the top fold photo. I relax back against the chair and sigh with pleasure. Keeping hold of the precious newspaper, I luxuriate in the sight of my time's blue sky. I used to complain about all our rainy days, the too-many cloudy days, but we have so much sun. I close my eyes; its warmth heats up my eyelids. I let my eyelids lift and sit up. I flap the paper to read the front page, the oh-so-delectable front page of a real newspaper, not a horridly named continuous issuance, a real broadsheet covered in stories by reporters who have real independence.

A breeze flutters it, blows fallen leaves into my face.

I cough and gasp and spit out stems. As I'm trying to pull leaf bits off the end of my tongue, I hear a soft, "Hi."

I look up and see a strange woman staring at me through the side of a barely visible white *Egg*-like ship. She moves forward enough for me to see her whole self. She isn't wearing white, yet I know this *Egg*, this ship, can only be from the first time. 3011.

She beams and widens her eyes.

Royal blue.

"They're real," I say stupidly.

She laughs, a light, happy laugh. She says to me, "My eyes are real. You recognize?"

She isn't wearing a bikini. Instead she is wearing a cerulean flowing tunic that is longer in back than front. In back, it ends at her knees, in front it ends just below her hips in fat pleats. The neckline is a discreet V edged in a band of a darker hue. The wrist-length sleeves are tight yet obviously not constricting. Her legs are encased in loose yet form-fitting navy blue trousers that drape softly over her matching shoes. Her hair is long and pulled back in a pony tail. Tendrils stick out around her face. Like the men's clothes, hers has no seams, no buttons, no zippers. And probably no Velcro. Light flashes from her ear lobes as she shifts her weight. Most remarkable of all, her face looks normal for her age. It's in better condition than mine—and it should be with all those nanobots inside them cleaning up toxins and free radicals and keeping DNA happy and new—her maturity is in the shape of her face, the structure of her bones, the bloom of her skin. She looks relaxed, blessed—she has the body language of a free woman.

I smile back, "I recognize you."

She nods. "Thank you. We *all* thank you."

She steps back, her *Egg* conceals her from me, and then it too is gone.

I watch the empty space for awhile. I flap my paper again and read today's news.

ABOUT THE AUTHOR

SHIREEN JEEJEEBHOY is a Toronto-based author, blogger, and photographer. She is the author of the award-winning biography *Lifeliner: The Judy Taylor Story*, *She*, and *Concussion Is Brain Injury*; two short ebooks; articles for print media and online sites; and she is working on her next few novels. She holds a B.Sc. in psychology from the University of Toronto.

You can visit her website at http://jeejeebhoy.ca and subscribe to her blog posts to receive a free poetry ebook.

A Plea: Did you enjoy *Time and Space*, enough to tell others about it? If so, please leave a review on the online book retailer of your choice—it's the best way to support the work of an indie author like me. Honest reviews by readers are invaluable to authors, and I would love to hear from you. Thank you!

Please enjoy the peeks at my first novel *She* and my first book *Lifeliner* on the following pages, and don't forget to keep an eye out for my next book.

SHE

CHAPTER ONE

THERE WAS ONCE A WOMAN

TIRES HISS AGAINST the road. A gentle bump bump at high speed wakes her up. She stretches against the confines of the seat belt and blinks open her eyes. Pitch night engulfs the car. The glowing numbers on the dashboard clock draw her eyes: 12:54.

"Wow, I can't believe the time." She yawns, "Did I really sleep that long? I can't believe it's that late. Did we run into heavy traffic? That sucks. I thought leaving so late in the evening, we'd miss the Toronto-bound traffic. I guess not, eh?" She smiles at the driver, but he looks stoically ahead. Her eyes drift past the clock again and suddenly widen. "Hey! Do you know what time it is? It's almost summer solstice time. How cool is that, being out in the country at the exact hour?" Still no response.

Sighing, she looks out her window and frowns. Not only are they late, but for that matter, where are they? This country road doesn't look like Highway 10. Pickets of a prim wooden fence fly by, the ground at its feet rising into view and disappearing. The fields beyond vacuum the meagre starlight, and the car's beams cannot penetrate into their depths. She leans toward her window and cranes her neck to look up at the sky. It's a moving charcoal surface with white glitter winking here and there. The moon is nowhere in sight.

She asks him as she continues to stare out the window, "Where are we?"

"I thought we'd take a shortcut."

"Meaning you don't know," she laughs. He smiles faintly as he continues to stare straight ahead, his hands resting in the ten to two position on the leather grey steering wheel of their car. The amber glow of the dashboard lights up the front of his face like some sort of eerie jack-o-lantern. She watches him for a moment.

"Well, I guess we're somewhere in the country. Traffic must've been bad, eh?"

He shrugs one shoulder. She sighs. She's fully awake now and sharing space with a statue.

"I guess it wasn't so bad for you that I dozed off, eh? Silence is golden and all that," she grins. "Well, I can be silent ... sometimes." She chuckles and then stretches again. "That nap did me good. I feel so awake now and refreshed. I'm raring to go, and I can't wait till tomorrow, I mean today. I have all these song ideas bouncing around in my head. This was a great idea of yours, going on this road trip, it's got me going again, and I love visiting those cute Ontario towns." She twists round to the left to check out the back seat, to make sure all the goodies they bought are still there. Pies and jugs of maple syrup sit side by side with pints of fresh Bing cherries, her favourite. She untwists herself and settles back in her seat. She watches the hypnotic yellow line as it snakes ahead.

"I can't wait to dive into those cherries. They were my favourite fruit growing up. Did I ever tell you that? I used to look forward to the end of school because that's when Grandmother would buy them. And I'd make a big mess, and she'd get so mad." She laughs at the memory. "Now I can make as big a mess as I want." She falls silent for a moment. "I was thinking: they're too good to make pies with. I'd rather eat them fresh like that, but it's almost strawberry season. Maybe we can go up to Andrew's Scenic Acres and pick some berries. I'm in the mood for making strawberry rhubarb pies or maybe mixed berry pies if the blueberries and raspberries are out too. We have enough room in that chest freezer, I'm sure. I gave it a big cleanout the other day. What do you think?" she asks rhetorically. She savours the thought of a strawberry rhubarb pie with crumble topping. Those are always a hit. And they freeze so well. She can almost smell them baking and taste their sweet tartness. She smiles; her eyes focus on the road again.

She looks past the yellow line, past the boundaries of light the car beams create, into the darkness coming toward them, a forest on the right. The hairs on the back of her neck lift up; her stomach flutters.

"Uh, where are we really?" she asks as she sits up straight, tensing her body. He stays silent.

Her nerves feel taut. She urges, "We need to stop and turn around. Now, if you don't mind."

The car doesn't slow down. His eyes don't flick up to the rear-view mirror or down to the speedometer.

Her chest starts to contract. "Look, I know you're all into exploring the side roads, but this doesn't feel safe, and it's really really late. Let's drive home on a faster road. Let's turn around and go to Highway 10."

He says nothing.

"Could you please just stop the car, turn around, and go back to Highway 10."

"We're fine." He stretches the word out. "Stop being so paranoid."

"I'm not being paranoid."

"You are," he replies. The slight put-down in his voice works. She feels silly. They're just trees.

Those trees are beside them; ahead their mates on the left loom. They fill the front windshield more and more. It's 12:56 a.m. She wants to be the one in the driver's seat badly; instead she's being driven inexorably toward the forest, where starlight cannot penetrate. She shifts her gaze back down to the road, to the familiar yellow ribbon and the dusty edges of the asphalt where road meets grass. But then the edges vanish into the shadows cast by the trees standing shoulder to shoulder, leafy branch merging into leafy branch, creating a light-sucking toothy maw. She feels the air hold its breath. Her breathing speeds up. His body remains still.

The trees close in on the other side, only a sliver of rectangular sky between the two forests breaks their starless black.

She leans toward him, her thick, shingled hair falling against her cheek, trying to get away from the trees on her right, jostling his arm.

"What are you doing?" he snaps at her.

"Can't you move closer to the yellow line?"

In response, he steers toward the right.

"Stop it!" She struggles to breathe evenly.

"I'll stop it when you stop being silly."

She leans forward to look up through the windshield, her hair gleaming in the reflected dashboard light, searching for that sliver of glittering sky, looking for the one opening in the lightless claustrophobia without.

"Would you get a hold of yourself. We're fine. Don't worry." He tries to nudge her away with his elbow, but she resists.

She cannot move back to the upright position; she just cannot separate herself from him. She looks ahead, focussing on the end of the forest, even though she cannot see it, where the fields re-emerge beyond the headlights, willing them to arrive there as fast as possible. But their speed drops to 70 kilometres per hour. She begins to see the individual trees, the shrubs sticking up among them, the rocks laying among their bases. The sky is morphing, undulating, changing degrees of grey-black shades. Clouds are rolling in.

"Why are you slowing down?"

He doesn't answer. "Of course not, why need he?" she thinks angrily. He's proving his point. He doesn't usually treat her this contemptuously. Her anger fades into loneliness as memories arise of how he used to always treat her with consideration and respect and love. She remembers the first time they shopped together, how he had insisted on carrying the grocery bags. Or how when she had lost her keys for the umpteenth time and was becoming mighty annoyed about it, he'd used his carefully modulated voice to calm her and focus her memory on those keys. Within minutes she'd found them. But lately, ever since his annual spring camping trip up near the Bruce Trail with his buddies, he's become moody. Grim. Many, many days, he has been his old cheerful self, making her laugh so hard that she snorts water out her nose, or he has run errands by himself instead of interrupting one of her songwriting sessions. But on this weekend's road trip, he'd once again become serious, become watchful of her as darkness inhabited his face. She doesn't understand this change in him and towards her. It's like he's decided that she has to prove her worth over and over again.

She wants to grab that wheel and take back control. But she can't. She's in his hands.

Sinking down into the shadow of her seat, still leaning on him, her eyes reach the level of the clock. It flips to 12:57 a.m.

The landscape flashes sickly neon green. The car heels to the left as a wind screams out of the forest like a ghastly, whirling Northern light, and slams into its right side then dances up on to the hood, on to the roof, down beside them. The car's back fishtails out. She squeezes her eyes and senses the car turn one way then the other. Even through her closed eyelids, she senses the chartreuse-yellow lightning inside the whirlwind. She squeezes her eyes tighter until they hurt. They're speeding up; they're driving to the left; they slow. She opens her eyes to see him manhandling the steering wheel until they're aiming straight down the road again, but the wind, with its ever-changing neon-green-bottom border, with its dancing gold-green veins, streaks alongside and in front of them. They can't outrun it. He presses the accelerator, trying anyway, as she clings to his right arm, as she puts her head between her own arms. Glass cracks in front of her. The cracks glow green. She scoots closer to him and squeezes her eyes so tight, she sees red. Cracks fracture her side window, and she can't help opening her eyes to look toward the sound. Air moves all around her, pushing at her, raising the hair on her arms, throwing up the hair on her head, fluttering her T-shirt, turning her skin sickly green. Suddenly she sees nothing. She closes and opens her eyes and still sees nothing. Panic attacks her. And then they shoot out of the trees and are between open fields. She sees again. Sobs rack her, and she can't stop them.

"There's a patrol up ahead. I have to pull over," he says.

Her sobs quit suddenly. She sits up, wipes her eyes, smoothes her hair off her face, straightens her Black Sabbath T-shirt. The car rumbles off the road to the gravel shoulder and crunches to a stop. He pushes the window button and his window hums down. A policeman with a bright wand in his right hand and a reflective vest walks toward them; the officer leans in, his eyes keen on them. She returns his look emotionless.

"Good evening sir, ma'am. How are you this morning?"

"We're fine officer. I wasn't speeding."

"No, you weren't sir. That's not why I pulled you over. We're the Akaesman patrol."

"The what?"

"Will you step out of the car sir, ma'am. We need to ask you a few questions."

She obeys. Or tries to. All her muscles seem to have seized up; she looks down puzzled, feeling old. Using her hands and her arms as leverage, she turns herself towards the open door, puts her feet on the ground, stands up, and leans on the open car door, apperceiving her balance, before straightening her flared black jeans and walking over to where the policeman has joined a woman standing a metre or so in front of what looks like the back of a white ambulance sitting next to the black and white police car.

"Did you drive through the forest sir?" the policeman asks him.

"Yes."

"Did anything happen?"

"Like what?"

"You tell me sir."

Slowly he shakes his head.

The policeman stares at him for a few seconds, and then turns to her.

"You ma'am. How are you feeling?"

She considers that for a moment. Shocked maybe.

The woman who had been standing there watching them walks over to her, while snapping on blue nitrile gloves. She takes a penlight out of her pocket and flashes it in her eyes. She flinches. The woman is unfazed. She reaches round and lightly squeezes her neck muscles, moving down to feel the top of her shoulders.

"Follow me."

She obeys.

"Please sit here," she gestures to the step at the back of the ambulance. From there, she can see the reflective letters on the side of the police car: "Akaesman Patrol. To Guard and Save." Weird.

She feels a cuff being fastened around her left arm, and then the rhythmic pump, pump as the woman inflates it. Air hisses out before the cuff is ripped off. A stethoscope is pressed against her chest and then her back. She finally looks at the woman as she straightens up and speaks to the policeman: "It's mild, but definitely."

He nods and faces her fiancé again.

"Sir, you did experience something back there, didn't you?"

She watches her fiancé stare back nonchalantly, but he's no match for an officer of the Akaesman Patrol.

"We might've."

"You did sir. I want to know what it was."

He told him all, even how she was whining about turning back.

"You should've listened to her sir. Stay here." He walks over to the patrol car, the gravel crunching under his dusty black boots. He opens the driver's door, gets in, and slams it shut.

They wait.

He gets out with a clipboard and walks over to her.

"OK ma'am, I'm sorry to have to tell you that you probably had a run-in with Akaesman. Now it doesn't look too serious, some sprains, but I must ask you to read this form and sign it. Then go see your GP tomorrow." He looks at his watch. "Today." He writes, his pen scratching the paper on the clipboard. Then he hands the clipboard over to her. The woman aims a flashlight at it, but it's too much to read. She must be tired, and so she pretends to read it. His finger extends into her view, pointing to where she should sign. She signs. He flips the page up and asks her to sign the copy. She signs and hands it back to him. He presses down on the clip handle and releases the top piece of paper. He hands it to her. She takes it, but he doesn't let go until she looks up at him.

"Go see your GP ma'am."

She nods.

He still doesn't let go. "See your GP, your family physician."

She looks up into his face and says, "I will."

He lets go. She carries the paper back to the car, where her door is still open. She gets in awkwardly and drops the paper on her lap, wondering why she has to see her family physician. She reaches back for the seat belt, and pain ratchets up her neck. She pauses and then turns her entire body right to get at the seat belt, pulls it toward herself, turns her entire body to the left, and stiffly aims for the seat belt clip. Click. She sits back, sighing. And waits, staring at her fiancé, yet not seeing him as he strides back to the car. She hears his door open, his booted foot twisting on the gravel, his jeans sliding against leather; she hears the slam of the door, the feel of the car softly rocking in response, the slither of the belt as it's pulled, the click of it going home, the key being turned, and the engine roaring excessively to life. They accelerate onto the asphalt, the wheels spitting small stones out, and drive for home.

Keep reading for a peek at the fascinating true-life story about the woman who could not eat ...

LIFELINER

CHAPTER 1

BACK IN ONE HOUR

"I'M SO LUCKY to have a family, adopted or not! I'm so lucky to be alive!" Judy Ellis Taylor tells her three school-age girls out of the blue on this chilly September morning. They roll their eyes, having heard this before many a time.

Judy didn't know her biological parents, a twenty-three-year-old nursing-student mother and a twenty-seven-year-old painter father, nor did she care to. To Judy, her real parents were Marjorie and Percy Russell. Shortly after her birth on March 26, 1936, they had scooped up the little round-cheeked, black-haired baby and taken her home. At first, Marjorie hadn't wanted to adopt this baby. Only six months had passed since their second adopted child had died suddenly; but Percy talked to Marjorie gently and persistently until he convinced his devastated wife that she could adopt again, that she could have her dream of children, children who would live. She acquiesced, and they adopted Judy from a Presbyterian home. To help ensure that both their girls, Joyce and Judy, their first and third adopted children, would have the best chance, they moved from Rosedale to a large house in the valley of York Mills, where violets flowed up to the door in springtime. It meant a one-hour drive to his engineering job, but Percy made it sweeter by bringing home chocolate éclairs. Meanwhile, Marjorie anchored their family life with big weekly Sunday lunches after church.

It was a good decision, for Judy thrived on life. She attended the prestigious Bishop Strachan School during her junior-high years and joined the young people's group at St. John's Anglican Church. At thirteen years old, this healthy, mischievous girl pledged herself to Christ at Camp Gay Venture in Haliburton—she didn't explain why to anyone, just did it—and became a camp counsellor at the same time. Like a mother bird, Judy took charge of the little girls at the camp, including Sandra, a small seven-year-old. Judy especially loved teaching the little ones to ride. But being Judy's pupil was not an easy thing: she had a tendency to kick her charges out of the nest if she felt that they could handle it, plus she had a penchant for practical jokes.

One sunny day as the group cantered together, Sandra's black horse (known as Blacky) threw her off. Sandra sniffled on the ground, feeling sorry for herself, while the others milled around. They expected Judy to pick her up, dust her off, and plop her back on her horse. Instead, she steered her horse over and, looking down from her great height, demanded, "Well? What are you going to do about it? I'm going back to the barn. You can either walk or get on your horse and follow me." She gestured to the others to follow her and rode off.

Sandra howled. Some of the kids looked back, but not one slowed down. They disappeared toward the barn. Sandra stopped, mouth open. No point howling anymore. She closed her mouth. She stood up, climbed onto Blacky, and trotted back to camp, where Judy was waiting. "Well, if you hadn't done that, you probably wouldn't ever have ridden again," Judy informed the little girl. "Now take Blacky in and groom her."

That fall, Percy decided that Judy would be better off at his (and my) alma mater, Jarvis Collegiate Institute, near the heart of Toronto, and had her transferred there. She did reasonably well. By age seventeen, she knew what she wanted out of life: to find a husband and have a family.

Judy joined her girlfriends at the church picnic near Fenelon Falls that summer, hoping to find a husband. She did. Her friend introduced her to her boyfriend's buddy. Cliff Taylor was a taciturn, slightly older fellow with a sudden smile and a shock of dark hair. He had to grow up quickly after his mother had tried to kill him along with herself, leaving him alone with his alcoholic father while his younger sister was shipped off to boarding school. By age sixteen, he had dropped out of school to work. He developed a philosophy of paying his own way with cash only. He didn't believe in credit cards or debt, except for a mortgage perhaps. Unlike Judy, he didn't live in the genteel areas of town, but he had become successful in sales and was doing well monetarily. Still, the educated, well-off Judy clicked with this man from the wrong side of the tracks. He loved her with a devotion that drove him to cross the threshold of a church, a feat he vowed never to repeat after their marriage on July 27, 1957, in St. John's Anglican, and she loved him with a strength he could count on.

Cliff bought a new house for his bride, and they settled comfortably into Scar-borough life, spending weekends up at the cottage near his father's place in Bobcaygeon, Cliff paying for everything in cash, as usual, and Judy looking after their growing brood: Cyndy, Julie, and Miriam. Judy had grasped her dream. With her family complete, she went on the birth control pill, a fairly new drug back in late 1966. She was wildly happy and having fun.

But God wasn't impressed with Judy's life plan. He gave her the gifts of toughness, generosity, kindness, healing, advocacy,

and teaching. Her dream was too mundane for those gifts, and
He would call her to travel to unfamiliar places, places so dark,
frightening, and unexpected that she would have no choice but
to trust in His faithfulness to her.

Stomach pain was the first intimation of the change to come.
The stomach pain was so bad that, after three months, it forced
her to see her general practitioner (GP) in February 1967.
Despite X-rays, blood tests, and referrals to specialists, nothing
revealed the source of her pain, although by 1970 her insatiable
appetite and loss of weight clued one of her specialists, a
gastroenterologist, into the fact that she might have
hyperthyroidism. She joked to her girls that she could run up
and down the road at ninety miles an hour, making them laugh
while she hid from them the wrenching pain deep inside her.
By the summer of 1970, her endocrinologist irradiated her
thyroid. Perhaps things would settle down now, Judy and Cliff
hoped.

But the pain squeezed harder. Her doctor prescribed
morphine; Cliff and Judy hid that, too, from their girls, or so
they thought. Family conversations took a strange turn. The
talkative, joking Judy suddenly would stop mid-sentence; they
would all pretend she hadn't and would gamely continue on the
conversation without her. Suddenly, she'd pop back up and
finish her sentence. Unfortunately, she would soon space out
again, and cries of "Mom? Mom!" from her girls would go
unheeded. Frightened, the three dared not ask about this
phenomenon when she resurfaced from wherever she'd been,
and they pretended that everything was normal. Judy had
deceived herself into thinking they hadn't noticed, clenching
her teeth against the truth, fighting both the pain and the
effects of the morphine.

Wednesday, September 23, 1970, dawns cold. The pain had
increased during the past weekend. She had spent the time at
the cottage, lying balled up on her bed while the children

played with their dog, Goldie, under the sunny fall skies. Back at home, she had pushed herself to get through Monday and Tuesday, but today, Wednesday, she calls her GP. With Cliff by her side, she dials his number. He's on vacation. His partner takes her early morning call. He instructs her to call her endocrinologist, the one who irradiated her thyroid. She calls him, but her symptoms are outside his field of specialty, he informs her. She hangs up frustrated and decides to soldier on. "I'll be fine," she assures Cliff so that he will leave for work and not worry about her. She has toughed it out for over three years; one more day will not be so hard.

But Cliff feels unconvinced. He writes down his work number and commands her to call him.

Later that morning, after her family has left, Judy's neighbour Frances comes over for their usual cup of tea and chat. After one look at Judy, Frances runs to fetch her next-door neighbour Fran. They return to find Judy lying on the chesterfield, wearing shorts and shivering. Fran dashes into the bedroom and grabs a pair of slacks and a blanket. Judy—the one who always does things for herself, who never discusses her health, who never talks of her ailment—now lets her two neighbours bundle her up.

Fran asks her, "Where's the pain?"

Judy points to, but dares not touch, her sore stomach and confesses her whole story.

Fran thinks that maybe it's appendicitis and is livid at the doctor's inane advice. They should call Cliff, she asserts, and she takes the slip of paper with his work number on it and calls while Frances offers Judy some tea.

Judy cannot abide the thought and turns her head away. Fran suggests that she make lunch for Judy's girls at her place. Judy nods.

Frances has to go back home, but Fran stays. Judy feels maybe a visit to the bathroom will help. She rises carefully from the chesterfield and leans gratefully on her neighbour's arm for the short walk down the hallway. But the bathroom visit doesn't help. The pain hangs on, her nerves screech at her every movement. She lies back down on the chesterfield with relief.

It's eleven o'clock. The phone rings. Fran picks it up. It's Cliff, calling her back. "I may be wrong, but that wouldn't cause what she had, right?" she asks him, referring to Judy's hyperthyroidism.

Cliff doesn't know; he says it's all incomprehensible to him, this illness stuff.

Fran gets off the phone as lunch is fast approaching. She has to get it ready and bake cookies for her son and for Judy's three girls. "I'll ask Frances to keep an eye on you till after lunch," she tells Judy. She runs out the door under the scudding clouds and light rain to Frances's place. Although Frances has her own four kids to make lunch for, she pops over several times and takes messages from a worried Cliff. He's coming home early, and she lets Fran know this when she returns after lunch.

At 5:30 PM, Cliff barrels in from work. He watches Fran leave with a worried backward glance at Judy. He unwraps the fish 'n chips he'd picked up on his way home and coaxes his wife to eat at least a little bit. Fish 'n chips. The last meal of her life. If only they had known, he would've gotten something nicer.

Fed and off the couch, Judy takes a deep breath and throws her affliction out of her mind. Life cannot stop just because my innards are screaming, she thinks. Her girls need new running shoes, groceries need to be bought, for it's Wednesday night, grocery night. She tells Cliff to get the car ready, and she steels herself for the drive to Parkway Plaza. There in the middle of the grocery store, she sways.

Cliff grabs her and half carries half walks her to the car with the girls running along beside them. Cliff rushes them home and settles his wife on the chesterfield. He whips across the street to ask Frances if she can look after the children while he takes Judy to the doctor's office.

Frances doesn't hesitate to say yes, and the two race back to his house. They wrap Judy up in blankets.

As Cliff carries her out the door to the car, Judy—ever protective and still trying to hide her illness—calls back to her girls: "We're just going to the doctor's. We'll be back in an hour."

GLOSSARY

antecedents (in 3011); antegenerations (in 2411) (generations that come before)
accept (understand)
attache (girls)
antique (old)
architecture (buildings)
architecting (building as in constructing)
assure I (really)
attathrall (attaboy)
awesum (awesome)
Barnacle idea (great idea)
birth chips
CEO! (God! in 2411)
charged curtain (similar to a *Star Trek* forcefield)
cloudlight (daylight or day)
cloudlightly (daily)
continuous issuance (newspaper)
coverers (reporters)
3011: do as in old generation do
dodo (outdated)

dogdroid (an android or AI dog)
drinks (sucks)
earth exchange (TSX)
ecologies (corporations)
even so (yes, or yeah?)
fraggiest (rockin')
Governor (God! in 3011)
green earth (the planet but more than the planet—like Earth
plus Nature with a capital N and environment)
greenhouse gas storm
habitat (thing)
habitants (people)
habitant base (medical database)
habitant wall
hoverform (platform)
I dig (like)
Iself (myself)
land Wealth
livre (ebook)
mabbe (maybe)
Mait-D (maitre D)
middle class
no green (no way)
not so (no)
novatastic
nutrition printers/grown food
Oh CEO! (oh God!)
Oh I C! (OMG)
Originals (aboriginals)
Parliament (God! in 3011)
personwalls (firewalls)
plegan (play)
Press (baloney)

proton replacement therapy
repropagated (3011 form of propagated)
sci Wealth
sire (father)
sugar (sweet)
the Wealth (upper class or wealthy class)
Thrall (lower class or working class, like serfs)
Wealth enforcement patrol (police)
you till (you know)
zetta